VINEET BAJPAI

THE GREAT DELUGE

www.VineetBajpai.com

PRALAY

THE GREAT DELUGE

ISBN : 9788193642405

Published by
VB Performance LLP
Sector 93A, Noida,
Uttar Pradesh - 201304, India
Email - vb@vineetbajpai.com
www.VineetBajpai.com

Printed and Bound in India by
Gopsons Papers Ltd.
A-2 Sector 64, Noida - 201307, India

Cover Design by
Munisha Nanda

PRALAY
THE GREAT DELUGE

www.VineetBajpai.com

To
Vedika, Aditi &
Vandita

DISCLAIMER

This novel is a work of pure imagination and fiction, written with the sole intention of entertaining the reader. While the content has several references to various religions, historical events, institutions, beliefs and myths, it is all presented with the only purpose of making a fictional story richer and more intriguing. The author is a believer in all faiths and religions, and respects them equally and deeply. He makes no claim to the correctness and veracity of any historical or mythological or contextual references used in the story.

NOTE FROM THE AUTHOR

The Dalai Lama once said, 'Great love and great achievements involve great risk.' Can't say about the achievements yet, but his point about great love is beginning to make sense to me. And that is because of the tens of thousands of readers of Harappa.

I wrote Harappa with creative abandon, penning down what my heart chose to. While I had written three business books in the past, Harappa was my first fiction novel. Therefore, I did not know what to expect from it. So I wrote with speed, courage and freedom. With the blessings of *Maa Saraswati,* the Goddess of Talent & Wisdom, the result was a book that made its way deep into the hearts of its readers.

Harappa became an instant bestseller. To my delight and gratitude, I was inundated with emails, Facebook messages and tweets, and surrounded by people at literature festivals – thousands of readers expressing their adoration for the book, its characters and its intensity. It has been one of the most fulfilling times of my life.

However, like Bruce Springsteen once said, 'Sustaining an audience is hard. It demands a consistency of thought, of purpose, and of action...'. When I began writing the sequel *Pralay*, the chains of love were tying me down. The love showered on me by my readers. It was then that it dawned upon me that *Pralay* will now have to live up to the expectations of all those wonderful people. That was my Everest to climb.

The book you hold in your hands has been written with a deep sense of affection and responsibility towards you - my reader. I sincerely hope you enjoy it as much as you appreciated Harappa.

And please keep sending the emails, the tweets, the online reviews and the Facebook messages. They are my fuel.

Utthishtha!

Rise.

Vineet Bajpai

THE STORY SO FAR...

Harappa, 1700 BCE – The devta of Harappa, the mighty Vivasvan Pujari, who has been revered for decades as the Surya of Harappa, is ambushed in a ruthless betrayal. His trusted friend and brother-in-law, the wise Pundit Chandradhar, succumbs to the malicious greed of Priyamvada - his beautiful wife, the Princess of Mohenjo-daro. Three blind black magicians from Mesopotamia, Gun, Sha and Ap arrive in Harappa at the invitation of Priyamvada and her evil man-at-arms, Ranga. The dark wizards poison the water sources of the city with their concoctions, driving its entire populace insane and violent.

In the midst of the chaos, Vivasvan Pujari is indicted in a false accusation of the murder of Nayantara, Harappa's most famous exotic dancer. The devta of Harappa is condemned to the mrit-kaaraavaas or the dungeons of the dead. His valiant son, the young Manu, joins forces with Pundit Somdutt, the chief architect of Harappa and the last remaining friend of Vivasvan Pujari. In the battle that ensues, Manu kills the vile Ranga in a spectacular duel. At the same time, the River of the Wise, the Saraswati, rises in unnatural and ominous spate, threatening to devour the whole of the Harappan civilization. Astronomers predict imminent doomsday. The devta's gracious wife and Manu's mother, Sanjna, becomes the target of the arrows of manic Harappan soldiers and breathes her last on the battlefield, dying in her son's arms. At the behest of Somdutt, and his closest friend, the beautiful Tara, Manu rides out into the mist with his mother's body in his lap. But even as he gallops into the haze, poison tipped arrows tear into the handsome Manu's back and neck.

The devta of Harappa is dragged and tortured like an animal in the Great Bath of Harappa. He is skinned by the mad soldiers, pelted with stones and spat upon by the maniacal citizens of the once glowing metropolis. The devta, the Surya of Harappa – Vivasvan Pujari - swears vengeance. A man once known for his glowing and God-like appearance now looks ghastlier than the Devil himself. He looks up at the sky and screams out his last, bloodcurdling words to the masses of Harappa -

Listen, you who are already dead. Listen, you congregation of corpses. Listen, you fools.

I am half-human, half-God!'

Banaras, 2017 (present day) – Dwarka Shastri, the 108 year-old mystic leader of the Dev-Raakshasa Matth (God-Demon

Clan) located in the ancient city of Banaras, is on his death-bed. He summons his highly successful, unusually handsome and supremely talented great grandson - the magnificent Vidyut to the matth. Before his departure from Gurgaon, Vidyut confesses to his beloved partner Damini and to his best friend Bala that he hails from an ancient and mystical bloodline of devtas. Upon reaching Banaras, Vidyut discovers that his arrival had been awaited for centuries. Among other loved ones like Purohit ji, Balvanta – the war General of the matth, and Govardhan - the clan's physician, Vidyut also meets his childhood friend Naina. Naina has grown up to be an indescribably beautiful young woman, and Vidyut feels an inexplicable, magnetic attraction towards her.

The great matthadheesh Dwarka Shastri reveals to Vidyut that their bloodline was the bearer of a primordial curse. And that Vidyut was the last devta, the prophesied saviour – not just of his own bloodline, of the matth or of Banaras – but of all of humankind. Just as Vidyut sets foot in Banaras, a mysterious man called Reg Mariani has a meeting in Paris with someone who is known not by his name but by his title – the Maschera Bianca. Reg hands over a note from his own superior, the Big Man, to the Maschera. The note has five words inscribed on it – *'Kill that bloody Aryan boy!'* The Maschera Bianca or the White Mask is Europe's most dread-ed crime-lord. An innocent looking yet masterful assassin named Romi Pereira arrives in Banaras.

The great Dwarka Shastri narrates the haunting story of Harappa to Vidyut, along with how a dark conspiracy hid the truth of the metropolis forever from Indians. He elucidates how the East India Company blew up the most precious remains of the lost civilization and deprived the sub-continent of its true, ancient glory. But most unexpectedly, the matthadheesh reveals to Vidyut that he is none other than the great Vivasvan Pujari – reincarnated 3,700 years later... to fulfill his ultimate destiny.

Events unfold rapidly including a daring but failed attempt on Vidyut's life, a magical moment where Naina presses her lips on those of a smitten Vidyut, the bubbly arrival of Damini at the matth, and an open invitation to the last devta by Romi - for a final confrontation on the Dashashwamedh ghaat. Ridden with suspicion directed at Naina, Vidyut unleashes himself on the mercenaries sent for him by the same veiled overlords who had hired Romi. Vidyut vanquishes the mercenaries singlehandedly, but not before getting shot at by his most trusted friend – Bala. Bala is captured, and the devta then goes after Romi across the dark ghaats of nighttime Banaras. The sophisticated assassin is held captive by Vidyut and bites into potassium cyanide – in his dying moments informing Vidyut that a force called the New World Order was coming for him...and for all of mankind.

DASHAVATARA

Dashavatara (daśāvatāra) refers to the ten divine avatars of Lord Vishnu, the God of preservation. According to Hindu mythology, Lord Vishnu descends upon this Earth time and again in the form of an omnipotent avatar, to restore cosmic order and establish the dominance of good over evil.

Matsya
(The Mighty Fish that salvaged all Creation)

Kurma
(The Turtle that helped churn the oceans for the nectar of immortality)

Varaha
(The Wild Boar that saved the Earth from drowning)

Narsimha

(The Half-human, Half-beast that slew an invincible demon)

Vamana
(The Dwarf who reclaimed two worlds)

Parashurama
(The Immortal Sage – the slayer of tyrants)

Rama
(The Prince of Ayodhya, the ideal man)

Krishna
(Warrior, lover, musician, statesman, creator, preserver & destroyer)

Buddha
(The Enlightened One)

Kalki
(The final avatar, the bearer of the blazing sword, the awaited…

the dreaded…)

PROLOGUE

'They are all going to die…' mumbled Manu to himself. 'And I will die with them.'

These desperate souls, these young men and women, the infants, the old and the destitute, this entire collective that I promised to protect forever, will be crushed like ants.

Manu now realized the ghastly reality of his daring enterprise fully for the first time. Till this horrifying moment of truth, he had been way too immersed in carrying out the bizarre yet fateful commandment of the mystical Master of the *ocean-tribe*.

The fiery young leader of this nearly deranged, ragtag architectural force froze as he saw the gigantic vessel tilt beyond the endurance of the twenty thousand jute chords and tree-vines holding it aloft. The violent, monstrous waves of the river-sea were pounding on the biggest ship mankind had ever built. And the vicious flood was going to sink it.

Does this murderous deluge know what irreplaceable cargo this last boat carries?

That the final, universally destructive flood was incoming was not hard to tell. The dark, reddish-purple clouds, that appeared like some insane celestial painter had dyed the skies with the color of stale blood, enveloped all of known Earth. The maddening roar of *Indra's* thunder and the unnatural tempest of violently lashing rain had now announced the apocalypse, the final end. Droplets the size of tiger fangs were falling from the skies, transforming into a piercing shower of agonizing water-arrows as they struck Manu and his devoted followers. Every drop hitting the skin of the *Manu-Shishyas* or *Manushyas* was like an invisible spear penetrating through. What this militia of valiant men and women was trying to tug at and balance on the furious waters was not a regular boat anyway.

It was the *last* boat. Not the last boat from a harbour. Not the last boat of a fleet. Not the last vessel to leave a port for the season or a sailor rowing away for the night.

It was the last boat for creation itself. It was the *nauka* (boat) where *Prithvi* (Mother Earth) herself was going to take refuge. Along with the seeds of all her flock.

It was the great warrior, priest, ascetic, philosopher and king

Manu's ultimate deliverance.

It was his ark.

Manu's Ark.

The fearless struggle of over one hundred thousand men and women against a vessel, the expanse of which even the Gods could not imagine, was a spectacle that had never been seen before on the planet. And would never be seen after, even till the end of time. Manu's gigantic ark was the size of a glorious city. But its purpose was the noblest that mankind could ever fathom.

It was a doorway. The only bridge of continuity. From a decaying ancient world…to the new dawn of resurrection. It embodied a fierce contest between Armageddon at the behest of nature and the survival instinct of man. Humanity was not going to perish without a fight – a fight that even the heavens would remember. But despite this heroic endeavor, a lot was going to be lost. Eons of precious and irreplaceable wisdom acquired by the human race was not going to pass through this portal of sorts between different universes, even though it was all going to unfold on the same planet. Ancient alchemy, medicine, aviation, occult sciences, architecture, weaponry and spirituality were all going to disappear forever, drowning in the aftermath of the great deluge, to the bottom of the mighty oceans in spate.

And yet the Ark was the last ray of hope for life, as *Aryavarta* knew it. Much as Man is dumbfounded by God's profound conceptions like the stars, the galaxies and the constellations being the symbols of His divine workmanship, the greatest of the Lord's creations is undoubtedly *life*. Magnificent, resilient...life. Beings that feel pain, give birth, weep tears and love boundlessly. Beings that mirror the image of the Gods themselves. And it was *this* creation that needed to be saved.

Above all.

·||ॐ||·

The thick, twisted, drenched ropes and vines were now cutting into the arms, necks and flesh of Manu's militia. The tearing force exerted by the ropes, harnessing the toppling boat as big as a floating city, was breaking their fingers, dislocating their shoulders and ripping into their forearms and biceps. Men, women and children fought on alike against the formidable onslaught of the unimaginable weight of their adversary. They were all made of destructible blood and bones, whereas the *Nauka* was made of heavy wood, reinforced copper and rock-stone – so enormous that the people pulling the ropes in the water could not even get a glimpse of the mast of this massive vessel, even if they looked straight up at the grotesque skies.

The *Nauka* was taller than Mount Sumeru and wider than the gory field that had hosted the *Dasarajna* or the decisive ancient Battle of the Ten Kings.

Manu was getting increasingly desperate. He pulled out the crooked seashell blow-horn that had been given to him as signaling gear, only to be used when caught in the midst of the worst calamity. And that time had come. Nothing could be darker than the imminent and painful demise of his devoted people. Manu wiped his face with his leather wristguard, took a deep breath and blew into the horn, which shrieked out in its horrendous and maddening call, nearly splitting open the stormy skies.

Standing atop a lone and eerie cliff that looked black as coal against the bleeding red sky, Manu covered his eyes against the whipping rain with his open palms, looking far into the misty horizon. He saw nothing. With every passing moment his despair was growing. He tried hard to hold back his tears of defeat, and once again blew into the twisted horn with all his might. The scream of the blow-horn was like the cry of an angry dragon, and the tens of thousands of Manu's subjects felt needles piercing through their eardrums.

Manu squinted his eyes to ward off the vicious sky-arrows and tried to look far beyond the mountainous waves. He hoped to see the faint silhouette of the One he believed was the true savior.

He saw nothing.

'MA...AATTSYA!' yelled Manu, now darting feverishly on the edge of the protruding cliff that was his observation post as well as control station for the gargantuan undertaking he was overseeing. His tired, afraid and hopeful eyes kept gazing at the far horizon of the devastating deluge. Raindrops lashed on his handsome yet battle-torn face. He was probably crying at the horror he could see envelope his ambitious enterprise. A sinking realization was making it impossible for him to continue battling this unnatural typhoon.

Had the only person he had ever trusted, aside from his own beloved father - the great Vivasvan Pujari, betrayed him? Had his friend, mentor, counsel, healer …betrayed him?

Had his beloved Matsya betrayed him?

'MAAATTTTSSSYAAAA…ARRGHH!' screamed Manu, looking up at the punishing firmament, his arms outstretched and his lungs ready to explode, as if he wanted the heavens to hear his desperate plea!

And then he saw it. In the endgame flood, riding the oceans' merciless surfs, he saw it.

Lok-naas, the biggest sea-monster that even the mighty creator *Brahma* could have envisaged, raised what looked like its enormous head in the distant waves. It was the first time Manu was witness to the faint outline of the fabled giant-beast.

And there he was, standing fearlessly between the hydra's gleaming eyes.

Matsya.

Somewhere near Rome, 2017

'DO YOU BELIEVE IT IS REALLY *HIM*?'

He was late for his only superior's customary public appearance. The Big Man from somewhere near Rome was uncharacteristically agitated this morning. The phone call he had received in the wee hours had left his nerves jangled. His hands shook as he raised the teacup to his holy lips.

Revered by millions as one of the highest priests on Earth, he was the guardian of the known world's greatest wealth and treasures. He was the spiritual God-man to the planet's most powerful men and women. He was someone who decided the fate of not just individuals or communities, but of entire continents. A text message from him could activate a nuclear payload or end the bloodiest, decades-old civil war.

The Big Man was not an ordinary man by far. He was one among the many lovingly disguised yet sparkling symbols of absolute power, unquestioned monarchy, superiority and global control. Yet a 34-year old lad from half the world away, had made this remarkable man nervous.

Really nervous.

This cold anxiety was not something the Big Man was accustomed to. He glared angrily at the junior priest who came in to politely remind the Big Man of his routine duty to his superior, who had already stepped out to greet the thousands of people gathered below the balcony of the palace of ultimate dominance. The Big Man needed to smoke some tobacco to calm his rattled soul.

After more than 1,600 years of ancient and haunting prophecies, the pious *devvtuh*, as the Big Man pronounced it, seemed to have finally arrived. And this was horribly bad news for everything the Big Man's golden palace stood for.

I must call Reg.

⚖️

'Good morning, your Holiness,' said the sophisticated Italian voice from the other side. 'You did not have to call me, Sir. I am on my way to you anyway.' Reg Mariani was sweating under his collar.

Very few people knew the Big Man as closely as Reg did. Which is why he knew he was speaking to the world's most powerful and most dangerous religious leader.

'Is your job done, Reg?' asked the Big Man calmly.

'No…no, your Holiness, it is not.'

'Then what purpose would your visit serve, my son?'

There was a momentary pause.

'As you say, Sir,' replied Reg, after clearing his tar-ravaged throat. For now, he was *persona non grata* at the palace of dominance.

'Present yourself for my blessings only once you have delivered on the critical task you have been entrusted with, Reg.'

'Yes, your Holiness.'

The Big Man now spoke in a tone that Reg was both familiar with and petrified of. He had often witnessed cruel and violent consequences of instructions passed in that tranquil yet ruthless tone.

'Remind the *Maschera Bianca* for me, will you, Reg? Remind him that his very existence depends on the grace of my prayers for him.'

'I will, your Holiness.'

'Remind him that his evil deeds are overlooked by the Lord only because he promises to serve a larger purpose. If he fails that divine objective, the world has no place for him.'

Reg froze. Only the Big Man could send such a cold-blooded threat to Europe's most feared Mafioso.

Reg was relieved as he heard the click of the phone line

being disconnected. He had seen the brutal outcome that several of the supposedly powerful men had suffered when they had failed the Big Man. Even though he had spent years in the service of His Holiness, Reg felt no safer than he did on the first day.

Even before he could heave a slight sigh of relief, his mobile phone rang again. To Reg's deep duress, it was the Big Man again. But this time he was not his cold, calculated self. He sounded uncertain, shaken.

'Tell me Reg, do you think it is really *him?* Do you think this boy is really the *devvtuh* of the prophecies?'

There were a few moments of silence again. Reg knew better than to mince words with the Big Man.

'Yes, your Holiness. I believe it is he.'

Reg paused, before emphasizing the truth he knew the Big Man dreaded hearing.

'The *devta* has returned.'

HARAPPA, 1700 BCE

RAIN OF BLOOD

Two hundred of the Harappan army's elite mounted troops rode at a fierce speed. Fifty of the piked cavalry galloped as advance guard. Fifty swordsmen rode as rearguard and a hundred archers on horseback pounded on either side. In their center tumbled and raced along the heavy, wheeled cage, pulled by sixteen thoroughbred horses. Made of solid stalks of the hardest wood and thick copper bars, this impregnable cage was custom-built to hold in captivity a pride of lions. Only this time the prisoner was not one of the big cats. In his current manifestation, the prized captive was something far more savage.

The crazed cavalry was a fearsome sight. These Harappan warriors were now on the brink of complete insanity and uncontrollable blood-thirst. Their eyes were red and wid-

17

ened, nearly unblinking. Their mouths salivated froth like rabid wolves. They all grunted like beasts as they rode, their collective growl adding to the viciousness of the clouds of red dust rising from the hooves of their violent charge.

Armed to the teeth, each Harappan rider had a bone-cutting heavy sword strapped to his waist. The massive spears the advance guards swung in circles above their heads as they rode, could tear into the thick hide of even the one-horned rhino from the Far East. The archers' arrows were dipped in the blue poison of Harappa's war-alchemists. This was a select platoon of the finest Harappan soldiers, handpicked by the new queen. She could take no chances with the powerful prisoner bound for the *mrit-kaaraavaas* (dungeons of the dead). For one last time. Once there, he would never return alive.

But Priyamvada was under the same predestined trance of madness that curses the fate of most ambitious monarchs. When even the Gods had never succeeded in holding *Surya*, the Sun, captive, how could she?

·‖ॐ‖·

His head flew from his body and landed many paces away in the red dirt. The arrow came from nowhere, shot with extraordinary precision. The torso of the leader of the advance guard swung and galloped headless next to his comrades, his severed neck spouting blood like a small fountain.

Within moments another head was decapitated. And then another. And another. The confused and panicked soldiers started to break ranks, their eyes searching wildly for the invisible attacker. A master archer had decided to pounce on this armed caravan like a cat in a henhouse.

Despite being among the finest warriors of the Harappan military, none of these demented fighters stood a chance in front of the Pujari family's very own slayer of demons.

Their very own protégé. Manu's closest friend and his greatest military commander.

The beautiful. The valiant.

Tara.

Much as they were intoxicated with the dark venom that the sinister wizards Gun, Sha and Ap had mixed in the water sources of Harappa, the cavalry of the metropolis was not one to be undermined by a lone archer without a fight, no matter how skillful he, or in this case, she may be. A trained and ferocious combat outfit, the hundred mounted archers spotted the direction from which the hidden assassin was assaulting their troops. Without breaking their gallop, these expert bowmen stood up in their stirrups and unleashed a shower of arrows in the direction of the attacker. Tara had no choice but to take refuge behind a boulder.

But the attack had begun. The daring rescue of the great devta, Vivasvan Pujari, had begun.

'Like we planned, our first objective is to unchain the devta,' Somdutt reminded his handful of combatants, moments before they were to launch themselves into the heat of the clash. 'Once he is free, not one of these beastly soldiers will survive. The devta will vanquish them all singlehandedly.'

'But my Lord, pardon my audacity…the devta looks nothing more than a flayed lump of meat!' exclaimed one of the young fighters.

They could see beyond the copper bars of the massive crate on wooden wheels. The devta lay lifeless on the floor of the cage, his body tossing and bouncing with every bump on the road. There was no skin left on his once glowing body. The wooden walls of his confinement were smeared with his blood. He *was* a lump of raw flesh.

'Believe me, my brave friends. I have seen the mighty Vivasvan Pujari in the face of worse odds,' responded Somdutt. 'While I agree his present state is perhaps beyond human endurance or imagination, I continue to repose my faith in his unfathomable power. He cannot be defeated unless he chooses to be. He cannot be killed till he decides so himself. He cannot be beaten in battle, unless it is by an adversary he loves.'

His bunch of followers was listening. He knew he did not have much time. And Somdutt was aware that they only had a short window of opportunity on these red planes to deliver their sworn mission.

'All I ask from you, the bravest of warriors in all of Harappa, is that you unlock the massive cage that holds the devta.

Cut open his stifling chains. And the savior will rise. He will liberate all of us. And all of cursed Harappa.'

The Harappan soldiers were now scattered all around the heavy cart carrying Vivasvan Pujari. Tactically placed archers of Tara's combat unit had joined her and they were together wreaking havoc on the Harappan riders. Within moments of Tara's initial attack, over two dozen of the deranged cavalry had been annihilated - heads tossed off or chests torn open by merciless arrows. Their bestial rage was on the rise. Though their effectiveness had been radically diminished.

Losing all sense of direction and purpose, baffled by the invisible enemy and the rain of warm human and horse blood all around them, the mad riders began to collide into one another. One of the horseman lost balance, got entangled in the other's stirrup and flung off his horse like a pebble shot from a catapult. Only to be trampled to a mash of flesh and bone by the riders behind him. One angry soldier lost whatever little sanity he had left and stabbed his spear into the neck of a fellow rider that had come dangerously close. The extraordinary marksmen had achieved their mandated goal. There was fear and chaos in the Harappan ranks.

And a large part of the seemingly invincible cavalry, was trying to flee.

Knowing well that this was their only chance, the fifteen warriors from Somdutt's small platoon charged their mounts into the heart of the Harappan troops, like a pack of wolves among sheep. Swinging their swords, slashing and beheading at will, Somdutt's young fighters were battling their way to the cage that held their beloved devta.

Tara's archers had now left their positions and were riding into the wet crimson field to assist their comrades.

But this was not going to be easy. Amidst the bold and so far one-sided rescue raid, one of the senior Harappan commanders began rallying back his troops. A giant of a man with his face painted red and black, his shining eyes reflected both his lunacy as well as his cruelty.

'Fight baaaaack…!' he yelled out to his disarrayed troops in a hoarse and bloodcurdling command, swinging his massive spear wildly from its handle-end, making it impossible for any attacker to approach him from even a distance. 'Fight back, you cowards…!' He was charging towards the wheeled cage. Several of his fierce soldiers turned their horses and began following their commander with renewed lust for killing.

For now, this was anybody's fight.

Somdutt spotted this formidable and demented adversary from a distance. Two of his young fighters were now very close to the cage, and moments away from freeing the fallen devta. But the gigantic Harappan commander was now galloping towards the center, and Somdutt knew his brave fighters would not be able to resist this veteran beast and his trained troopers. He was too far to intervene himself. He turned to his best bet.

'Taraaaaa…!' screamed Somdutt.

Tara dodged a spear by falling back on her saddle and in the same motion stabbed the gut of an attacker with the dagger she held in her left hand. Her right hand wielded a battle-axe. Tara was ambidextrous and could fight equally well with either of her arms. She turned to Somdutt and even in the middle of what appeared to be a red cloud that had descended on the battlefield, she followed his eyes. Tara realized instantly what the erstwhile Chief Architect of Harappa was drawing her attention to. The monstrous commander and his men had to be stopped!

Tara took the shortest route to intercept the mad commander, even though she had to tear through a thicket of enemies, blood and gore. An ace rider and an accomplished pupil of the great Vivasvan Pujari himself, the golden Tara was a warcraft magician. She weaved her way through enemy soldiers like a shark through water.

'Eeeyyyaaaaaahh…' Tara screamed as she first stood on her horse's saddle and then pounced on the giant Harappan commander. For a few moments Tara appeared to be flying in the air, her long-axe ready to plunge at the throat of her target, her beautiful, blood-washed hair flowing behind her supple body.

But this enemy was stronger and more skilled than the rest

of them. The giant commander sprung up on his horse and greeted Tara with his muscular leg ramming into her diaphragm. Tara was deflected mid-air, and she crashed to the ground, breathless and stunned.

The monster with his face colored red and black in battle-paint was quivering with anger. The reek of blood in the air and the screams of disemboweled, dying men was making him delirious with animal brutality. He threw away his headgear, tore down his own armor to display his astounding, brawny frame. He was truly a fiend. He slapped his own face violently, growled like a goblin and drew out a spiked mace-on-a-chain. He swung it violently to pop open Tara's head.

The spiked mace landed an inch from Tara's temple, as she rolled over on the red mud to avoid the strike. The spikes dug into the soil soaked in blood, and took a moment to get pulled free again. This was enough time for the Tigress to counter attack. She pulled out two shining needles from her hair with her arms across her face. Both of the killer needles were dipped in lethal poison. She charged towards the monster like a slippery serpent, but his powerful arm shot out and grabbed Tara by her throat. His arm was so long and strapped with such thick copper armor, that Tara could not reach any part of his flesh despite her frenzied and valiant efforts. His grip was tightening and Tara felt her life being sucked out.

Till something happened that she had never even imagined.

The monster's mouth opened wide in a suffocating gasp of extreme suffering. To her disbelief, Tara saw a bloodied human claw and then an entire human forearm emerge from the gut of the giant commander right under her eyes. Someone had clawed through the mad monster's entire girth with his bare hands, ripping him open.

As the agonized monster's dying grip on Tara's throat loosened, she got a glimpse of the creature that had performed this ghastly killing. Half the length of his arm was buried into the gut of the now already dead Harappan commander. It was the most inhuman killing Tara or anyone on that battlefield had ever witnessed.

A man drenched in blood, skinned beyond recognition, with one eye melted and the other eye shining like that of a primordial *Brahma-Raakshasa*, stood behind the corpse of the commander. It took Tara a few moments before she realized whom that was.

Her eyes darted to look at the wheeled-cage.

Its thick door was creaking heavily, wide open. Its massive locks were shattered to pieces.

Vivasvan Pujari was not a devta anymore. He appeared to be more evil, more ghoulish than even the darkest *raakshasa* described in the ancient scriptures.

Despite trembling with fear at the grotesque gutting of his commander, one of the slain giant's men attacked Vivasvan with his machete. With the ease of a master warrior, Vivasvan dodged the attack, grabbed the wrist of the attacker and rammed his elbow into his face, splitting it open instantly. The Harappan soldier crumbled to the ground. But the slaughter was not over. Vivasvan Pujari slowly pressed his knee down on the fallen soldier's back, picked up his machete and like a skilled surgeon sliced the man's forehead from temple to temple. The pinned man screamed in pain as blood poured down on his face from the deep gash on his brow. And then, to everyone's shock and disbelief, Vivasvan Pujari grabbed the soldier's hair and tore out his scalp right up to the back of his shoulders. The soldier writhed with unbearable agony before succumbing - not to the injury but to the extreme pain he was systematically subjected to.

Within a moment Tara found herself regretting what they had just done. She exchanged a quick glance with Somdutt, and they both seemed to be thinking alike.

He, who should not have been freed, had been freed.

The Sun had set on Harappa forever.

Banaras, 2017

MRITYUNJAYA

The white Mahindra SUV of the *Dev-Raakshasa Matth* heaved and sped viciously through the packed streets of nighttime Banaras. None other than Balvanta, the warrior-chief of the matth, was at the wheel himself. He knew the clock was ticking.

The lanes and roadside shops were bustling with activity even at this hour, packed such as to not allow so much as a bicycle to find its way comfortably. That was Banaras in its usual, lazy sprawl. But the city and its inhabitants found no difficulty in paving the way for this jeep turned ambulance. While no one knew who was inside this swerving and dashing vehicle, it seemed as if everyone did.

It was Vidyut.

·‖卐‖·

His head nestled in the lap of a nervously panting Naina, Vidyut coughed and sputtered blood every now and then. After two bullet injuries, a savage gash that tore open the flesh across his chest and hours of intense battle, the wounds were too grievously threatening even for this phenomenon of a man.

Vidyut, the prophesied protector, the last devta…*was dying.*

·‖卐‖·

'Drive faster…!' yelled Naina, as she saw Vidyut's breathing turn uneven. Till they found him on the *ghaat*, no one at the matth was aware of the bullet wound Vidyut had suffered at the hands of the assassin, Romi. The matth physician Govardhan had stayed behind to tend to the injured Sonu and other fighters of the monastery. That was a big mistake. Vidyut was now gasping for every wisp of air, clearly struggling to stay alive. Naina snuggled his head into her arms and was looking at him with the tears and the passionate intensity of a woman completely in love. She could not lose him. *Not again.*

'We are losing him,' muttered one of the matth warriors accompanying Balvanta and Naina in the jeep.

'No, we are not!' snapped back an angry and desperate Naina. 'He is Vidyut! Don't you remember? He cannot die!'

Everyone in the vehicle knew Naina was wrong. Vidyut was

breathing his last.

Naina whipped out her mobile phone and dialed Govardhan, the miraculous healer of the Dev-Raakshasa matth.

'Govardhan dada, we are still a few minutes away from the matth. But Vidyut doesn't seem to have that much time. He is going, dada…he is going to go…!' Naina was now crying unstoppably as she managed to utter those words into the phone.

'You have to bring him to me, Naina. Stay calm and try to get him here as fast as you can,' replied Govardhan in a quiet yet tense tone. He knew what was at stake.

'But he won't last, dada!' screamed Naina into the phone. She was nearly hysterical with anguish.

Govardhan remained composed.

'Tell me what he is like, Naina.'

Balvanta turned for a moment towards Naina, as the jeep slowed down in the middle of a bustling crowd.

'We all love him as much as you do, Naina. We all know what Vidyut is prophesied to do. Not just for the matth, not just for Banaras…but for the whole of mankind.'

Naina was listening. *No one can love Vidyut as much as I do.*

Balvanta continued, 'Just listen to what Govardhan is saying, and do your best, my dear.'

The beautiful and brave Naina nodded. She knew she couldn't lose hope. Not at this time.

Govardhan repeated his question, 'Tell me what his symptoms are, Naina.'

Naina wiped her tears and observed Vidyut carefully.

'Dada, he is gasping for air and his entire body is burning with high fever.'

'Keep sprinkling water on his forehead, Naina,' replied Govardhan. 'Give him another injection of Tranexamic Acid just the way I told you. Do not let him sink into complete unconsciousness. Keep talking to him, no matter what. What else…?'

'His lips are dry and he is…'

There was silence for a moment.

'Yes Naina, what? Go on…' urged Govardhan.

'He…he is mumbling something, Govardhan dada,' replied Naina after a few nervous seconds.

'Mumbling what? You must listen to what he is saying!'

Naina leaned forward and put her ear against Vidyut's flickering lips. She could not make out what he was saying.

'I…I can't understand anything…' she exclaimed, making sure that both Govardhan and the passengers in the jeep heard her clearly.

'What is he saying, Naina?' enquired a visibly panicking Balvanta. They were now just about five minutes away from the matth. But it seemed like forever.

Naina bent down and strained her ears. She could finally catch a couple of words that Vidyut was uttering.

'...*trayambakam...pushtivardhanam...maamritaat*...'

After a few seconds of confusion, she looked up at Balvanta. She had disbelief written all over her face. *How could someone in such deep trauma and a semi-conscious state have the faculty for this?*

'Naina, you have to tell us...what is Vidyut mumbling in this state?' enquired Govardhan.

It took her a moment or two before she could speak.

'Dada...' said Naina.

Balvanta, Govardhan on the phone, and the warrior from the matth, were all listening with utmost attention.

'Govardhan dada...you are not going to believe this,' continued Naina. 'Vidyut is repeatedly chanting the all-powerful *Maha Mrityunjaya mantra.*'

Everyone froze. How could someone on his deathbed have the streak of consciousness left for something as powerful as this?

The *Maha Mrityunjaya* intonation was believed to be the ultimate protector against death. It was the Almighty *Shiva*'s invocation against *Yama* or the God of Mortality.

Even moments away from death, the devta was fighting. On the narrow streets of this ancient city, standing on the bridge between this world and the next, Vidyut was invoking the Lord of Kashi Himself. He was calling Shiva for help.

Vidyut was determined not to die.

Not today.

East of Harappa, 1700 BCE

'THESE DROPS OF WATER... I OWE YOU'

The vultures cawed and circled their prey persistently. They could sense a feast coming their way.

It had been twenty-eight hours since the badly wounded young man had been riding, without food and little water. His deep injuries were festering. He was on the verge of passing out because of the uncontrolled blood loss. His mouth was dry and his lips were parched. He should not have lasted this long.

But something was keeping him alive.

Manu was not going to die without offering the last rites to his dead mother he had been carrying on the lap all this while.

Manu owed this to his beloved mother. He owed it to Sanjna.

'Ride east…look for the Black Temple…'

Those were the last words Manu had heard from his father's loyal friend, Somdutt. He had been riding eastwards, all day, all night. But he could not risk stopping at villages or huts. He could not ask anyone for help or for directions. He knew that Priyamvada, the new queen of Harappa, would have unleashed a massive manhunt for him.

But now the journey was becoming hopeless. Manu knew neither he nor his beast could trudge on much longer. His beautiful mother's body was also showing signs of its mortal, natural vulnerability. *'Ride east…'* was too vague an advice. Yet Manu was sure that the wise Somdutt would not offer him a suggestion without a clear motive. But nothing had presented itself so far. No Black Temple. No help. No hope.

Manu was now a pitiable spectacle covered with blood and dust. He pulled out his leather flask. The last few drops of water were left, enough only to wet his lips one last time. These counted drops might give him a few more hours of survival, he hoped.

The vultures would have to wait.

The land was arid till wherever the eyes could see. Manu was the lone rider for several miles around. Warm, dusty winds blew across the plains constantly. Manu wet his fingertips and rubbed them gently on his mother's eyes, lips and forehead, with the same tender love with which a mother caresses her newborn. Just as he was about to upturn the near-empty flask into his thirsting mouth, Manu noticed something far out in the horizon. It looked like a tiny grey speck, but Manu felt he could see a human shape. Lying lifeless on the dry land.

The young warrior-ascetic nudged his tired horse and cantered towards the seemingly lifeless body far out. He had let his mother down a day ago on the battleground at the outskirts of Harappa. He was never going to let anyone else down again.

Manu was convinced that he was hallucinating due to his rotting wounds and the dehydration. As he rode closer to the figure, he rubbed his eyes. What he was seeing looked less like a man and more like the scales of a big fish! As far as Manu had seen during his grueling gallop over the last nearly thirty hours, there was no water body anywhere close by. How could a giant fish get swept so far inland?

But as Manu drew nearer to the fish, he was startled. It was indeed a human, lying unconscious. Dressed in strange attire that made him resemble a fish, his body was wrapped in a cloak made from dried fish scale. The unfamiliar jewelry he wore was all made of seashells and fishbone. And let alone his clothing and trinkets, even from a few paces away, he smelled of the sea!

·||ॐ||·

The fish-man was slumped facedown on the ground. He looked lifeless. Manu noticed his skin had a bluish tinge. It either meant that he was poisoned. Or that he was dead for a long time.

Manu's immediate urge was to ride on. He had enough to worry about already. He anyway carried one precious body that needed to be cremated. In a matter of a few hours, he was probably going to be the second *body* himself. He could not take the burden of a third one.

But then, he was Manu. Son of the great Vivasvan Pujari. He was not one to leave anyone behind, man or corpse, disrespectfully.

Even as Manu was weighing his options, the man in the fish-skin robes moved. He was alive! Manu dismounted immediately, after settling his mother gently on the saddle. He bent down and slowly turned the man over. As Manu caught the first glimpse of the unconscious man's dust ridden and sunburnt face, he could not take his eyes away. Even in this near dead state, it was the most exquisitely handsome face Manu had ever seen. There was something extraordinary about this man that Manu could not comprehend. Within moments, he sensed the pain of his deep wounds subsiding. A serene calm was seeping into him and he felt the familiar peace he had experienced when he had touched the feet of the *Saptarishi*. Only this was even more intense. Even more divine.

Manu was still dazed, but he knew he had to do something

quickly if he wanted to save this man. There were no signs of any wounds on this fish-man's bluish skin. He was clearly dehydrated. Manu used a few drops from his water flask to moisten one corner of his robe. He then dabbed the wet cloth on the man's cracked lips.

'Water…' muttered the fish-man as he regained a bit of consciousness.

'Please…water…!' he repeated, before Manu could respond.

Now Manu was faced with a choice. He could drink the last few drops left in his flask and live for a few more hours. Hopefully even find the elusive Black Temple. Or he could offer the water to this dying man and save him. But that would mean certain death for himself.

Without a moment's hesitation, the son of Sanjna and Vivasvan Pujari lifted the man's head and poured the last few drops of water into the fish-man's mouth.

·‖ॐ‖·

The bluish man touched Sanjna's forehead and stroked it like a loving father.

Manu stood next to his horse stupefied. As this fish-man had opened his eyes and smiled, Manu's whole life had flashed in front of him. His childhood laughter with his doting father, his playful memories with his loving mother, his cherished moments with Tara, his battle with the scoundrel Ranga… everything. And more. He seemed to be reliving flashes from times and places that he did not even recognize. They were probably sights from his lives before this one. Manu felt all his pain, thirst, hunger, angst...all simply vanish just as this blue skinned man cast his eyes upon Manu's face.

Who is he?

The fish-man had been unexpectedly rejuvenated with just the very little water he had consumed. Without saying a word, he had got up and walked towards Sanjna's body. He looked at her with so much love that Manu broke into heavy sobs that he had been holding back for hours. The man touched Sanjna's forehead tenderly and stroked it a few times. Manu could not say whether he was daydreaming or it was all really happening, but with every stroke Manu saw his mother's slowly decomposing body return to what it had been like at the time of her death. The gentle smile on her face was back, her skin glowed again and she emanated the soft fragrance that Manu recognized as his mother's.

'She is now ready for her last ceremony,' said the fish-man in a deep, loving voice, as he turned to look at Manu.

Manu was overwhelmed. He was now certain that this was not an ordinary man. With one glance he had healed Manu, physically and spiritually. With a few strokes of his palm, he had reversed the decay of his beloved mother's mortal body. Or at least that was what Manu felt and saw. Whether these were real occurrences or the delirium of a tired and dehydrated young man, who could say?

'Who are you?' Manu asked the fish-man whose long, beautiful brown hair accentuated his godly appearance.

The man grinned. Almost instantly Manu felt the raging hot winds transform into a cool breeze. The burning fields around him were now overcast with pleasant clouds. Before Manu could react to this sudden change in the weather, he felt the patter of tiny raindrops on his face.

He knew it was the bluish man who was doing all this. Manu turned to him, only to see the man walking away into the cloudy dawn.

'Who are you, O mystical one?' Manu shouted out to the man.

The man in the fish robes turned and laughed at Manu, without stopping his walk.

'Remember, O great devta, you must reach the Black Temple. Ride towards the rising Sun and you will find it,' said the man in his soothing voice.

How does he know about the Black Temple? I never told him anything.

'But who are you, *Arya*?'

'Don't call me 'Arya', O king. I am indebted to you. These drops of water…I owe you. From now till the end of time, I am your friend. And I have a name.'

'And what would that name be, my dear friend?' shouted Manu louder, as the man kept going further away.

The blue man turned briefly, smiled at Manu and shouted back with a short wave of his hand.

'You can call me what everyone in this land calls me.

You can call me Matsya.'

Banaras, 2017

BATTLE OF THE EXORCISTS

Damini had dosed off on the chair next to Vidyut's bed.

Vidyut had been brought into the matth in a comatose state two nights back. Govardhan had not spared any effort, working tirelessly to pull his devta out of danger. He had even called in Dr. Shashi Dikshit, a renowned surgeon and a friend of the matth. It was a powerful concoction of Ayurveda, modern medicine, loving prayers and potent *yajnas* that had kept the devta alive.

It was the hushed exchange of words between Dr. Dikshit and the great Dwarka Shastri that woke her up.

'Dwarka Shastri ji, this is a big relief. Vidyut will survive this brutal onslaught,' said Dr. Dikshit. 'In fact…in fact…I am a bit dumbfounded.'

Damini shut her beautiful eyes in a prayer of gratitude. Her Vidyut was not going to leave her.

'What is bothering you, doctor *saahab*?' enquired Dwarka Shastri. He probably knew what the doctor had in mind. But as always, he played along.

'*Guruji*, Vidyut's recovery is abnormal. In my twenty-five years as a surgeon, I have never seen anyone heal so rapidly.'

Dwarka Shastri was listening, with a faint, almost unnoticeable smile on his face.

'His tissues are healing at remarkable speed. His response to both herbal and allopathic medicine is astonishing. While I can see he is an exceptionally fit man, his body is fighting back with vigor like I have never witnessed before. It is like he is superhuman!'

'He is,' replied Dwarka Shastri simply.

The grandmaster folded his hands in gratitude to the doctor and left. Leaving the surgeon gasping for a more palatable explanation.

'He is,' whispered Damini happily under her breath.

'My Vidyut *is* superhuman.'

'Do you know how and why your great grandfather fell terribly ill, Vidyut?' asked Purohit ji, as he dutifully peeled an orange for his adored devta.

Purohit ji's son, Sonu, was also well on his way to recovery. He had not only found his health, but also his innocent sense of humor back. This allowed the revered Purohit ji to focus his attention back to the Shastri scion.

'No, Purohit ji,' replied Vidyut. 'I assumed it was old age catching up. May the Almighty grant him a much longer life, but he *is* over a hundred years now.'

Vidyut was recuperating rapidly. While still on the infirmary bed, he was fully conscious and back to his alert self.

'As soon as you are well enough Vidyut, you must spend more time with our grandmaster, the great Dwarka Shastri ji. You both have a lot to catch up on.'

'There is nothing more I want than to be with Baba, Purohit ji,' replied Vidyut. 'But he is a hard man, don't you agree? He speaks at his own pace. He reveals only as much as he wants to at a particular time. No one can rush him. At least not me!'

'You are the only one who can make him do as you please, Vidyut,' said Purohit ji with a tired smile. 'At least make him confess to the lethal battle of exorcism he fought to protect you.'

It took Vidyut a few seconds to grasp what he had just heard.

'Sorry…did you say battle of exorcism, Purohit ji?'

Purohit ji arranged the orange slices neatly on a plate.

'Yes, Vidyut. Your great grandfather did not fall prey to a natural disease or any age related illness,' stated Purohit ji matter-of-factly.

'He almost died combatting the world's most powerful black-magician.'

·||ॐ||·

'A very dangerous and accomplished occult practitioner from half the world away had unleashed two exceptionally powerful beings from the netherworld on you, while you were still in Gurgaon, Vidyut. These foul spirits would have killed you and pulled your soul into the dark realm had it not been for our great master. Dwarka Shastri ji saved you from this long-distance exorcist attack. He nearly gave up his life to protect you.'

Vidyut was as angry as he was stunned. He knew his great grandfather loved him dearly, no matter how detached the pompous old man attempted to show himself to be. But, until now, Vidyut was not aware that the grandmaster of the Dev-Raakshasa matth had fought a battle to the death - just to defend him.

'Who is doing all this, Purohit ji?' enquired an agitated Vidyut. 'Who is trying to kill me? Before I left for the Dashashwamedh ghaat that day, Baba mentioned something called the *New World Order*. What is that and why are they our adversaries?'

'The *why* you ask is a very complicated question, Vidyut. The answer to that only your great grandfather can and should give you. But I can tell you *who* was the fierce opponent in this vicious battle of exorcists.'

'Okay…?' Vidyut insisted that Purohit ji goes on.

Purohit ji looked into Vidyut's eyes and spoke flatly.

'Dwarka Shastri ji is one of the most consummate *taantrics* to have ever walked this planet. Imagine what it would take in a challenger to nearly vanquish him. This is not an ordinary soul. He is a spiritual overlord and is second only to our *matthadheesh* in skill and ethereal power.'

Vidyut was listening intently. Purohit ji continued.

'It was a fearsome night. Our *gurudev* Dwarka Shastri ji appeared to be perturbed right from the early evening as we witnessed violent winds sweeping through the matth. None of us could sense anything sinister but as the strength of the gusts increased, our matthadheesh suspected at once that it was not a natural occurrence. He confided in me that as per planetary positions, it was an exceptionally vulnerable time for you, Vidyut. Someone who had command over both western as well as eastern astrology had chosen the perfect hour to turn you into a living puppet.'

Purohit ji was now gaping into nothingness, recollecting that ominous night stroke by stroke.

'Gradually the colour of the moon turned a ghostly red as the menacing winds gave way to a blinding dust storm. Tens of thousands of birds of all kinds began cawing against the bleeding dark sky in a cackle so loud as if a hundred evil witches wept and guffawed at the same time. As the night grew darker, dogs began to howl like a pack of angry *bhad-maanas* (werewolves). And then, we heard it. Distant bells from the guardian temples surrounding the periphery of Banaras were all chiming at once. The mystical *sadhus* of all those ancient shrines were awakened to the threat, just as Dwarka Shastri ji was. They were tugging the chains of their temple-bells, raising the alarm to save their savior, even as they all beckoned their collective army of pious spirits. The blackest hour, for which the concentric spiritual construct of Banaras and the Dev-Raakshasa matth had been built, had arrived. It was now that the skies above the ancient city were set to become the arena for planet Earth's biggest battle of the exorcists.

Those abhorred and awaited for centuries, had finally come.'

Vidyut could feel a thin film of cold sweat all over him. But he did not want to interrupt Purohit ji with any sudden reactions. He kept his questions to himself for now and listened quietly.

'Within moments the great matthadheesh was heading towards his grand cottage, fervently chanting counter-attack *mantras* from the darkest recesses of the *Atharva Veda* and other ancient occult scriptures. He was probably summoning his own ethereal militia. The grandmaster's cottage housed his most powerful companions, and he was seeking their assistance in what he knew was the ultimate battle of his life. But he was late. Even before he could reach his spiritual fortress, a bolt of red lightning struck from the sky directly upon our grandmaster. It was like hellfire being spewed by the skies. For a moment we all stiffened, for we were sure we had just witnessed the end of our beloved leader. But, lo and behold…as the smoke cleared we were stunned to see the mighty Dwarka Shastri standing his ground firmly, his legs pillared like ramrods and his long white tresses flowing in the wind. His giant *trishul* (trident) glowed orange after bearing the brunt of the otherworldly attack.

The great battle had begun.'

Banks of the Indus,
West of Harappa, 1700 BCE

A-SURA

In the dark of the night, his horse galloped with the haste of a storm. Smeared from head to toe in a green paste of *tulsi*, *lohabaan* (myrrh) and other ayurvedic herbs, only his lone eye shone in the nocturnal blackness like those of a prehistoric wolf.

A massive scimitar hung from his waist-belt. His very own, very dreaded sword – the *Ratna-Maru*. His saddle was strapped with a hundred arrows and a powerful bow slung across his torso. His lost eye was covered with a leather flap, to shield the empty socket from the ever-increasing, violent winds that now swept across the vast plains incessantly.

Vivasvan Pujari was riding to the camp of his once sworn

enemy. He was riding to the demon-king, Sura.

·‖卐‖·

He could not believe his ears. The name his watch guard had taken, was one that Sura both admired and feared.

How could this be?

'Are you sure…? Are you sure this is the name of the visitor?' enquired Sura again.

The soldier was now nervous. One rule that everyone in this behemoth of an army knew was that the great Sura was not to be angered. Ever.

How a man of such diminutive stature could appear so indescribably domineering was something most people who met Sura could not understand. His skin was fair but he perpetually smeared it black in the ashes of his burnt enemies. Known never to even sleep without being fully armed, he drank his daily copious volumes of wine from the skull of a desert panther he had killed with his bare hands. Known to enjoy the company of beautiful women, particularly the wives of his fallen foes, he never took a woman by force. He waited till they fell for, or more likely pretended to fall for, his raw and irresistible charm. Those of them that didn't were fed to his pet wolves in public spectacle. That made him more irresistible to the next set of widows he claimed. He beheaded a massive beast every morning for meat meant for his savagely loyal soldiers. Not one of them ate breakfast unless it came from the sacrificial sword of their master. His court of law had a simple rule. Any criminal he condemned to the death penalty had a redress mechanism. He could battle the king himself to the death. But in case of losing, it would mean an execution so brutal that would disturb generations to come.

A man known for a gaze so piercing that it could tear deep into the heart of a human if he looked hard enough, Sura was a God to his people.

He was a demon for everyone to the East of his dominions.

·‖卐‖·

This legendary demon-king began his life as the son of a cobbler in the great city of Mohenjo-daro. After summarily slicing off the leg of a nobleman who had kicked his father in the face for a faulty shoe-stitch, Sura had left the city with a band of seven loyal friends. He had thought the matter would end with his departure. When the news of his parents being sent to the dreaded mrit-kaaraavaas reached his ears, Sura knew they would never return alive. And he was too weak then to rescue them from this gruesome fate.

He swore vengeance. Not just against the city that wronged him and his parents, but against all of *Aryavarta*. Sura took a vow that he would decimate the prevailing order for good. His seven followers joined him. As months and years passed, Sura rose from being a highway bandit to a dreaded warlord of the hills. His band grew into a militia and then slowly into a tribe. His army came to be known as the most cruel and invincible across the known world. And unlike the glowing

Harappan way of life, Sura's army was a savage force. The only reason they took male prisoners was to burn one of them alive every day, to anoint themselves with the ashes of the fallen foe as a daily ritual. King of every speck of dust across the entire Hindu Kush ranges, Sura was a living legend.

To put a seal of opposition to the very way-of-life of Aryavarta, Sura made his massive tribe take an oath that they would never speak a name from Aryavarta in its true form. Their hatred would be embodied in every word they spoke. They would speak the un-language, the *a-bhasha*. They would call the ultimate form of enlightenment and the Creator *Brahma*, A-brahma. Even though they worshipped Him as the supreme God just as their Aryavarta counterparts did, they would never address Him by His Harappan name. Their God was now *Abrahma*.

The same God was now worshipped under two different names by two different cultures. But He was one. Always was. Always will be.

And in this very un-language, as the years passed and his legend spread, Sura and his army of followers were themselves renamed. Worshipped as Gods by their subjects and loathed as fiends by their neighboring colonies…

They were now…the *A-suras!*

'Yes, my lord. This is the name he asked me to convey to

you,' said the guard, not once raising his eyes to meet those of his mighty king. 'And your highness, I must inform you that...he is brutally disfigured.'

Sura's sparkling eyes were now darting from one point on the ground to another. He placed his wine skull on the table next to his makeshift throne and turned to his friend and *senapati* Prachanda, who had stopped devouring a roasted camel-leg as soon as the name of the visitor was announced in the large tent.

'Kill him without a moment's delay, Sura,' advised Prachanda. 'You remember what he did to us the last time we met...'

Only Prachanda could address the great king Sura by his name. And only Prachanda could risk reminding him of his humiliating defeat.

'I remember vividly, Prachanda...' snapped Sura. 'I remember he crushed our armies with a handful of warriors by his side. I remember he rode away with my finest *ashvas* from the mountains. I remember he trounced both you and me with his sword!'

Sura took a big gulp from his skull of intoxicating nectar.

'But I also remember...that he spared my son's life,' spoke Sura again. 'I also remember that he did not touch any of our womenfolk and treated them with great reverence.'

Prachanda was listening. He could not disagree. He knew Sura was right.

'I remember how he waited for me to pick up my sword again, every time I fell to the ground during our duel. I cannot forget that he simply walked away when he could have beheaded me.'

Sura turned to his childhood friend and the commander of his armies.

'He is not an ordinary man, Prachanda. No ordinary man can beat both you and me with such ease. He is a devta! I have seen it in his eyes. There is an uncanny twinkle of benevolence in them, even towards his enemies.'

'You are right, my king,' replied Prachanda, recollecting everything that Sura had just said clearly. 'But he is still our enemy, Sura. He is the only barrier preventing you from becoming the king of the whole world!'

'Yes he is. Yes he is...' mumbled Sura. He suddenly turned to the guard and gave his orders.

'Bring the visitor in. And bear in mind that he should be treated with utmost respect.'

'Yes, my lord,' bowed the soldier and left to escort the mysterious and repugnant visitor in.

·‖ॐ‖·

Sura and Prachanda could not believe their eyes. What stood in front of them was not the devta they remembered with awe and fear. Covered with a green paste that had now turned brown because it was now mixed with so much blood, this man looked nothing like the glorious warrior-ascetic they had met last on the battlefield.

Sura looked closely into the eye of the visitor. It was staring back at him with disturbing brutality. It was he, all right. But something was different. Frightfully different.

What happened to him?

'Welcome to my humble camp, O great a-devta,' greeted Sura, after holding back his gasps and shock at what he was seeing.

'Welcome, O great Avivasvan Pujari.'

Banaras, 2017

BRAHMA RAAKSHASA

'Do you know what a *Brahma Raakshasa* is, Vidyut?' enquired Purohit ji.

'I am not very sure Purohit ji, but I believe it is a contorted being, cursed to endure suffering for centuries,' replied Vidyut.

'You are close. A Brahma Raakshasa is a monstrous being that is neither here nor there. A Brahma Raakshasa is not fully dead and not fully alive. He is neither a resident of the underworld, nor of the material world. It is a transient state for the cursed spirit of a very profound mystic who, despite all his knowledge and wisdom, sinned terribly in his lifetime. He is condemned to suffer for millennia together, in a hideous, ghostly form.'

As he uttered these words, Purohit ji's gaze turned to something outside the window. Vidyut realized he was staring at the cottage of the great matthadheesh.

Without taking his eyes off that mystical chalet, Purohit ji continued.

'You know Vidyut, there really *is* a Brahma Raakshasa residing in the villa of our grandmaster. I saw him that night. For years we felt his presence. But that night, Dwarka Shastri ji unlocked and summoned the otherworldly beast to his aid. I…saw him…' By now Purohit ji was in a partial stupor.

Vidyut put his hand on Purohit ji's shoulder and tried to calm the old priest down. Purohit ji appreciated the gesture immediately, tapped Vidyut's hand and offered a bleak but reassuring smile.

He cleared his throat, took a sip of water from a glass and continued with fresh resolve. Vidyut needed to know everything.

·||ॐ||·

'The ritual intones of a hundred necromancers emanating from his cottage were bloodcurdling. It was a chilling hour, for each one of us in the matth had seen our gurudev enter the cottage all by himself,' continued Purohit ji.

'We saw Dwarka Shastri ji enter his villa alone, but within moments the whole place erupted in a strange, outlandish glow. It seemed like hundreds of sacramental fires had been lit at once. And then in one great flash, the whole of

Banaras went dark. Every light bulb, every street lamp, every TV screen...why, even every cooking fire went out in a black puff. It was like an evil, cosmic djinn had blown away every source of light for tens of miles. There were only two things visible thereafter - the unnerving glow of the taantric fires from the grandmaster's cottage, and the red streaks of thunder-flash raining from the sky.'

There was silence for a long time in the quiet nursing room of the matth. Vidyut was dazed. Purohit ji was lost in the macabre memories of that haunting night. A matth nurse entered the room with Vidyut's meal, but was turned away by a polite but firm shake of the head from the devta.

'But Purohit ji, if they were coming after me, why did all this begin to happen here, in Banaras? I was hundreds of miles away!'

'Long distance exorcism is a very old and accepted practice, Vidyut. Some legends have it that western clerics, Pope Pius XII in particular, attempted it on none other than Adolf Hitler himself, at the peak of World War II. Convinced that Hitler was the Devil incarnate, they unleashed intense remote exorcism on him. No one can say for sure what the outcome was; except that folklore has it that one of the high priests from the Vatican was almost killed in this ritual. They say the demon in Hitler was too powerful to dislodge.'

'Wow! Hitler?? Who would have imagined that?' gasped Vidyut with disbelief.

'It is recorded in several texts related to Hitler, the World War and the church. Later Vatican exorcists, including Gabriel Amorth, said the long-distance exorcism failed because the subject was not physically present in front of Pius XII. That, of course, is a western notion. Our ancient dark-arts suggest no such barriers.'

'This is all so fantastic and so terrifying, Purohit ji. But my question still remains. If you say the attack was on me, why did all this happen here in Banaras? Why not where I was, in Gurgaon? And while I am a novice as compared to my great grandfather, I would not have been overpowered easily in this battle of occult.'

Purohit ji nodded vigorously, in agreement with Vidyut's last statement.

'Yes, you would have given them a hard fight, Vidyut. But you would not have beaten them. Remember who Dwarka Shastri ji is. You are an accomplished taantric no doubt, but you are no match for your great grandfather. Moreover, our matthadheesh did not fight that battle alone. He had help from hundreds of profound taantrics and *rishis* of Banaras, who joined this decisive battle from their ritual pits, temples, homes, ghaats and cremation grounds. It was a powerful glimpse of the proverbial battle between good and evil. They all fed Dwarka Shastri ji with the illumination of their lifetimes of penance. They all knew, mankind could not afford to lose this battle.'

Vidyut could now picture that perilous night. The Dev-Raakshasa matth and the grandmaster Dwarka Shastri's hut being the epicenter of the spiritual counter-attack, while hundreds of occult practitioners from around the primordial city joined forces via pre-practiced chants passed-on from generation to generation, resonating like the shielding voice of God across the black skies.

Scores of generations of the priests of Banaras had been preparing for this dark night. They knew they could be sacrificed in this merciless mayhem. And yet they were there, fighting fearlessly. Over hundreds of years they had lost their social sheen. Revered once as the sentinels of the moral code of living, sacred teachers for whom even kings left their thrones in welcome, these sadhus and rishis were now no more than emaciated, third-grade citizens living in penury. Segments of materialistic, westernized and irreverent society had abandoned these vital guardians to the dustbins of *grih-pravesh*, birth and death ceremonies. Unwanted essentials that had to be invited to perform the formalities many metropolitan Hindu families found to be nothing more than a tick-box. Little did they know, that even till this day these sidelined God-men were their most potent line of defense against the dark powers. They were going to lay their lives that portentous night.

What were they trying to protect?

'By the time gurudev emerged from his cottage, he appeared like a monster himself. He looked much bigger than his own size and walked like a zombie. Locks of his hair flew in the wind like white serpents. But most of all…most of all what struck terror into our hearts was the venomous blue blaze streaking out from his eyes. We knew we were not looking at our grandmaster. It was someone else in him.'

'Who was it, Purohit ji?' asked Vidyut plainly. His mouth was dry.

'It was the Brahma Raakshasa in our grandmaster, Vidyut. And he could not have penetrated gurudev's being of his own volition. Dwarka Shastri ji had summoned him into his body, as his final move to counter the attack of the two exceptionally powerful black, vindictive spirits.'

There were a few long moments of silence in the room. Eventually, Purohit ji spoke.

'Before the skies cleared suddenly and Dwarka Shastri ji crumbled to the ground lifeless, we heard him raise his trishul, turn his glowing blue eyes to the blood-moon and scream these last two lines...'

Purohit ji was now animated, attempting to recreate those last moments of havoc. With fear clearly visible in his eyes, he raised both his arms upwards, threw his head back and screamed out words that were in a language Vidyut had never heard him speak before.

'Eu o bani da cidade sagrada, Agostinho!'

'Eu o bano dessa terra sagrada, Cristovao!'

Vidyut did not understand the meaning of these lines, but he knew it was something sinister. And he could gather that this was Portuguese.

'What do these lines mean, Purohit ji?' asked Vidyut, now nearly giddy with anxiety.

Purohit ji replied simply. 'It means the following, Vidyut –

I banish you from this holy city, Agostinho!

I banish you from this sacred land, Cristovao!'

The Portuguese marauders from the 16th century Goa *Inquisition* had come back. The two cruel executioners, who had been killed by Vidyut and Dwarka Shastri's ancestor, the great Markandeya Shastri, had been summoned back.

In fact, they had never fully left.

Bithynian City
(Modern-day Turkey),
325 AD

THE COUNCIL OF NICAEA

'*Non lasciare che questo accada, Imperatore!*' whispered the hood-ed monk.

'Do not let this happen, Emperor!'

Walking beside the bejewelled horse of none other than the most powerful king on Earth, Advait Shastri implored with the monarch. He knew that the all-powerful king had not fully grasped the long-term implications of what had just been decided in the secret meeting held after the main Council of the three hundred Christian bishops was over.

'Leave before I get you arrested,' mocked the sovereign, as

he waved to the cheering masses of the very kingdom he had conquered not too long ago. He could not help but smile at the vacillating and herd mentality of human beings.

They are predisposed to being governed by a single ruler. Under one law. By one Order.

Advait was a friend, and someone the emperor admired immensely. 'Meet me at my camp, you petulant boy,' he said with a wry smile to his young friend from the plains beyond the Hindu Kush mountains. The monarch looked formidable.

Constantine the Great was a man ahead of his times.

·||卐||·

He looked undoubtedly like he was sent to rule the planet. Constantine sat crossed legged on his ornate chair, still decked in his golden armour. His powerful jawline, his sharp nose and his curly hair made him look like he was Alexander of Macedon born all over again.

He probably was.

Advait entered the royal pergola. The opulence of Constantine's regal lodging was unimaginable. Studded with rubies, diamonds and emeralds, the emperor's tent was nothing less than a symbolic umbrella of wealth and power. Constantine sat there with a golden cup of wine in his powerful hands. He was a force of nature.

The monarch got up to welcome Advait, and with him stood

up the entire imperial council. The emperor permitted them to sit with a little flick from his two fingers, without turning to look at any of them. His councilmen were aware that Constantine kept regular contact with mystics, priests, warlords, pirates and wise men from all corners of his vast kingdom. And far beyond. But they were all stunned when they saw the great conqueror embrace this mysterious young man with the warmth of an old friend.

Sensing the affection between the king and the hooded visitor, the royal cupbearer proceeded to offer the guest a golden goblet of the fine wine Constantine and his councilmen were consuming.

'My powerful but pessimistic friend does not partake of wine,' announced the monarch with a teasing smile and a raised eyebrow, as he gestured for the cupbearer to stand back. He oozed unquestioned authority in every move he made.

'And he does not eat meat either!' continued the emperor, turning to his councilmen. 'Yet I assure you, he can push back a raging bull by its horns and shoot an arrow to find its mark two miles away.'

He now turned back to Advait. With both his hands on the shoulders of his friend, Constantine added, 'One more thing. He is closer to the Lord than any of us here.' The king's voice was soft with admiration and fondness.

'You are kind and generous, O mighty Constantine,' replied the visitor as he pulled back his hood in a sign of respect for the great ruler. Two things took everyone in that tent by surprise - the uncommonly handsome face of the young visitor, and that he dared to address the great Constantine by his name!

·‖卐‖·

They were now in the private pavilion of the king. What they spoke about was going to change the fate of the world forever.

The Council of Nicaea was summoned by Constantine as a gathering of Christian bishops from all over his enormous dominions. Religious strife and violence had marred the Roman Empire for the last three hundred years. Ruthless persecution of sects and apostles at the hands of the rulers had only made Christianity stronger. The monarch had waged continuous wars to consolidate his colonies, and was now determined to put an end to all religious discord – starting with opposing groups within Christianity itself. He was going to bring everyone on the same page when it came to beliefs and philosophies.

But Constantine had a deeper plan. The main Council was followed by a smaller assembly, behind tightly closed doors. It is here that Constantine shared his vision with the highest priests, generals, treasurers and advisors. A world vision for when he was gone.

He aspired to leave the planet secure in what he believed was a governance and social order for eternity. He believed that differences in faiths and dogmas were the greatest threat to mankind. After decades of wars, bloodshed and conquests, after ruling over people of diverse cultures and civilizations, after observing the violent streak inherent in humans at very close quarters, Constantine had formed a firm opinion. The world needed to be controlled by one force, one supreme power – that transcended the borders and Gods created by quarrelsome societies and lustful individuals. It needed to be governed by a novel and perpetual order.

A new world order.

·||卐||·

'But *this* was not the purpose of this congress, O king!' insisted Advait. 'You sent for me saying you needed me to counsel you on matters related to bringing factions of priests together.'

'So you think I could have explained this ambitious design to you via an emissary, Advait?' responded Constantine. He stood resting against a counter made of ivory and gold, twirling an empty, diamond-studded cup in his fingers.

Advait sighed. 'Tell me again Emperor, what will your grand plan achieve?'

Constantine was quiet for a moment or two, but his face twitched with passionate hope. He kept the glass aside and pulled a luxuriant stool to sit face to face with Advait.

'Don't you see, my friend…mankind is killing each other more savagely than ever before. The cruelty of humans finds new reasons to hate and murder one another every day. They kill in the name of God, in the name of faith, in the name of patriotism, in the name of creed, for land, for gold…whatever quenches the blood-thirst of insatiably ambitious scoundrels. The blood of millions of innocents is spilled just to fuel one man's ascension to a golden throne.'

'Haven't you fought wars for years, defeated and killed thousands to become who you are today, Emperor?' asked Advait plainly. He respected Constantine. But he was not willing to let a king, who ruled by the force of the sword, offer profound sermons on the viciousness of human beings.

'I knew you were going to point that out,' replied Constantine without even a hint of irritation. 'Yes, I have fought and vanquished enemies for years. Which is why the futility of violence and conquest is clearer to me than to anyone else. And I have to make arrangements to leave this world as a better place than what it was when I was born. If we let everything go on the way it is, the day is not far when we will face extinction at our own hands. And I, Constantine the First, will not let that happen.'

'Your purpose is noble, Emperor. But the edicts you have passed are not the way to achieve that goal. Human beings are not sheep. It will never be possible to take away their liberty. You cannot control their free will. You cannot suppress their instincts.'

'Of course I can!' retorted Constantine, displaying a glimpse of his unreal self-belief. 'Didn't you see those thousands of people showering me with flowers? These are the people whose homes and cities I torched not so long back. And today, they bow to me. They celebrate me. Don't you see Advait, that human beings can be moulded, that they can be governed?'

The king got up, paced up and down his tent in deep and excited thought. Advait noticed Constantine's powerful fist clenched the handle of his sword. The conqueror's mind was on fire. After a few brief moments, the king sat down to face the young warrior-priest from Aryavarta again.

'Imagine Advait…a world without war. A world without violence. A global, unified creed, free from the bondage of religions, liberated from the division of nations…'

The monarch's eyes were now looking far beyond Advait. They were the eyes of a visionary who believed he could change the world.

Only this time, the king was making a mistake. *A very big mistake.*

·||卐||·

It was the first light of dawn streaking into the royal tent that reminded Advait of his long journey back home.

After a whole night of debate, Advait was certain that nothing could stop Constantine from executing his master plan for the human race. It is impossible to stop a man who thinks he has become as omnipotent as God.

'Your plan is very dangerous, Emperor. It will concentrate extraordinary power in the hands of a few, who if corrupted, will emerge as the most vicious evil on Earth.'

Constantine nodded in agreement. He walked up to his friend and put his hand on Advait's shoulder.

'Which is why I have called you here, my noble friend. If the New World Order deviates from its noble purpose, your clan is the only one that will be able to stop it. You have been guardians of the world's most precious secret for centuries. I know you will be able to restore order.'

·||卐||·

Advait bid farewell to the great king. As he was about to step out of the Emperor's tent, he turned around.

'You are among the handful of people who know the secret of the Black Temple, Emperor. You know what it guards. Then why…?'

'Yes, I know,' replied Constantine. 'Which is why I am doing what any devoted servant must do.'

East of Harappa, 1700 BCE

MAA...

As guided by the fish-man who called himself Matsya, Manu had ridden eastwards, carrying his mother's body with unabated love and care. Refreshed as much by being in the vicinity of this strange, divine man, as he was by the cool showers, Manu had a creeping realization.

He was not going to die today.

And that meant he would get a chance at revenge. Without letting the thought overpower his present duty, Manu let his desire for vengeance simmer under the surface.

I will annihilate Pundit Chandradhar and Priyamvada just the way I killed that rogue Ranga.

He had been riding for hours again, without having found anything in the dusty plains that surrounded him. Only now he was nowhere near despair of any kind. Something told him that if Matsya had given him directions, they had to be right.

Another hour passed and Manu noticed the blurred outlines of grey hills in the horizon. They could not be more than a few miles away. Hills could mean food, water and most of all...temples.

As he rode closer and closer to the rising hills, Manu realized that the mounds were taller than he would have expected to find in these lands. The height of these mountains should have made the ranges visible from much farther than where Manu spotted them. He recognized that it was only the fresh, unseasonal showers that had made them noticeable. On a regular day, in these semi-barren lands where rain was a rarity, these hills would be nearly invisible. The haze of dust and rising heat from the burning earth hid these mountains behind a natural curtain.

·‖卐‖·

They were running in his direction. From a distance Manu could see scores of men and women coming towards him. As they drew closer, Manu could see four of them carrying a cot meant for the demised.

All of them were carrying weapons. Both women and men appeared to be fit and trained in the art of war. Manu could see that in their strides and in their muscular built. Yet all of them had simplicity and love written over their tanned, glowing faces.

Who are these people?

Manu's gallop had now slowed down to a trot, as he saw these people dressed in black robes slowly surround him. He felt no fear of them. An accomplished warrior himself, Manu had the sharp instinct of a soldier. He could sense hostility from a distance. Here, he found none.

An old woman, with a face as beautiful as his own mother's, walked up to him. She had snow-white hair, blue eyes, a sharp nose and unusual poise. Clothed in flowing black robes that fluttered in the moist breeze, she was probably eighty years of age, or more. But she walked and spoke like someone half that age.

'Welcome, Manu,' she said in a soothing voice. 'Let us take care of Sanjna now.'

Manu was overwhelmed at meeting someone he intuitively felt he could trust. He was tired, wounded, emotionally shattered and burning with hatred. He simply nodded in gratitude, burst into tears and kept crying as they took his mother and placed her on the cot.

He dismounted, bent down and kissed Sanjna's face again and again. 'Ma…my Ma…my beloved, Ma…I will see you soon, Ma…don't be afraid, Ma…I will join you soon, Ma… Ma…My Ma…' was all he kept saying.

As they lifted her, he realized this was the last time he was going to see his mother's face. 'Maaaaaa…!' screamed Manu, as he crashed down on his knees, fell facedown till his forehead brushed roughly against the ground. The mourning son repeatedly slapped the earth with both his hands in extreme anguish. They were taking her away for her last rites.

Even in death Sanjna had not left her son's side.

But now she was finally going to go.

It was his first meal since he last ate a morsel of rice back at Somdutt's camp over two days ago, moments before he had witnessed an arrow pierce through his soldier's head. Manu was slowly raising his fingers full of rice and vegetables to his mouth. He was eating just enough to survive.

The kind, white-haired woman entered the dimly lit cave of grey stone that Manu was lodged in. The nights in this dry, hilly terrain were as cold as the days were hot. Manu was recouping by a small fire. The physicians of this mysterious settlement had tended to him all through the day.

It was a miracle that Manu was alive. No one in that battlefield that he rode out from could have ever imagined that someone with three deeply pierced arrows and a lethal sword-wound could live to see another day. It seemed like some unknown force was keeping the son of Vivasvan and Sanjna alive.

She fed him with her own hands, just like his mother used

to even till he was eighteen. She stroked his head, which now had a bit of hair growing. Her eyes looked at him with the gentleness of a mother. When Manu indicated gratefully that he had had enough nourishment for now, she kept the rice bowl away.

'You must rest now, my son,' she said lovingly, as the graceful old lady got up to leave. 'Tomorrow I will take you to the Black Temple.'

'Thank you, my dear lady...for everything...' said Manu. He had never felt more grateful to anyone in his life. His mother's cremation had been consummated strictly as per the *Sanatana* (Eternal) rites prescribed in the scriptures. This meant the world to him.

The lady smiled. 'Rest now, Manu,' she said, as she turned towards the exit of the cave.

'My lady...' called out Manu.

She turned. 'Yes, my son...?'

'How did you know my name? And how did you know that my mother's name was Sanjna? I never told you...' enquired Manu.

The elegant godmother smiled.

'Our friend Matsya informed us,' she said simply.

Manu was confused. 'Yes I met him. But how...how could he have reached you before I did?' he asked. 'I was on a horse and he was on foot. I rode straight to these grey mountains. There is no way he could have gotten here first!'

The lady grinned, walked up to Manu and touched his cheek lovingly.

'Matsya doesn't need to *reach* anywhere, Manu.'

'Sorry I don't understand, my lady…' said Manu looking up at her serene face.

She laughed kindly and turned to leave once again. As she reached the door of the cave she looked back at Manu.

'Matsya doesn't need to reach anywhere, because he is *everywhere*, Manu'.

Banaras, 2017

THOSE MEN IN WHITE ROBES

'I'm going to kill him, ' said Sonu, fuming with rage.

This was the moment Vidyut had been waiting for. Battling for his own life first and then confined to a nursing bed, all Vidyut could think about was the grisly betrayal by his most trusted friend. He needed to know why Bala had stabbed him in the back. He needed to know how Bala was connected to all that was going on around them.

The lack of answers to these questions was killing him and he wanted to hear everything from Bala. The pain of disloyalty was far more insufferable than the bullets that had torn deep into Vidyut.

·‖卐‖·

Balvanta pushed open the heavy door of the matth prison.

Vidyut was still recovering from his grievous injuries and slowly limped in to the dark cell.

Sonu flicked on the loud switch of an overhead lamp. In a blinding flash it filled a tubular portion of the black space with glaring white light. Under that dazzling light sat the muscular man, tied to a metallic chair. Despite his bondage and the hostile cell, he appeared to be in deep meditation. Not in the familiar yogic way. But like he stood at an altar, his fingers clasped, crossing each other. His head was bowed in reverence.

Vidyut had never seen this before. In the several years they lived and laughed like brothers, Vidyut had not seen Bala meditate before.

Who is this man?

'I am going to smash his face into a pulp!' exclaimed Sonu, as he charged forward towards the tied man. But he stopped midway. Bala had suddenly opened his fiery eyes and stared at Sonu. That was enough to dampen the enthusiasm of the young man. There are few things more chilling than the I-see-you glare of a caged tiger.

Vidyut walked towards Bala and sat down on the chair across the steel tabletop that separated them. The two old friends, the two brothers joined at the hip, the duo that looked like they could conquer the world, sat staring at each other.

·‖卐‖·

'*Why*, Bala?' asked Vidyut.

Bala looked into Vidyut's honest eyes for a few seconds, and then burst out laughing. It was the familiar, hearty merriment that Vidyut so loved over the years. Only this time, it was an unsettling laughter.

It took Bala a minute to compose himself. He was bordering on lunacy, in the way he was acting delirious, though completely unprovoked. Or maybe this was who he really was.

'Why, Bala? Why did you try to kill me?' asked Vidyut again, unfazed by the display of madness.

'Sorry…? Did you say I *tried* to kill you?' retorted Bala, his eyebrows raised in amazement.

Vidyut stayed quiet. He knew he had got the man to talk.

'Who are you, Vidyut? Are you a God? Are you a devta? Are you some naïve boy or some wicked conjurer?' hissed Bala in a melodramatic tilting of his head. The cold hate Vidyut had seen in his eyes at the ghaat when Naina overpowered him, was back.

'I tried to kill you, Vidyut? I *tried* to kill you? An ace marksman who can shoot a pigeon from two hundred meters; who can find the head of an enemy soldier from a mile away; a deadeye who has never missed a target…missed your heart from 8 feet? And you say I *tried* to kill you??'

He was right. And Vidyut knew it. Bala was not one to miss

his mark from point blank range. He was a trained com-
mando, a shooter par excellence. Almost instantly, an eerie
realization dawned upon Vidyut. Bala had purposefully kept
Vidyut alive!

'And not just me, Vidyut,' barked Bala. 'Even Romi was not
going to kill you till the prophesied hour. He had stuffed just
enough mercury fulminate into that zippo lighter to injure
you. The mercenaries were going to mutilate you, which they
couldn't, but even they were under strict instructions to keep
you alive, you devta!'

·||卐||·

'Get me some rum, Video…'

Matth members in that dark chamber scowled at this ridicu-
lous request from their captive.

'Get me some rum and untie my hands, man,' urged Bala.
'You know I would not stand a chance in front of you, even
with this broken condition you are in.'

Vidyut gave a weak smile. Bala laughed again. 'Come on,
man. You know I need my drink!'

Vidyut nodded at Sonu. The young lad let out a groan of
protest, followed by a disapproving stare at their prisoner.
But he left right away to obey his devta.

·||卐||·

He had gulped down two double shots of rum in less than

a minute. Heaving a sigh of relief, Bala poured a third one for himself.

'I was not going to let them kill you, Video,' said Bala. 'That was my precondition.' He was looking straight at Vidyut, with the accustomed sincerity that Vidyut trusted with his life. But he had had enough.

'Aw, shut up, Bala!' Vidyut exploded.

'You knew what was going on all this time! You knew a master-assassin was after my life. You knew there were trained mercenaries that day at the ghaat. You knew I was not supposed to leave Banaras alive!'

'No, I didn't!' Bala barked back. 'Romi was sent to kill you no doubt, but not just yet. I was told the mercenaries were there to overpower you and capture you. They had assured me that you would live through this episode. You are supposed to live till the prophesied hour!'

Vidyut could see Bala's eyes glinting with moisture under the hot, overhead white light.

'I shot you because there was no other way, Vidyut. You are unstoppable and you know that. You crushed over a dozen trained killers in a matter of minutes. What choice did I have? They were watching…'

There was silence in the dim chamber, which now smelled of strong military grade dark rum.

Finally Vidyut spoke. 'Who are *they* that you keep referring to, Bala? Who are you working for?'

Bala looked up at Vidyut. The devta notced both amusement as well as mortal fear in his erstwhile friend's eyes.

'You really don't know anything, do you, Vidyut?' asked Bala. His brave eyes were now wide with fear.

·‖卐‖·

'You know nothing about me, Vidyut,' said Bala, as he washed down his fifth drink. Vidyut permitted him this indulgence, as he wanted Bala to sing.

'I know you for years, Bala. You were like family to me,' replied the devta.

'Rubbish! You don't even know where I come from. I was not born into a powerful family of spiritual God-masters like yours, Vidyut. I was born to a bloody nobody!'

Vidyut was listening. As were Balvanta and Govardhan.

'Coconut climber. That was what my father was - a poor, famished, helpless coconut tree climber, from a remote village in Kerala. We were tribal, Vidyut. Living off the land. Or should I say, dying off the land...'

Bala took another big gulp from his glass and continued.

'We slept hungry most nights. Or drank a revolting gruel of a local seed soaked overnight in water. We had clothes that barely covered my mother's dignity. Home was a leaking hut and meat was what we stole from recently dead animal carcasses. It was poverty beyond imagination. It was a sub-human existence. We could enter no places of worship. We were thrashed out of even funeral kitchens. There was no medicine when we fell ill. My little sister died in front of me, rotting on the mud floor with diphtheria. And no one came to help us. We were living and dying worse than animals.'

The prison cell was quiet. Bala's eyes were gazing deep into his glass, as if reliving every horrible moment he was recounting. The gnawing wounds of abject poverty and irreparable loss can only be hidden. They never fully heal.

'And then one day, *they* came. Those men in white robes, walking straight into our pathetic huts and embracing us like no one had ever done before. They fed us, clothed us and cleaned us. Do you know what it feels like when someone offers you acceptance and hope, after the whole world around you has only subjected you to humiliation and hunger, Vidyut? Of course you don't! You don't even know what it is like to stay hungry for three days at a stretch. What would *you* understand?!'

Vidyut did not know how to react. Bala was right. Vidyut was not aware of anything about Bala's childhood beyond perhaps some incidents here and there narrated by Bala himself. Nor did Vidyut have an idea that his friend turned foe's background was so scarred.

'I did not know all this, Bala. And I can only imagine the pain that you went through. But that still does not explain why you would join forces with murderers and conspirers.'

'Because for once I wanted to be on the winning side!' screamed Bala, smashing the table with his powerful fist.

'Don't you get it, you bloody divine boy - for once I wanted to win, goddammit!'

The ex-military man was now panting with rage and emotion.

'The day they took my parents and me into their place of worship, the day they told me that God loves me too, the moment they changed our names and welcomed us into their community, I swore I would do anything for them. Live and die for them. Blindly. They were the only ones who spotted talent in me. They were the first to trust me with their secrets, even if that meant my leading their violent missions. Even as I grew up amongst them and sensed a larger, almost unimaginably ambitious design in the whole set-up, I never broke my oath.'

·||卐||·

Suddenly Sonu came rushing into the cell. He was panting. And he appeared nervous.

'Vidyut dada, we need to leave. *Now*. The grandmaster has summoned us all in full strength to the outer periphery of the matth.'

Balvanta, who was standing in a corner all this while, turned to Sonu. 'What is the matter, son?'

Sonu looked like he was going to suffer from an acute anxiety attack any time. He was now perspiring profusely.

'*He* is here, Balvanta dada...' said Sonu, as he swallowed a visible lump in his throat.

Balvanta and Govardhan had barely exchanged glances, when a dull, rumbling din made the floor under their feet tremble. This was followed by a rhythmic, sky-shattering thunder of metal clashing in a distance.

DDHAAKK! DDHAAKK!

THWANNG! THWANNG!

DDHAAKK! DDHAAKK!

THWANNG! THWANNG!

Vidyut was completely bewildered. He looked at Balvanta and Sonu enquiringly. At this very moment, Bala broke into a wild and nervous laughter. 'He is here! He is here!' he started chanting feverishly.

DDHAAKK! DDHAAKK! THWANNG! THWANNG!

DDHAAKK! DDHAAKK! THWANNG! THWANNG!

The noise grew louder, as Vidyut saw the faces of Balvanta and Sonu distort with fear and anger. He knew something was not right. If his great grandfather had summoned all his physical and spiritual troops to the matth's outer sanctum, something was really, really not right.

'What is it, Balvanta dada?' yelled Vidyut above the maddening roar of the thuds and twangs.

Balvanta paced hurriedly towards Vidyut to help him up. As he struggled to get back to his feet, Vidyut noticed Bala had gone into a trance again. His bald head was sweating under the gleaming light and his eyes were rolled up completely, showing only a sliver of white. He looked like a goblin in demonic penance.

·||卐||·

'It is *him*, Vidyut. The most threatening creature in all of Banaras. In fact the most dangerous demon left.'

As Sonu tied Bala's hands again and they prepared to leave to join the great matthadheesh, Vidyut turned to Balvanta again.

'Who is it, Balvanta dada? Who are you referring to with such fear and awe?'

Balvanta looked at Vidyut and explained in one sentence.

'It is who Dwarka Shastri ji believes to be the last raakshasa on planet Earth.'

Vidyut was straining himself to grasp every word Balvanta was uttering. He had heard of himself being called the last devta. *But the last raakshasa??*

'He has come with his six hundred and sixty six manic followers,' continued Balvanta.

'It is none other than the ruler of the *smashaans* (cremation grounds); the deity of the dead; the maha-taantric – Trijat Kapaalik!'

Banks of the Indus,
West of Harappa, 1700 BCE

THE DEATH OF
EVERY SON

'Think again, O great a-devta,' asked Sura again. 'Is this really what you want?'

'Yes, I am sure,' replied the rusty, cruel voice. 'I drew the maps for the mountains of brick and bronze with my own hands. A minor variation in the construction plan will alter the course of the *Saraswati* completely. And the glorious city of Harappa will be wiped out forever, cleansing Prithvi of all its maleficent inhabitants.'

Prachanda was skeptical of all that he had heard so far. It was their dreaded archrival, the tallest commander of the Harappan armies, the demi-God that had vanquished them in battle – sitting in their tent, asking for assistance in what was going to go down in legends and folklore as the most ruthless undertaking in the history of time. The only thing that was compelling him to believe the incidents narrated by Vivasvan Pujari was his inhuman condition. No ordinary man could have survived such pitiless punishing of the body.

'For a moment suppose we agree to help you, and put our armies and beasts at your disposal. What then? What is in it for us?' asked Prachanda. 'What use would we have for a vast graveyard?'

Vivasvan Pujari looked up at Prachanda with unhidden disdain. The man once known as the Surya of Harappa, was not accustomed to debates with lesser men. Sura sensed this tension. Without a moment's delay he intervened.

'All Prachanda means to enquire, O great Avivasvan Pujari, is that once such large swathes of Aryavarta are swept away in a deluge, what will I have left to rule over? What use is an empire without its subjects?'

The fallen devta was quiet for a moment. He then responded, systematically and clearly. He knew what the *Asura* wanted to hear.

'You can call it an empire without subjects, or you can look at it as being the unquestioned ruler of the world's most fertile lands. Lands that you can then populate as you like, build into cities as you please and rule over under your own order. Isn't that what you always wanted, Sura?'

The demon king was pleased to hear these words. This was *indeed* what he always wanted.

·||ॐ||·

He ate flesh of a roasted goat right from the bone and glugged down several skull-fulls of the Asuras' dark wine. Vivasvan Pujari had never tasted meat or touched an intoxicant before in his life. He was now making every effort to forget who he was. He was slowly killing the devta in him. And feeding the beast.

'There is one more offering we will need from you, O a-devta,' said Prachanda carefully, as they dined together over a feast of meats and liquors.

Vivasvan raised his bloodshot eye to look at both Sura and his military chief.

'You are going to get everything anyway. The lands, the rivers, the ruins, the treasures…what more can you want?' he asked.

'A-Saptarishi,' said Sura suddenly, referring to the holy Seven Sages.

And then he said something Vivasvan Pujari was hoping never to hear.

'We want the heads of the Asaptarishi.'

·||ॐ||·

'Our victory will never be complete unless the Asaptarishi meet with the same fate as every Harappan ,' explained Sura to a shocked Vivasvan.

87

'This cannot be,' replied the wounded devta. 'You will have your kingdom. Your empire will span all of Aryavarta. You will rule almost the entire known world, Sura. Leave the Saptarishi alone.'

'We both know that as long as those tricksters are alive, my rule over Harappa will never be guaranteed. These sages govern the rivers, they direct the winds, they speak to the beasts and even the mountains crumble as per their will. No, Avivasvan, we must kill them.'

'Enough, Sura! This is not a discussion that I am willing to indulge in. The Saptarishi are not warriors. They cannot defeat your massive armies. They are simple sages with no interest in the material world. And above all, they are the proverbial sons of the Saraswati. God knows what devastating destruction will strike Aryavarta if we try to harm them,' explained Vivasvan Pujari, assertively and logically. The truth was that in his heart he loved the Saptarishi deeply. They were the last thread connecting him to the Creator.

Prachanda knew Sura well enough to know that his king wanted him to be the tough negotiator now. He decided to up the ante.

'And why are you so protective of these sages, O great a-devta? What have they ever done for you?' taunted the commander of the Asura army.

'Careful, Prachanda,' replied Vivasvan, without looking up from his plate.

'No really, what affection do they have for you? Would you have been in this pitiable state if they were with you? Would your family have been murdered like dogs if the Saptarishi cared even one bit…'

Even before Prachanda could complete his sentence, the devta had pounced across the regal dining table, drawn his ominous blade and stuck it against the throat of Sura's military chief. The blue *lapis lazuli* handle of his dagger was smeared with his own perpetual bleeding.

'Not a word about the Saptarishi! Not a word about my family!' hissed Vivasvan Pujari threateningly into Prachanda's ears.

·‖卐‖·

'My apologies, O mighty a-devta. Prachanda is a fool,' said Sura politely, as he gently held Vivasvan Pujari's arm and slowly moved it away from Prachanda's jugular.

This is no ordinary man, as I always knew. He is surrounded by thousands of my troops, but he is fearless as a lion.

The men once again took their seats and Vivasvan Pujari slid back his powerful battle-knife into its scabbard. Prachanda thanked his stars. He knew he had come an inch close to meeting his evil maker.

'Do not take our counsel otherwise, A-Surya of Harappa,' began Sura, as he poured more wine into his guest's drinking skull.

When he saw Vivasvan Pujari's anger had subsided visibly, Sura threw-in his next set of dice. He knew the devta was vulnerable. This world spares no opportunity to manipulate a shattered heart and to exploit a defeated man. It extracts the last drops of life and hope from the broken, to add bricks to its ruthless palaces of ambition. But Sura was making a mistake. Yes, Vivasvan Pujari's heart was broken. But he was far, far from being defeated.

·‖ॐ‖·

'As we have heard, the Asaptarishi can change the course of rivers. They can command the clouds to rain and read the minds of men,' said Sura cautiously. By now he had made sure that the devta had consumed countless skull-fulls of his supremely intoxicating wine.

'So all we are saying is that we cannot help but wonder why they did not come to your rescue, O mighty a-devta...'

This was not the first time this question had cropped up in Vivasvan's mind. He had brushed it away each time, convincing himself half-heartedly that the Saptarishi must have got a reason. But every time this biting question came back to him. And now even Sura was raising it.

'They did not come to your aid when you were framed as a murderer. They did not intervene when you were condemned to the mrit-kaaraavaas. They also ignored you when you were assaulted at the courtroom,' continued Sura, now almost certain that this slow poisoning was working.

The last devta of Aryavarta had stopped eating. His head was bent in deep angst over the rich dinner table and his fists had tightened. Sura's verbal venom was showing its effect.

'Be that as it may, why did they not come to salvage your beloved family, especially when they knew you were not with them? They are perceivers of all the realms of time, as I hear. Nothing could have been hidden from them,' added Prachanda, this time very carefully.

'And your wife, O a-devta…we had heard so much about her piety that she was the only one we had liberated from our a-bhasha. She was the only one we called by her true name – Sanjna.'

Lying came easy to the demon king.

·||ॐ||·

'She died of a poisonous arrow wound. This was not the kind of end that a lady as pious and as devoted as she was meant to meet!' whispered Sura into the ears of a now sobbing devta.

Vivasvan Pujari could not help but agree with everything that Sura and Prachanda were saying. He could not hold back his anger and clawing dismay against the Seven he thought would have come to his aid. His fists were now on top of one another on the table, the devta's forehead resting on them. He was weeping profusely. He was convinced now that he had been betrayed. Betrayed by those he loved and trusted the most.

'And we hear your son, the handsome boy Manu, fought valiantly,' said Prachanda, now almost melodramatically, circling the table like a vile midget. His eyes were sparkling with the lust of a monster that knows it has cornered its prey.

'Three arrows pierced through him, you said...three arrows!' exclaimed Sura. 'What a valiant young man! He must have remembered you in his last moments, as he would have fallen off dead from the horse he fled with. He should be avenged with the death of every son in Harappa!'

Vivasvan Pujari was now trembling with hate. His soul mate, his beloved wife had died on a battlefield she was never meant to be on. His son had ridden off in a wounded state so grave that Vivasvan's friend Somdutt had submitted his tearful condolences. His whole life had been shattered to pieces in a matter of hours.

WHERE WERE THE SAPTARISHI WHEN MY WORLD WAS COMING TO AN END?

Banaras, 2017

TRIJAT KAPAALIK

It looked like the army of *shaitaan* (Satan) himself. Thronging the Dev-Raakshasa matth right from its arched stone gateway to the precincts of the *raakshasa khand*, the *aghori* taantrics of Trijat Kapaalik swarmed every inch. The local administration, the police and the people, all emptied the streets where Trijat and his violent band marched in procession. In several cities and towns scattered across the map of the world, law enforcers avoid taking religious and spiritual cults head-on. This is done, at times, at the behest of political bigwigs. But very often, it is an outcome of real veneration.

Dressed in nothing but animal hide, their long hair was matted into thick locks, turned orange-brown in colour over years of gory, polluted living. All 666 followers of the feared *maha-taantric* had sunken eyes that gave away decades of opium and *charras* consumption. Their bodies and faces were smeared with white ash from the burning pyres of the cremation grounds. Their mouths looked like they had all just drank blood, a crimson red from chewing tobacco and *paan*. Over a third of them carried massive spears, tridents and shields made of hardened leather. Their ornaments were made of human and animal bones. But worst of all, each one of them appeared to be under a wild and inexplicable spell.

Just the mere sight of Trijat's militia was enough to curdle the blood of even the most brave hearted among men.

·||ॐ||·

Aghora is an advanced and revered form of tantra. It finds its ancient origins in the worship of Lord *Rudra*. Believed by its practitioners to be a shorter route to unbridled spiritual power and even enlightenment, it has been deeply entrenched in the Indian spiritual landscape for thousands of years. Apart from complex devotional rituals, propitiations and interaction with *pret-aatmas* (unholy spirits) from the netherworld, it involves post-mortem sacraments that would repulse anyone uninitiated into their mystical world. The aghoris resorted to cannibalism and even intercourse with cadavers in order to achieve the occult goals only they understood. Yet this mysterious sect has been respected from a distance by millions of Indians.

However, like all forms of power, Aghora also corrupted some of its most gifted mystics. Once an aghori taantric accomplished proficiency of the highest degree, he could wield boundless influence over souls and otherworldly beings, who then served him like slaves. Angry spirits in the form of *pishachas*, *chudails* and *daakinis* could extinguish an enemy in the most effortless and cruel manner. This made these aghoris priceless allies to unscrupulous politicians, industrialists, movie stars and other men of power.

Trijat Kapaalik was the undisputed king of aghori taantrics that had abandoned the path to God for the lure of worldly wealth and dominance. He was known to be so powerful that just one step from him into a graveyard brought it bustling to *life* – though not as we know it. His punishing *saadhanas* or penances had taken him from the freezing caves of the Himalayas, to the darkest taantric monasteries of Bengal and Assam. He spent months together in various smashaan ghaats, chanting unnerving hymns and intonations, summoning the dead. As decades passed, Trijat or 'the one with three locks of matted hair' became Trijat Kapaalik – the latter part of his name being attributed to the human skull or *kapaal* that he carried strapped on his trident staff at all times. His feared followers laid the biggest and most domineering camps at holy congregations on the banks of Indian rivers. And it was at one of these *melas* or carnivals where a mysterious Italian man had approached Trijat many years ago.

Dreaded by taantrics, priests and ordinary folk alike, Trijat Kapaalik soon earned various titles like *Masaan-Raja* or ruler of the graveyards. His followers spread the word that Trijat had such a massive army of ethereal beings, that he was actually worshipped by the demised. This earned him the title of *Mritak-Naath* or the deity of the dead.

And yet the Masaan-Raja, the Mritak-Naath, the maha-taan-tric Trijat Kapaalik feared one man on Earth.

He dreaded the greatest taantric on the planet. He feared the great matthadheesh, Dwarka Shastri.

Vidyut saw his great grandfather standing tall at the center of the raakshasa khand. His flowing white and saffron robes, his rich long hair and his monarchical gaze were matched equally by the mighty trishul he held in his right hand. A light drizzle punctuated the surreal scenario, and the indomitable matthadheesh looked like a conqueror at the head of his army, staring into the face of a formidable adversary.

Vidyut walked as fast as he could with his crutch, in order to join his Baba in what could turn out to be anything from a simple exchange of words, to a violent clash of men and mantras. He was relieved when, from a distance, he spotted Naina positioned next to the grandmaster already. By now the matth's heavily armed warriors had tactically surrounded the quadrangular khand and riflemen were in position on all the watchtowers and perches of the holy complex. The highest priests of the matth were now also on the scene, equipped with their *kamandals* (vessels for consecrated water). Balvanta was walking shoulder to shoulder with Vidyut, his shocked initial reaction giving way to proud belligerence.

DDHAAKK! DDHAAKK!

THWANNG! THWANNG!

The terrifying, earthshaking smashes and jangles continued unabated, by now a deafening roar. Vidyut saw what it was. Hundreds of Trijat's manic disciples were thumping the staffs of their tridents on the ground in unison, followed by a synchronized double slamming of the metallic trident-heads against their battle-shields. The effect of this aggressive war cry was horrific.

'*Pranaam*, Baba,' said Vidyut, touching the feet of his great grandfather as he reached the center-stage of the impending confrontation.

'TRIJAAAAAT…' screamed Dwarka Shastri, his voice re-verberating even across the din of the tridents and shields.

'ENOOOOUGH!' he continued.

In a fraction of a second the entire assembly froze in pin drop silence. Even the Masaan-raja's men could not ignore a command from the grand old matthadheesh.

After a few moments, in the deathly quiet of the large gathering, all that could be heard was the sound of firm footsteps. This was accompanied by the jingling of heavy *ghun-groo* or ringing-anklets and the rustle of thick garlands of bone-jewelry. The ash-smeared aghoris slowly parted in the center to make way for their overlord.

And then he appeared. In all his glory.

The Masaan-raja!

East of Harappa, 1700 BCE

THE GREATEST KING

At the break of dawn, his horse was saddled and laden with weapons of all kinds that he had borrowed from the black-robed men and women of the mysterious mountain – scimitars, daggers, two hundred arrows, a battle axe and two spears made specially for long-distance, lethal attacks. Scorching with hate, dazed at how everything he held dear had been agonizingly obliterated in a matter of three bleeding days, Manu prepared for his final assault. He was going to ride into Harappa. Alone.

He was going to save his beloved father. And he was going to assassinate the princess of Mohenjo-daro. Along with her husband and his very own uncle.

The spears he carried had two names etched on them in

blood.

First was of Priyamvada the ambitious - the first queen of Harappa - who destiny was going to forever banish into the black depths of oblivion. That was going to be her final punishment.

And the very wise Pundit Chandradhar – a man who history was to label as the fool that succumbed to an evil woman's trickery, only to abandon righteousness and prudence…and who condemned a whole civilization to its untimely demise.

A spear hurled by the strapping young arm of Manu Pujari was not going to miss its mark.

'And where, may I ask, are you going?'

Manu stopped as he heard this voice. He had just about mounted his steed that these words summoned him from behind. He knew instantly whose magnificent speech this was. It was the voice he was longing to hear again.

He turned his horse around slowly, looking exactly like the marvelous warrior-prince that he was, his eyes already moistening with strange devotion towards the divine spectacle he expected to see.

And he was right. It was *he*.

Matsya.

He glugged down Manu's entire flask of water.

The son of the Surya of Harappa stood there dumbfounded; his eyes locked at this *man* who made him sense the presence of his mother, his father and God – all at one time. In just his second meeting with Matsya, Manu seemed to have found a friend, a brother, a teacher, a confidante, a critic, a deity, a magician, a warrior, a preacher, a savior...*everything!*

What Manu felt for Matsya today was not the only time it was being witnessed by Prithvi or Mother Earth. Several immortal tales of worthy devotees and their divine deities were going to shine like beacons across myth and legend - a forest-dwelling, omnipotent 'monkey' and the perfect prince who was the model for mankind; a gentleman archer par-excellence who lost his nerve in the face of battle with his own kin, and his spiritual reviver who spoke the ultimate truth for millennia to learn from; apostles who suffered inhuman torture just to propagate the word of their shepherd who gave his life to leave behind the message of love; or a believer who was willing to sacrifice his own son for his Lord.

It was this very eternal bond between the devotee and the deity; between the human and the divine; between the worshipper and the Creator - that has kept this world, and all the others, going since the beginning of time.

Manu dismounted slowly, strangely delighted that it was the second time Matsya had partaken of his water. He folded his hands and bowed deeply to the divine fish-man.

'Where are you setting-off to, O great *king*?' enquired Matsya again.

Manu was once again taken aback at the manner in which Matsya had addressed him.

'It appears you mistake me for someone else, O Matsya,' replied Manu. 'I am no king.'

'Oh, but you are! You just don't know it yet.' Matsya was smiling again, in his typically beautiful, mysterious way. He continued, 'we are who we are destined to be - at all times, across all universes, beyond the limitations of human senses and perception. You are the greatest king of this planet already, Manu.'

Manu smirked in bemused irritation. Maybe Matsya was not so divine after all.

'What you say will never come true, Matsya. I am going to rescue my father, avenge my family…and leave this land forever to be an ascetic.'

'Hmm…interesting. And *who* would you be seeking when you become…what did you say…an *ascetic*?'

'I will seek the Almighty, the Creator, of course…'

'Even now you *seek* the Creator, Manu?' Matsya's eyes twinkled with childlike naughtiness combined with enigmatic power. 'Maybe He seeks you!'

Manu was trying hard to grope for meaning in the ambiguous words of the blue-skinned mystic. The cool morning breeze was bringing life to the surroundings. The mountains behind Manu appeared to be rising from the Earth like black titans against the pink, early-morning sky.

'Why don't we learn to value what we have close to us, O son of Sanjna? Sometimes what we pursue is not far away.'

'The Surya of Harappa is dead.'

Manu's mouth went dry as he heard these words from Matsya's mouth. But something inside him was refusing to believe them.

'This cannot be. My great father…the mighty Vivasvan Pujari, cannot be killed. Not by an ordinary foe…not by ANY foe!' retorted Manu.

Deep down, however, he knew the odds were stacked steeply against his father. Manu's last hope was to rescue Vivasvan Pujari. But after his own escape from the battlefield at the insistence of his comrades, the survival chances of Somdutt, Tara and their last few men were almost non-existent. As far as he knew, there was no one left to rescue Vivasvan Pujari.

My father died without a single friend in all of Harappa.

'How…did my father, the great Vivasvan Pujari, meet his end?' asked Manu. By now his tears had all but dried up. He had endured such limitless physical and emotional suffering in the last few days that his pain had now begun to metamorphose into a hardened soul.

'The Surya of Harappa succumbed to his wounds…and to his hate,' replied Matsya.

Manu slumped to his left knee, rested his arm on his right leg and lowered his head, mourning and praying in silence for his departed father.

He had not noticed that not once had Matsya taken Vivasvan Pujari's name. He never said Vivasvan Pujari was dead. He only informed Manu that the 'Surya of Harappa' was no more.

And he was right.

Only Matsya knew what he was doing. And for the victory of *dharma* over *adharma*, of good over evil, He would do this over and over again. Millennia apart from this day, He would tell a sparring father that his only son had fallen in battle, when it was really a war-elephant that had been killed. Today he was informing a warring son that his beloved father was dead, when, in fact, it was Vivasvan Pujari's *goodness* that had perished.

Only Matsya could glance far into cosmic time. He was engineering the preservation of this universe's greatest creation – the human race.

Manu was needed for a far greater cause than his own vengeance.

Banaras, 2017

KAPAAL ARPAN

'*Bhakt Trijat ka pranaam sweekaar karein, gurudev!*'

'Please accept salutations from your devotee Trijat, gurudev!'

As he said these words, Trijat Kapaalik drew wide semicircles with his arms before joining them in a grand *namaskaar* to the matthadheesh. Melodrama was Trijat's perpetual companion, but never did it temper the ferocity of his chilling presence.

'What brings you here, Masaan-raja?' asked Dwarka Shastri.

'Just the desire of your *darshana*, gurudev,' replied Trijat deviously. 'But please don't call me that. As long as you are in Kashi, who can rule the netherworld but you?'

Suddenly Trijat's gaze shifted to Vidyut. He glared deep into
Vidyut's eyes, his head tilted crookedly to one side. It was
now that the devta fully beheld the maha-taantric.

Trijat was a fearsome sight. Not very tall, he still appeared to
be a giant of sorts. Nearly ten inches were added to his height
by the massive, conical bun in which his matted brown hair
was arranged on top of his head – a popular coiffure among
the taantrics. The rest of his hair was separated into two sets
of thick locks, long enough to reach well below his waist.
His eyes were meticulously made-up with a deep red ver-
million paste, making them glow starkly against the rest of
his white, ash-smeared face. His long beard had streaks of
grey hair, the only indicators of Trijat's age. He wore several
garlands of human teeth, bones and fingernails, interspersed
with animal bones and astrological gemstones. He donned
over twenty large rings on his thumbs and fingers, which
ominously clasped his long, black, fire-burnt trident. But the
ghastliest feature of Trijat's macabre persona was the human
skull fastened to his staff. The skull had all its teeth intact,
and its mouth was open as if it were guffawing hideously.

·||卐||·

'Send your great grandson back to where he comes from,
gurudev,' said Trijat politely, his overpowering eyes menacingly defying that fake courtesy.

Dwarka Shastri was stunned upon hearing these words. He
could not believe that Trijat Kapaalik could dare to take
Vidyut's name. Even before the matthadheesh could react,
Balvanta lunged forward at the maha-taantric, half-drawing

his gleaming machete. Vidyut held him back by the arm, but even as he did that, Trijat's militia responded in an unexpected way. Two terrifying looking women with messy, entangled hair slowly stepped forward and positioned themselves next to the Mritak-naath. The faces of these petrifying twins looked morbid like those of corpses, but their bloodshot eyes were looking provocatively at Balvanta, challenging him to make a move.

Vidyut could swear these two were the most horrifying creatures he had seen in real life. While Trijat's entire band looked like goblins, the spine-chilling appearance of these two dwarfed them all. They looked like they both would have been beautiful girls before they transformed into this ghastly avatar. They reminded Vidyut, Naina, Purohit ji and Dwarka Shastri of the description of *pishachinis* in the occult scriptures. They breathed heavily, as if under the influence of a dark spell or that of a powerful intoxicant. Their eyes were rolled-up, and mouths perpetually open. Their bosoms and legs were clothed in dirty rags of leather, with the rest of their bodies rubbed with cremation ash. In a moment Vidyut could decipher that the twisted tattoos on their arms and necks were the most terrifying verses from the dreaded *Garuda Puraana*, the ancient scripture that spells out the horrific punishments doled out to the dead in hell. Blunt sickles still stained with coagulated blood dangled from the waists of these two demented beings.

'You have crossed your boundaries by uttering the name of my great grandson Vidyut from your foul mouth, Kapaalik.

If you were not a worshipper of Rudra, today you would have joined your army of the dead.'

Dwarka Shastri was trembling with rage.

'Forgive me, gurudev. I only speak of his safety. Vidyut is the saviour, isn't he? He should not be subjected to the risks that lurk all around this matth.'

Trijat was once again looking straight at Vidyut. It was as if he was trying to assess whether Vidyut was really what he had been told. For all his darkness and sins, the Masaan-raja did possess powers unknown to ordinary humans. After a few brief moments, he took his eyes away. The inexplicable honesty and radiance on Vidyut's face were disturbing him. He was convinced.

It is he.

'Leave now, Trijat,' growled Balvanta.

Trijat turned to look at Balvanta, and broke into a mad laugh. His men responded with their typical act of aggression.

DDHAAKK! DDHAAKK!

THWANNG! THWANNG!

Suddenly Trijat stopped laughing and raised his hand. His followers immediately obeyed their overlord. The crashing reverberations stopped instantly.

Trijat turned back to Dwarka Shastri, placed his black trishul between himself and the great matthadheesh, and pulled out the ill-omened skull. Raising the skull to the level of Dwarka

Shastri's eyes, he bowed and offered it to the grandmaster.

'*Kapaal arpan sweekaar karein, gurudev,*' he said.

'Please accept this skull-offering, gurudev.'

Dwarka Shastri did not flinch.

'Leave now, Trijat,' he said.

Trijat Kapaalik looked up with a jerk, evidently hurt. It was yet another dramatic act from the maha-taantric.

'You refuse my greatest offering, gurudev?' he asked, pretending to be startled and disappointed. 'You turn down my *kapaal arpan?*'

'Leave!' roared the matthadheesh. Vidyut put his arm around his Baba, hoping to calm him down. He noticed that the two devilish sisters had quietly vanished into the crowd of aghoris. He was relieved, to say the least.

Trijat stared back at Dwarka Shastri, with hate and defiance written all over his face. It was for the first time since he had entered the Dev-Raakshasa matth that Trijat had shown his true color.

'*Kapaal arpan toh hoga aaj, prabhu,*' hissed Trijat. '*Kapaal arpan toh hoga…*'

'The skull-offering will happen today for sure, my lord.'

Vidyut could not understand what Trijat meant. Even the great Dwarka Shastri was bewildered. But he knew this was not something to be taken lightly. Trijat was *never* to be taken lightly.

The Masaan-raja, the Mritak-naath, the maha-taantric, Trijat Kapaalik bowed reverentially to Dwarka Shastri and turned to leave.

·‖ॐ‖·

'We must speak,' said Dwarka Shastri to Vidyut, as the army of aghoris made its way out of the compound.

'Yes Baba, I have been looking forward to that very eagerly. There is so much I need to know and hear from you.'

The matthadheesh nodded. 'Join me in my cottage after dusk today, my son.'

'Sure Baba, I will be there,' replied Vidyut. 'But I have one question for now…'

Dwarka Shastri stood listening.

'What did this Trijat fellow mean when he said that *kapaal-ar-pan* or the skull-offering will happen today?'

The matthadheesh looked worried as he replied, 'it means something terrible is about to unfold, Vidyut. Trijat Kapaa-lik is an extremely dangerous man. We should be on guard.'

·‖ॐ‖·

Vidyut and Balvanta decided to continue their conversation with Bala. Sending Sonu ahead to unlock the prison cell, they followed in silence. The meeting with Trijat Kapaalik had been taxing for everyone. The only thing that Vidyut was relieved about was that Bala was talking freely. Even after everything that had happened, something told him he would be able to bring his old friend back into the fold of righteousness.

As they reached the corridor outside the prison cell, a shivering Sonu greeted them. He looked like he had seen a ghost! Even before Vidyut and Balvanta could ask him anything, Sonu rushed to a corner and vomited repeatedly.

The door of the cell was half open, with an eerie glow from the overhead lamp illuminating a part of the corridor. Vidyut was looking at Sonu with concern when he felt Balvanta tapping on his shoulders. As Vidyut turned, Balvanta silently pointed to the lock of the door. It had not been unlocked with a key. It hung broken.

Has Bala escaped?

Both Vidyut and Balvanta now rushed to the prison cell and Balvanta kicked the heavy metallic door open, his machete ready for an attack.

What they saw froze their nerves.

The prison floor and walls were sprayed with blood, a terrifying evidence of the violent struggle that would have ensued there.

Under the cold white light of the overhead lamp, the steel table that Bala had used to place his glass of rum, was dripping with human blood. And there, on top of the table, clearly displaying the work of blunt sickles – it sat.

The decapitated head of Bala.

Its eyes were rolled up completely and its mouth was open like the skull on Trijat's trident.

Vidyut now understood. Those words were ringing in his mind.

'Kapaal arpan toh hoga aaj, prabhu...'

'The skull-offering will happen...'

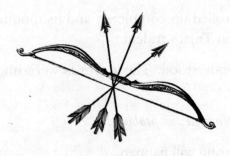

Harappa, 1700 BCE

THE MOUNTAINS OF MAYHEM

He stood atop the highest mound of brick and bronze, stalking the Harappan soldiers and workers like a hungry vulture waiting for a feast. The night was dark, and Vivasvan Pujari was going to cast his first die of revenge – a die soaked in blood.

·||卐||·

Climatic conditions across the vast Harappan settlements had been deteriorating rapidly ever since the first tremble of the Earth and the violent upsurge of the Saraswati had unleashed itself on the unsuspecting plains and its millions of dwellers. The days began to last only a couple of hours, as fearsome nights engulfed a large part of the daily cycle. The Saraswati swelled in size inexplicably with every passing hour, its ocean-like waters flooding hundreds of bankside villages and drowning thousands of peasants and livestock. Hardly anyone referred to the River of the Wise as the Saraswati anymore. Her name had changed and stuck. She was now the *Rakt-Dhaara* – the Blood River! Thunder, lashing rains and unabated dust storms crippled life across known Aryavarta. Everyone was convinced that someone among them had committed a very dark sin – and the Gods were going to strike them down with their wrath. Little did they know, that by being the spectators of and accomplices in the torture of the devta, they were all perpetrators of unpardonable decadence.

Intoxication from the defiling potion of the Mesopotamian black-magicians, Gun, Ap and Sha, was now beginning to wear off. Even though not fully back to their peaceful and dignified selves, Harappan citizens were gradually getting released from the cruel savageness that had consumed them over the last three days. Murmurs of the injustice meted out to their Surya could now be heard from various corners. Even tears of repentance were now flowing from some eyes. But it was all too late. Sanjna was no more. Manu was presumably dead. And the Surya had now contorted into a grotesque harbinger of destruction and death.

The plight of the now helpless Harappans was painful. On the one hand they could see their end approaching, and on the other they had nowhere to go. They knew that without a life-giving river to support agriculture, fishing and even drinking water, it was impossible to establish a new colony. Travellers, who rode a couple of hundred *yojanas* to the east, had always returned with tales of drought and dust. There was no escaping their ghastly fate. Mothers held their little ones close through the shrieking nights. Fathers assembled frantically to find a way to save their loved ones, only to return frustrated. Every home, every temple of Harappa was now turning to yajnas and prayers, begging the Gods for forgiveness and redemption.

But the Gods were not going to yield. These erring humans had tried to black out their Surya in a collective fit of madness.

And the darkened Sun was stalking them from a high perch, preparing to burn them with his fury.

·‖卐‖·

'At least a thousand of them,' said Prachanda to Vivasvan, shouting at the top of his voice to be audible in the violently windy night. 'And this is the night shift. During the day they are more than double of this.'

Vivasvan nodded, without worrying too much about the numbers Prachanda was cautioning him about. His eye was marking his targets – Harappan soldiers that were in tactical positions around the construction site more than two hundred meters below, the area illuminated by industrial torches and bonfires struggling to stay lit in the storm. Over the last three days he had made the mistake of holding back his real supremacy in inflicting mortal damage, and had lost everything in the bargain. He was not going to repeat that blunder. Harappa was going to face the full heat of the devta's declaration of war.

'I will do the *bhanjee*, the advanced vertical leap,' said Vivasvan.

Prachanda and his handful of men went numb for a moment as they heard these words. The plan was to capture the material, equipment and workers that were building the mountains of brick and bronze under orders from Pundit Chandradhar, the new king of Harappa. This ill-fated king was following the plan originally envisioned by Vivasvan Pujari, to use man-made ranges to divert the ominously shifting Saraswati. But what use is a blueprint without its masterful architect?

'Bring me the longest ropes of animal hide that you have. We have very little time,' continued Vivasvan, ignoring the expressions of disbelief on the faces of his newfound aides.

'But Avivasvan, this fall is too steep. No one has done the bhanjee jump before from such a height. Either the rope will give way or you will smash into the ground at the speed of an arrow!'

Bhanjee or obstacle leap was a known practice in Harappa, and even in the kingdom of the Asuras. It was used primarily for stealth assassinations. But the height, from which these jumps were made with a leather rope tied to the waist of the attacker, was never more than the top of a tall tree or the roof of a three-storied building. What Vivasvan Pujari was proposing to do was unheard of, and far too perilous.

·||卐||·

He was ready. A rope that he had carefully measured and tied to his waist himself was anchored around a massive block of brick and bronze. His left thigh had a quiver stuffed with lethal arrows, each arrow gently glued at its tip to the quiver – so as to not fall out unless pulled by the devta.

'As soon as I hit the ground after my third or fourth rebound, command your foot soldiers to surround the entire area. Kill the soldiers that resist and chain up the rest. They will also be harnessed into this massive project.'

Prachanda and his men nodded in agreement.

Before jumping off the cliff, deep down into the heart of the Harappan troops, Vivasvan Pujari decided to unleash panic in the enemy ranks. To the awe of the asura troops by his side, Vivasvan pulled out four arrows at one time. He masterfully placed them on his bow, took aim and shot all the arrows at once. Even while the first volley of arrows was in the air, the devta pulled out and shot another four. And then another. The lightning speed and accuracy of his archery was dazzling for the asura soldiers and their senapati Prachanda. In a flash the devta's arrows had found their mark, and twelve Harappan soldiers were pierced through. They fell from their high and low vantage points together.

The devta now took a few steps back and then raced off the edge of the cliff, jumping and flying down as gracefully as a diving hawk. As he dropped at increasing speed pulled by the Earth's gravity, he shot two more torrents of arrows, finding his mark with every shot. There was instant commotion in the Harappan troops, as they saw their soldiers crumbling all around them. And suddenly some of them saw a one-eyed ghost that pounced on them from the sky, only to vanish in a jiffy! Now all hell broke loose. Labourers carrying bricks and pulling stone blocks now dropped everything and began to flee. More arrows came shrieking out of nowhere, unnerving Harappan infantrymen that were on duty.

Prachanda was watching the proceedings with fear and admiration like he had never felt for anyone before. Not even for his valiant king Sura.

'He is one against one thousand, and yet he is winning!' he whispered to himself.

'He is truly half-human, half-God...'

·||ॐ||·

It was all over in less than one movement of the Sun-clock. Vivasvan Pujari had decimated nearly a hundred soldiers even before he finally cut himself loose using his sword and landed on the ground. He was surrounded by twenty or more Harappan soldiers, all of whom he hacked to pieces in a matter of moments. The haste at which the devta wielded his sword made it nothing more than a blur for the enemy – the last blur they ever saw.

Sura rode-in into the center of the scene, with his soldiers now beheading or tying-up their Harappan counterparts. The short and swift battle had been won.

The asura king dismounted and walked up to Vivasvan Pujari, who was leaning against a boulder, his arms resting on his sword that stood proudly in front of him. The Ratna-Maru was dripping with blood.

'You are beyond comparison, O great a-devta!' said Sura as he bowed to Vivasvan Pujari. There was no one else in the world Sura had bowed to before. 'History will never forget you.'

'History is precisely what I am going to erase, Sura,' replied Vivasvan.

Sura knew what Vivasvan meant. He let the devta continue.

'No one is going to remember me. But more importantly...

No one will ever know what happened to Harappa.'

·||ॐ||·

'So what is the plan now?' asked Prachanda. They were gathered around a crackling bonfire.

'Bring the head engineer of this site to me,' said Vivasvan.

In a few moments a middle-aged man, looking terribly frightened, was brought before the devta. He knew who Vivasvan Pujari was. Everyone in Harappa knew who Vivasvan Pujari was. The head engineer vaguely remembered seeing the Surya of Harappa being skinned alive at the Great Bath a couple of days ago. As if from a scene of an indistinct dream, he somehow pictured himself pelting this great man with a stone. He remembered laughing manically, delighted at the prospect of the great Vivasvan Pujari dying an animal's death. And here he was, in front of the Surya, full of reverence and repentance. It wasn't the poor man's fault. When the invisible hand of the universe etches misfortune on the pages of mankind's destiny, even the pious are consumed by the venom of immorality.

Vivasvan noticed the man shivering with fear and asked him gently, 'what is the objective of this massive undertaking, my friend?'

The trembling man replied, 'to…to…to deter the course of the Rakt-Dhaara away from Harappa, my lord.'

'Good,' said Vivasvan. 'There is just a small change of plan.'

Everyone was listening, including the head engineer.

'From this moment on, instead of diverting the Saraswati away from Harappa, we will make sure we turn it *towards* the wretched city!'

Banaras, 2017

'WE MADE HIM A MONSTER'

The beautiful, pillar-like dome of the Dhamek Stupa at Sarnath stood right in front of them. Despite being a sanctum of peace and spirituality, it was somehow failing to offer any balm of respite to the two shattered minds and souls that sat facing it.

Damini was inconsolable, frightened and distraught. Vidyut sat motionless, his face cast in stone.

'Vidyut, promise me you will not do anything silly in your anger,' insisted Damini. She could see Vidyut was burning with rage.

Vidyut did not respond. Damini could see his teeth clench in indignant fury. She knew that by committing the grisly act of a brutal murder in the precincts of the Dev-Raakshasa matth, Trijat had thrown the gauntlet towards Vidyut.

And she understood Vidyut too well to know that he was not going to let it go.

⦁‖卐‖⦁

Along with Bodh Gaya, Kushinagar and Lumbini, Sarnath is among the four primary pilgrimages believed to have been recommended by the Buddha Himself. About 13 kilometers from Varanasi, it is the site where Gautama Buddha gave his very first sermon. Vidyut had promised Damini that he would take her to this beautiful and holy place. Never in his wildest nightmares had he imagined the circumstances of this visit.

They sat crossed-legged on the grass of the sprawling lawns of the premises, lost and disoriented. Vidyut was unable to get the nerve-wracking sight of his misguided friend's severed head staring into his face with dead, white eyes.

Why did we tie him up? Bala could have saved himself! Why did we tie him up?

The incident had shaken up the whole of the Dev-Raakshasa matth. Never in its history of hundreds of years had the matth's security been breached so summarily and so violently. Fear had seeped into the hearts of its inhabitants, and the great Dwarka Shastri was nursing a deep, uncharacteristic guilt. He was crestfallen that he had let down not just his brilliant ancestors who had led and protected the matth against even marauding forces of cruel, bigoted sultans, but also the vital duty destiny had entrusted him with. Vidyut had to be protected at all cost! And if Bala could be beheaded right under the noses of the matth leadership, was Vidyut safe at all??

The God-Demon monastery was now in counter-attack mode. One of the first and immediate edicts of the matthadheesh was that Damini had to be sent back to the security of her Gurgaon metropolitan home and life. Her half-hearted protests were ignored, given that Vidyut was firm as well on the decision of her return. A trained fighter of the matth was dispatched to Gurgaon without Damini's knowledge. Her mandate was to ensure Damini's safety from a close but invisible distance.

Their trip to Sarnath was going to be Damini's last day in Varanasi.

For now.

·||ॐ||·

Damini slipped her fingers between Vidyut's, looking lovingly at his tense, handsome face. In just a few days their whole world had turned upside down. From her dashing, successful and famous boyfriend till just a week ago, Vidyut had transformed into this so-called savior or *messiah*, destined to protect something that was critical for the entire human race! He was at the epicenter of murders, exorcism, taantrics, bullets, assassins, spirits and hidden foes. It was all unfolding at a pace that Damini could not fully assimilate.

She had left everything on faith. The limitless, infinite, indescribable faith she had on one man. Her man.

Vidyut.

'*Kuchh toh bolo*, Vidyut…say something, na…' she said.

Vidyut knew he had just one more hour with Damini, before he dropped her to the airport. He had so much to share with her. His heart was burdened with sorrow, remorse and anxiety, and he knew it was only Damini who could understand everything he was going through. Only she who would *hear,* and not just listen.

'We made him a monster,' said Vidyut, looking far into the stretch of the Sarnath shrines.

'What do you mean…?' asked Damini.

'We made him the monster he became, Damini. I heard his story. The rotten reality of his childhood and everything we subjected his family to…'

Damini was confused. Not privy to the last conversation Vidyut had had with Bala, she was unable to comprehend who or what Vidyut was talking about.

Vidyut continued. Damini let him. She knew he needed to speak his heart out.

'We are the oldest, the most ancient religion in the world. In fact we are not a religion at all. We are the way of life of this glorious nation, this beautiful subcontinent. We discovered the zero, the value of the mathematical *pi*, martial arts, surgery, medicine, chess, politics, yoga…we were writing the profound Vedas when the West was living in caves and hunting for raw flesh! We created the *Varna Vyavastha* or the

Caste System as the most prehistoric and efficient form of division of labour – a vital construct for the development of an economy. But look how we corrupted that most evangelical concept of all.'

'Sorry Vidyut, I understand you are talking about Hinduism and the division of the society into castes. But how is that an efficient or evangelical structure? Isn't it the worst form of inequality?'

'Of course it is! Of course it is, Damini…' replied Vidyut fervently. 'But this was not how it all began. If you read our scriptures, each of the four broad castes of *Brahmins* (priests & teachers), *Kshatriyas* (warriors & protectors), *Vaishyas* (merchants & businesspeople) and *Shudras* (workers & artisans) are believed to have emanated from a distinct body part of Lord Vishnu! How can any caste, creed or community that finds its genesis from Lord Vishnu Himself, be inferior to any other?'

'Please be clear, Vidyut. I think I know what you are saying, but please explain a little. And I have no idea how Bala is connected to all this.'

Vidyut sighed. He turned to Damini and kissed her softly on her forehead. It was out of nowhere, but he could not stop himself from expressing his love for her. She tightened her grip on his fingers, and raised her pretty eyebrows, urging him to continue.

·||ॐ||·

They were now walking towards a famous sweetmeat shop, a short distance outside Sarnath. Vidyut had gushed about the delectable *gulaab jaamuns* of this shop a couple of days ago, and Damini insisted that she wanted to try the delicious *mithai*. She was not one to enjoy sweets too much, but she wanted to keep Vidyut engaged in some silly niceties somehow - anything that drew him away even momentarily from the darkness of the previous evening.

'Varna Vyavastha or the caste system did not propound or champion any form of hierarchy whatsoever. Each section of the society was considered to be equal and vital to the harmony and progress of the people,' continued Vidyut, as they walked in the bright sunlit afternoon.

'Well, that's news to me,' said Damini. 'I always thought that Brahmins were supposed to be the highest order of caste, followed by Kshatriyas and so on…

Vidyut laughed and shook his head in amazement.

Even someone as well informed as Damini has these misgivings!

'No, Damini, there was no such distinction. It was simply division of labour, to encourage specialization and expertise for the benefit of the society at large. Consider this – in a company like my own, which department is more important? Marketing? Software programming? Human Resources? Or Finance?'

'Okay baba, I understand…' replied Damini, grasping fully what Vidyut was trying to explain. 'But then how did this system of equality and economic specialization change into an exploitative set-up?'

Vidyut turned to Damini, his eyes widened in disbelief at her naïve question, as he spoke.

'Just how a religion propounded by a Shepherd who sacrificed himself for the message of universal love, unleashed the most brutal and inhuman religious crusades! Just how a Prophet's word of love and humanity is being distorted by some people to spread violence and hate, Damini. Don't you see? It is the greed for power and wealth that distorts great ancient vision into quagmires of shallow vested interests?'

Damini was listening carefully, absorbing every word Vidyut was saying.

'I am not defending what Bala did. But why blame him alone when he was actually the victim of societal decay? Blind execution of the caste system, in a way that leads to the exploitation of one community by another, is not Hinduism. It never was. This ruthless subjugation of any caste or any community is nothing but moral and social corruption! And it not only defiles the name of our great way of life, but also brings misery to fellow humans. Bala was just at the receiving end of this perversion, and he took the only way out he saw.'

'I understand, Vidyut,' said Damini after a few moments of pause, as they walked silently. 'But will you try to get this whole episode out of your mind? I know it will not be easy. But it is important for you to put it behind you.'

Vidyut stopped and turned towards Damini.

'This is not about me, Damini. It is not just about Bala either. This is a larger issue that we face as a nation, as a people. There was a long phase in our history when Brahmins and Kshatriyas were oppressing the Shudras or *dalits* as some people call them. Those were dark and deplorable times. But now see what is happening. Politicians are exploiting and fanning those old scars. As a result now sizeable sections of the so-called lower castes are voting en masse, bringing corrupt individuals to power - simply because they belong to a certain caste! Democracy, which is the heart and soul of our great country, is succumbing to caste-based fault-lines. Buses are being burnt and massive rallies are being called in the name of caste even today, when all of us Indians should be focusing on uprooting poverty, illiteracy, malnutrition and so many other challenges we continue to face. But no! We are busy fighting each other based on caste, religion, language, state and what not. And if this keeps going, more Balas will emerge as the noxious by-product of this perpetual conflict.'

From a distance the shrines of Sarnath were visible, looking glorious against the bright afternoon sky. Vidyut pointed at them for Damini to see.

'We are standing where the Buddha stood one day, Damini, thousands of years ago. The Buddhists embrace Him as their very own. On the other hand, Hindus believe Him to be the ninth avatar of Lord Vishnu. Both communities love the Buddha. Both communities share Him and His divine legacy. There is no struggle, no clash whatsoever. It is this very assimilation, this very inclusiveness that makes us unique and makes our heritage immortal.

It is this very precious way of life that we need to protect, Damini.'

East of Harappa, 1700 BCE

THE BLACK TEMPLE

It was the most magnificent sight.

After riding for several hours in the constricted goat-trails and ravines of the grey-black mountains, their caravan emerged at an open clearing. From the serpentine route they had taken, it was clear to Manu that neither the great architects of this splendid edifice nor the black-robed guardians of these ranges wanted anyone to find it.

As Manu's horse emerged from the narrow crevice of the mountain they had just navigated through, his eyes got locked on what he saw. The domineering presence of the structure ahead made him breathless. The most gigantic and complexly carved doorway was cut into the massive black mountain across the plain. There it was, towering majestically high into the sky.

The Black Temple.

·‖卍‖·

Chiseled intricately into the hard, black rocks of the gigantic mountain, the doorway was more beautiful than anything Manu had ever seen before. His horse trotted aimlessly towards the Black Temple even as Manu felt hypnotized by the force emanating from it.

'Come with me, Manu,' said the gracious lady, the leader of the mountain guardians. 'Let me take you inside this holiest of temples.'

Manu dismounted and followed the lady. Something was drawing him towards the core sanctum of the shrine.

As Manu entered the great door, he comprehended what he had seen outside was not even a scratch on the surface of this mesmerizing temple. A few steps inside were all that it took for Manu to grasp the real architectural wonder that he now beheld in front of his eyes. To his utter shock he realized that the master craftsmen who built this temple - *had chipped and cut the entire mountain hollow from the inside!* Manu stood at the entrance of the most enormous hall he had ever set foot in. And it was the giant belly of the black mountain.

Manu was staring up at the high walls of the temple, turning his head and then his entire body around to fully capture the enchanting sight. The ceiling was so high that it faded into the darkness. Illuminated by hundreds of glowing torches, the temple was carved into beautiful pillars, arches, sculptures and prayer rooms. A series of staircases, carved out of pure rock at a dizzy height, connected the high corridors from one end of the hall to another.

But the most imposing and awe-striking feature of the temple was what sat at the center of the hall. Manu fell to his knees and folded his hands in devoutness and entrancement.

A colossal rock statue of Rudra or Lord Shiva, deep in penance, sat soaring into the heights of the stone temple.

Manu had never witnessed or even heard of such scale and grandeur of architecture. He had never imagined a statue of Rudra to be as brilliant as what was in front of him. To him it was all like a marvelous, fantastic dream. He was nearly giddy when he felt a hand on his shoulder.

'You look like you've witnessed Creation itself!' joked Matsya, as Manu turned to look up at him.

Giving in to an inexplicable urge of love and devotion, Manu got up and fell into the arms of Matsya. He was overwhelmed by the mystical grandiose all around him, and Matsya's shoulder seemed like a comforting cushion. The mysterious fish-man was taken by surprise, but he laughed in delight and held the son of Vivasvan and Sanjna in a tight embrace. It was hard to say who needed whom more. Perhaps divinity is no greater than its believer. One would not exist without the other.

'What *is* this place, O Matsya?' asked Manu, once he had resumed his composure.

Matsya walked a few steps around the hall, admiring the forceful, mysterious beauty that surrounded them.

'It is a safe-house for this planet's most priceless secret, Manu,' he said. 'It is the seventh temple of its kind built over the last one thousand years. Several more shall be built in the centuries yet to come. The secret that is hidden here must be shifted from time to time, in order to protect it till the prophesied day arrives.'

Manu was listening intently as he noticed that several men and women dressed in the same fish-skin robes as Matsya's had appeared around them. From the way they bowed to Matsya, it was evident that they were his disciples. They all looked gentle and kind, and smelled of the sea. Manu was perplexed.

There is no sea for hundreds of miles!

'After every cycle of *yugas* or eons is over, Creation assesses its own work as well as the collective conduct of Earth's only species that resembles the Creator. It then decides the course of action that is aligned with the longevity of life, as we know it. Sometimes what is needed is a complete purging, which is engineered through the indescribably powerful forces of nature. On some other occasions, a partial cleansing is required. An end to evil through the triumph of good.

That is when an avatar appears.'

They were now sitting in a circle at the feet of Rudra - Matsya, the fish-folk, the Godmother of the mountain-guardians and Manu. Matsya was responding to Manu's queries about the Black Temple and its significance. Even as Manu focused on what Matsya was explaining, he could not help but notice that some of the distant prayer rooms of the temple were glowing a soft blue in colour. This was different from the regular yellowish-orange radiance emanating from all the other cells, as a result of the ritual fires that were lit in them. One, two...three...he quickly counted. There were seven prayer caves that were glowing blue, cut high into the temple walls and connected with rock-carved stairs.

'But what right does the Creator have to decide on the fate of this world and its inhabitants? Who gives the Creator the authority to exterminate life on this planet as and when the Creator chooses? The purging you are talking about, isn't it cruel and unbecoming of the One we worship as the Almighty?' asked Manu.

Matsya smiled and looked at Manu with great fondness. His smile reminded Manu of the way his father, the mighty Vivasvan Pujari, used to look at him affectionately.

'So you want to debate and discover *Brahma-Gyaan* or the ultimate, cosmic truth over this huddle, Manu?' said Matsya. 'Don't you think the complexity of the universe, the laws of good and evil, the construct of *Rnanubandhan* or karmic-debt, the forces of creation and destruction...might be a bit profound to unravel all at once?'

'Yes of course, Matsya. I understand that sages and mendicants dedicate their lives in an effort to enlighten themselves with the final revelation of the cosmic order, and we cannot discuss it all here and now. All I am saying is that I have been a student of the insightful Vedas and other scriptures. For all their wisdom and brilliance, I have always found it hard to accept that a force above all we know, gets to choose the fate of humanity. How unfair is that?'

The gathering was silent after Manu said these words. Most of them were now looking at Matsya to respond.

'So you want to play a role in deciding the shared destiny of your kind, Manu?' said Matsya after a few moments of deliberation. He wasn't smiling.

Manu noticed that Matsya had used the term *your* kind, and not *our* kind. He let it pass. He also felt he could see Matsya's skin radiating the bluish tinge more than usual. He shrugged away the thought.

'Yes…yes, I think I would want to be instrumental in anything that is decided for me or my people.'

Matsya was now staring into Manu's eyes, as intense as he looked delighted. Manu felt the enigmatic fish-man's glare pierce through his head, reaching far beyond into an unknown horizon.

'Then be ready, O son of Vivasvan Pujari!' Matsya roared suddenly. 'Your chance is not far away!'

His eyes were blazing and his right hand was outstretched, his finger pointing straight at Manu, as he screamed out the bloodcurdling words.

'*PRALAY…ESHHYATI…!*'

'THE GREAT DELUGE…IS COMING…!'

Banaras, 2017

CONSTANTINE

Vidyut was complaining. He had reason to. And his great grandfather was perhaps the only person in the world he could shamelessly grumble to.

'You are *trikaal-darshi*, Baba, the viewer of all realms of space and time,' said Vidyut. 'I cannot believe that you could not foresee any of this. First, that Bala was going to betray me. And second, that Trijat Kapaalik's visit was not just for an exchange of pleasantries!'

Vidyut was pacing up and down the great Dwarka Shastri's room, expressing his angst visibly to the matthadheesh.

'Has Damini landed safely in Delhi?' enquired Dwarka Shastri.

Vidyut turned to the grandmaster irritably.

'Yes. Yes, she has!'

'Hmm...'

Vidyut was getting agitated now. He needed answers from his great grandfather. He needed quick answers, several answers.

'Baba, come on please...I need you to talk to me!' exclaimed Vidyut, looking at his beloved great grandfather with exasperation.

Dwarka Shastri was flipping the beads of the *rudraaksha maala* on his fingers. He was chanting his daily intonation of the very powerful *Hanumanaashtak*, the prayer of Lord Hanuman, like he always did in trying times.

He knew certain revelations and explanations were now overdue.

||ॐ||

'Who was Lord Rama, Vidyut?'

The scion of the Shastri clan, the prophesied saviour, the magnificent Vidyut was now much calmer, sipping on some *tulsi* tea. A few days had passed of him living at the matth and he felt much at home in the austere yet authoritarian cottage of his only living parentage.

'Baba, seriously? *That* is where you are going to start from?'

The matthadheesh grinned. Vidyut also spluttered out a short laugh, trying to not spill his tea. The air around the matth had been starkly tense for the last twenty-four hours. It was a respite for both the Shastri men to share a light moment.

'No, but tell me, Vidyut,' insisted Dwarka Shastri, 'who was Rama?'

Vidyut kept away his teacup.

'You're really asking me who Lord Rama was, Baba? You're asking me to define the *Maryaada-Purushottam*, the Embodiment of Morality, the Model of Mankind, the Ultimate God-King, Rama?'

'I'm not asking you to describe Him or to endorse Him. I simply want to know if Rama was human or divine.'

'He was an avatar, Baba - the incarnation of Lord Vishnu in a human form. You know all this so much better than I do.'

Dwarka Shastri nodded and continued, 'now tell me Vidyut, did Rama make a few mistakes during His lifetime? He was incorruptible, perfection personified…but did He not make judgment errors also?'

'Yes, He did, Baba. Despite being perhaps the most ideal of men to have ever walked on Earth, He made several mistakes. But wasn't that the very objective of an avatar? The Almighty did not need to take a human form to destroy the forces of evil in this world. If we go by the conventional or popular perception of God, God could have simply struck them down by lightning! But the larger purpose, the teaching of an avatar and its human-like struggles is to set an example for mankind...that even the Creator suffered when the avatar came to this mortal world. Whether it was Rama, Krishna or the Prophets, Gurus and messiahs of any religion or faith, they all combatted life like any ordinary human being, and yet left their everlasting mark behind. Here the entire discussion becomes very intricate, because some beliefs indicate that these avatars were meant to show humans how they can rise and become Gods themselves! But like I said, that is a far more complicated discussion for now.'

'Thank you for the detailed response, Vidyut. You are absolutely right. Having traces of divinity or spiritual evolution does not make one omnipotent, or all-powerful. Rama knew golden deer don't exist. Yet He chased one. Couldn't Rama see that it was actually a demon under the illusory golden hide of the deer?'

Vidyut was listening. He now knew what his Baba was trying to say.

'Nothing can stand in the way of destiny itself if it chooses for certain events to unfold as part of a pre-decided karmic scheme. If Lord Rama could make a judgment error, who is this mere mortal Dwarka Shastri? I am sorry I could not see it all coming, Vidyut. I could sense the presence of evil, but it was all under a strange veil,' said the matthadheesh, looking deeply disturbed.

Vidyut suddenly felt horrible at making his great grandfather, who was already reeling under guilt, stand trial for his failure to see through the dark deception that had seeped into the Dev-Raakshasa matth.

·||ॐ||·

'What happened in Constantinople, Baba?' asked Vidyut.

They had decided to take a walk around the lawns of the matth. It was also an effort by the great matthadheesh to reassure all the inhabitants of the monastery that everything was going to settle back to normal very soon. The grandmaster met his disciples and their families every now and then, smiling at them or raising his palm in *aashirvaad* or blessings. Vidyut playfully lifted a few of the children in his arms, making them laugh with joy and relief.

'What transpired in Constantinople was something that changed the world forever, Vidyut. And it was not exactly in Constantinople. It was about a hundred miles from the city, in a town called Nicaea.'

'Nicaea…?' whispered Vidyut. 'I have heard about Nicaea, Baba. It was where the great council of Christian priests had taken place, back in the 4th century. It was quite a milestone event, as it resolved some of the greatest debates within the believers of the faith.'

Dwarka Shastri was impressed, as always.

'You are quite well read, Vidyut,' said the grandmaster. 'Kartikeya and Pooja would have been very proud.'

The matthadheesh and his great grandson looked at each other momentarily with moist eyes. This was the first time Vidyut had heard his great grandfather mention his late parents.

'Thank you, Baba. Please go on...' urged Vidyut.

'Most people know about the Council of Nicaea and that it was a congress of Christian priests. But very few people know that Constantine held another clandestine meeting that very day. That secret and high-level group was gathered to discuss something that he believed was going to define the future of a peaceful, prosperous and conflict-free world.'

Vidyut was listening carefully, wondering immediately how his great grandfather knew anything about the hidden chapters of the Council of Nicaea. He did not have to wait too long.

'And even fewer people know that apart from his leading military Generals, high-priests, Roman and Egyptian mystics and the richest of merchants, there was one special attendee of that secret conference. One who Constantine trusted the most.'

It was hard for Vidyut to keep up with everything the matthadheesh was saying. Nicaea? Constantine? An emperor's secret manifesto?

Where is all this going? How are Constantine and his world-view connected to me?

Dwarka Shastri noticed the bewilderment on Vidyut's face. He knew it was time the last devta heard everything.

'What nearly no one knows is that Constantine's special guest at Nicaea that day had ridden thousands of miles from the East.'

Vidyut was listening with his eyes wide with anticipation.

'He was none other than our magnificent ancestor, the hooded warrior-sage, Advait Shastri.'

Harappa, 1700 BCE

HIS GREATEST SIN

It was time to deliver his end of the promise. Sura had kept his word and helped Vivasvan Pujari capture the mountains of brick and bronze. His army had also ring-fenced the construction site with thousands of fierce warriors, to ensure that Pundit Chandradhar and Priyamvada could not win it back. Therefore it was now Vivasvan's turn to keep his word. It was time for him to commit his greatest sin among all.

The erstwhile Surya of Harappa was going to offer Sura the lives of the very Saptarishi that he once worshipped like the Gods themselves.

Not aware that his valiant and beloved son Manu was alive, Vivasvan Pujari continued to seethe with uncontrollable fury. He was going to unleash such cruelty and hate that this world had never seen before. And would perhaps never witness hereafter.

He was going to permit the killing of the Saraswati's sons. Even someone of his wisdom failed to foresee the devastation that would follow.

Or maybe he knew.

·||卐||·

They made their way in the darkness, walking waist-deep through the freezing stream that gushed along the secret abode of the Saptarishi. It was a small band comprising fifty of Sura's elite, nocturnal troopers. It was the demon-king's idea to make a stealth approach towards the cluster of forests and caves where the Saptarishi dwelled. Vivasvan knew it was a waste of effort. The Saptarishi would know about their progress from even before they took their first step. But Vivasvan Pujari also knew, that the Saptarishi were not the kind to flee. The holy Seven would either bring the creeping twines of giant trees to turn into serpents and strangle their attackers in the darkness, or command hundreds of wolves to tear their flesh apart. Vivasvan did not care. His asura brigade was working incessantly towards building massive mounds that would withstand and direct the Saraswati's formidable flow towards the evil city of Harappa and its outskirts.

His work was done already. He was going to fulfill his promise to his vile comrade, and then give up his body in a final yogic ritual of ascension of the soul beyond the realm of flesh and blood.

Even now, even after everything that had revealed itself in the last few days, the great devta had not learnt the most vital lesson. Even now he had plans that he felt were going to fall in place as he envisioned them.

How can a heart filled with hate and a mind poisoned with vengeance ever hope to have the universe on its side? How can blackened souls embarking upon violence against the unarmed and the innocent, hope to ever enjoy the favour of the Creator? The violent shall always be punished first. Punished foremost.

·||ॐ||·

They now stood exactly where Vivasvan Pujari had met the Saptarishi last. It was a cold night and, unlike his last visit, none of the magical occurrences of singing rivulets and chirping birds presented themselves. There were no giggling pebbles or neighing horses. It was a chilling, black dusk.

'Find them!' commanded Sura.

The fifty fighters of the demon-king now unsheathed their menacing swords and began slashing their blades around wildly at every bush and every thicket. Sura himself was prancing around to look for even the remotest evidence of the Saptarishi's presence. But to no avail. They were nowhere to be found.

Just when Sura, Prachanda and their men decided to abandon their search and turned to Vivasvan Pujari with angry, enquiring eyes, they saw the devta staring in one direction. As they followed his gaze, they saw too. Those that seemed to have appeared out of nowhere.

The Saptarishi!

·||ॐ||·

'They are not in their bodies,' said the Surya of Harappa, his eyes still observing the Saptarishi from a distance.

Sura, Prachanda and their men could not understand what Vivasvan had just said. As far as they were concerned, the Saptarishi were right there in front of them. They moved forward cautiously, their scimitars ready to strike the divine sages down. Sura's breath was heavy with anticipation. He was going to destroy the last hurdle between him and the greatest empire anyone had ever ruled!

The Saptarishi were now only a few steps away. One of the sages sat cross-legged at the bank of the cold stream. The other was in a trance on a rock clearing ahead of them. Yet another was in deep meditation perched on a low hill, while the other was in penance under a lush tree. All seven of them sat no more than a few paces away from one another. All of them appeared calm and undisturbed at the approaching assassins.

'It's no use…!' shouted Vivasvan to Sura and Prachanda. He was still standing where he was when he saw the sages for the first time tonight.

Sura turned impatiently, as Vivasvan Pujari walked slowly towards him.

'It will be no use harming their bodies, Sura. They are not in them anymore.'

'What are you talking about, O a-devta,' the king of the asuras snapped back. 'They are all there! They are alive...but not for long, I swear to you!'

The demon-king turned to his men and yelled out an order that was routine for him, but one that stunned Vivasvan Pujari. Something the devta of Harappa had not anticipated.

'I need their ashes on my body tomorrow morning,' commanded Sura in his authoritative, gruff voice.

'BURN THEM ALIVE!'

THE NEW WORLD ORDER

'When a monarch becomes too powerful and perhaps too narcissistic, he begins to believe that he is the hand of God. That everything that the Almighty wants to implement will be done through him as God's medium. Alexander believed he was divine, till just before his early demise. The Egyptian pharaoh Ramasses II built enormous statues of himself to be worshipped as a God, and believed he was related to *Ra*, the Sun deity. Why, even as late as the Mughal kings we see this phenomenon. They gave themselves the title *Jahanpanaah* or Refuge of the World!' explained Dwarka Shastri, as they continued their walk around the monastery.

Vidyut was listening silently, attentively…nodding his head once in a while. He did not want to interrupt the flow of Dwarka Shastri's discourse.

'Constantine was no different. He waged war after war and conquered enormous territory. He began to consider himself above ordinary human beings, who, he started to believe, had a predictable pattern of social and political behavior. Just because he was able to unify a large empire comprising numerous smaller states under his suzerainty, he began to envision a unified world at large.

He identified religion as the primary cause of discord between people. He observed that while regions and territories can be annexed and forced into unification, the same was not true when it came to faiths and religions. Constantine was well aware of the rise of Christianity despite the full might and brutality of the Roman Empire. So in order to realize his dream of a cohesive world, he decided to begin with religion.'

'This reminds me of the Mughal king Akbar, Baba,' replied Vidyut. 'Even Akbar made an attempt to bring peace and harmony across his vast empire by rejecting the supremacy of any one religion and bringing together the best of all prevailing faiths. He even started a new religion, so to speak, called the *Din-i-Ilahi* or *Tawhid-i-Ilahi*.'

'You are right. But there is a key difference. Akbar did not try to compel people into his newly founded faith. He never used force. Nor intrigue. But that was not the case with Constantine. He first brought two factions of Christianity together in the official Council of Nicaea. That was an easy project for him. It was on the sidelines of this Council that he commissioned the most ambitious and far-reaching politico-religious campaign in the history of our species. He unleashed a dangerous and unrealistic quest to establish a *New World Order.*

·||ॐ||·

They were now back in the grandmaster's cottage. Even though the 108 year-old master and commander of the Dev-Raakshasa matth had shown remarkable recovery from his illness, he was still weak. He rested for a while on his stately bed, before coming back to their discussion.

'Constantine was a visionary no doubt, and his intentions were noble. Most importantly, he was among the handful of people over the last hundreds of years who were privy to the secret of the Black Temple. He wanted to do what he called 'God's work' by appointing himself as God's deputy!'

Vidyut did not hear the whole statement of Dwarka Shastri. The mention of the Black Temple *again* made him jump.

'Baba, before we proceed, you have to tell me what the Black Temple is! Balvanta dada mentioned it the other day at the ghaat. He said Naina keeps a satellite phone to stay in touch with the Black Temple. Then Romi was muttering something about it before he consumed that potassium cyanide pill. Now you allude to its secret that has remained hidden for hundreds of years. What is the Black Temple, Baba? How is it related to us? What is the secret it guards?'

'The Black Temple holds in its heart the last hope for mankind. But please have patience, Vidyut. If I have not told you about it, there must be a reason. In just seven days from now you will not only find out what the secret of the Black Temple is, you are in fact the chosen one to protect it till the moment of salvation arrives for all of us. Not just all of us in this matth. Nor just for everyone in the holy city of Kashi. But all of us on this planet, Vidyut.'

·||ॐ||·

'In his unreasonably high confidence or perhaps arrogance, what Constantine did not foresee was that great visions can be shouldered and realized only by men and women worthy of that burden. Being someone who had himself satiated all his desire for wealth, power and conquest, he attempted to build a framework that would survive beyond a few years only if none of the men involved in his grand scheme nursed any personal ambitions. How ridiculously naïve of a king who dominated a quarter of the known world in his time!' said Dwarka Shastri.

'It sure does sound silly, Baba. But what exactly was his grand design? What *was* the New World Order?' enquired Vidyut, now sitting right next to the matthadheesh's bed.

'*Was?* Did you just say 'was', Vidyut?' asked Dwarka Shastri, his eyebrows raised in amazement and mild rebuke at his great grandson's choice of words. 'The New World Order thrives like a ghost-shadow on this entire world, more powerful now than it has ever been. Isn't this what all the signs have been telling you, Vidyut? Isn't this what I cautioned you about on the fateful day you went to the Dashashwamedh ghaat to meet Romi Pereira?'

Vidyut figured he had made a mistake. But more than that he recognized how very sensitive his Baba was to the mention and treatment of this name - *the New World Order*.

'My apologies, Baba. That is not what I meant. Since we were talking about the times of Constantine, I meant to ask what his grandiose vision was? What was he trying to achieve through this Order?'

Dwarka Shastri nodded and continued.

'It was a bizarre, utopian dream. By a New World Order Constantine meant to rebuild the world, this time without barriers, without hate, without fault-lines and without identity wars between human beings based on ethnicities, nations, beliefs, colour or economic imbalance. The few years of peace he experienced in his own life of greatness and conquest were those when the people of his vast kingdom lived under one law, one monarch, one culture, one economy and most importantly, almost one religion. In his desire to do God's work and to make the world a better place after he was gone, Constantine laid the meticulous foundation for the world's most formidable underground organization in the history of the Earth. A brotherhood so powerful that it would pulverize humankind at large towards Constantine's great vision of a uniform world – one government, one economy, one currency, one military, one culture and one God!'

This was the most impudent world-view Vidyut had ever heard of. Anyone even attempting something like this had to be either a lunatic or a superhuman.

Constantine the Great was a bit of both.

·||卐||·

'How can anyone think up something so incongruous, Baba? It is a Herculean task to even keep a great nation like India under one unified identity, given the politically motivated separatist forces at play. But even if we take the politics away, how can human beings, richly diverse as they are, be whipped into artificial uniformity? How can free will, liberty, choices, preferences, aspirations and loyalties be permanently compromised? How can people be treated like sheep?' asked Vidyut irritably. He was finding it almost offending that one emperor could have the audacity to try and control the fate of not just the global populace of his own time, but also those that were to follow generations later!

Dwarka Shastri smiled wearily, not looking at Vidyut. He was glad his great grandson felt the same angst about this medieval madness that persisted till this day.

'Constantine's mandate to the first ring of the brotherhood that he commissioned at Nicaea that day was simply worded. To the first twenty 'brothers' he handpicked to carry out his determined design he gave a straightforward primary goal - to work incessantly, unstoppably and ruthlessly towards setting up a *one-world government.*'

'Now what on Earth is that, Baba? One-world government...? What set of madmen can ever imagine to achieve something as absurd as this?'

The grandmaster turned to look at Vidyut and smiled. But Vidyut could see his eyes were far from any cheer of any kind.

Dwarka Shastri now asked Vidyut something that was long overdue.

'Have you heard of the Nestorian Christians, Vidyut?

And of the Knights Templar?'

East of Harappa, 1700 BCE

PRALAY

'Your father did not just know about the existence of the Black Temple and its location, Manu. He was one of its principal guardians.'

Manu was now taking a tour of the grand temple with Matsya. The blue fish-man, who Manu had come to love dearly in such a short span of time, had requested for this walk-about with the son of Vivasvan Pujari. Even as they walked from one high corridor of the magnificent temple to another, catching glimpses of intense mystics and mendicants deep in penance in their intricately sculptured prayer cells, Manu could not get two things off his mind. One, what Matsya had said a while back, in the most uncharacteristic and frightening of tones, about the coming of a great flood. Two, the seven prayer rooms, quarried highest into the steep, black walls of the hollow mountain, glowing with a divine bluish hue.

'He never said anything about this temple, O Matsya,' replied Manu. 'Nor did mother.'

The mention of his father and mother choked Manu for a moment, but he let it go.

'But Uncle Somdutt yelled out something to me when I was riding out of the battlefield with mother, and that stuck in my mind as I rode for hours in a semi-conscious state. He asked me to ride eastwards, till I found the Black Temple'.

Matsya halted briefly and turned to Manu.

'You know you were destined to find this temple, do you not Manu? Similarly, this temple was preordained to find you! And from now on, *you* will be its chief priest, master and protector.'

This was all too overwhelming for Manu. The Black Temple, the overpowering, mammoth idol of Shiva, the minutely carved, titanic cave-temple, the prophecy of a great deluge, the glowing blue caves…and now this declaration from Matsya.

He sighed deeply, unhooked his waist-belt and pulled away his sword. Keeping it aside he sat down on one of the rock-cut stairways.

As he settled down and looked up, he saw Matsya staring at him with the naughtiest, most amused eyes! The marvelous leader of the fish-folk burst into a soft yet infectious laughter.

'Whaaat…?' exclaimed Manu, slightly embarrassed. He was half laughing himself now, but clueless as to what Matsya found so funny.

'You're so melodramatic…taking away your scimitar, collapsing down on these steps…ha…ha…ha' guffawed Matsya louder. 'And…and…I loved the way you sighed…O God!' Matsya was now laughing so loud that the whole gigantic belly of the mountain was ringing with his joyous hoot.

Before Manu could utter another word of merry protest, he developed goose bumps at what he witnessed. The echo of Matsya's laughter was darting across various arches and high walls of the massive temple sanctum and getting amplified. In a matter of moments Manu felt as if the whole mountain was laughing. Nay…not just the whole mountain, but also the entire universe. Every fallen leaf, every pebble, every bird, every animal, every wisp of tendril, every little gust of breeze, every ray of light, every newborn infant… entire creation seemed to be instantly immersed in the bliss emanating from Matsya.

This was it.

Manu got up slowly and walked up to Matsya, who was now wiping his eyes, wet with the moisture of his delightful mockery. Manu fell at his feet.

'You are Vishnu, aren't you? You can be none other than Lord Vishnu Himself, O Matsya…!' exclaimed Manu.

Matsya smiled, but he looked ready to break into tears. He bent down and lifted Manu up.

'You are Vishnu…' whispered Manu, staring into the eyes of Matsya with indescribable devotion. This time it was not a question.

'I am not Vishnu, O great king,' replied Matsya.

He wasn't.

Just as Rama and Krishna were not exactly Vishnu.

·||ॐ||·

'Vivasvan Pujari, Somdutt and even Pundit Chandradhar were some of the people who were aware of the presence of the Black Temple,' explained Matsya. 'All of them knew that this shrine holds a mysterious crypt that is of great importance to the future of the human species. But only your father, the mighty Vivasvan Pujari and his wife Sanjna, were in the know of the real secret.'

It always bothered Manu how Matsya referred to humanity strangely as *your kind* or *human species*. He never sounded haughty or judgmental. He did not even sound distant. But it was something that made him appear to be an otherworldly eremitic.

'What *does* this temple hold, O great Matsya? Why did Somdutt ji direct me to it? Did he know you were here? Did he know the black-robed guardians of these mountains would rescue me? And what did you mean when you suddenly erupted and announced the onset of a devastating deluge? We all can see that a great downpour engulfs the Harappan settlements. The Saraswati is in spate too. But we have always believed that the divine Saptarishi are her children and she would never do anything to harm them. I am sorry for so many questions Matsya, but bless me with your enlightening words.' Manu knew he was inundating the blue fish-man with queries, but he had no choice.

Matsya's eyes were peering deep into Manu's. But before he answered, he picked up a bucket made of seashells woven into a container.

'Bring me some water, will you please, Manu?' said Matsya, pointing at a stream gushing out from a corner of the temple. 'My people are thirsty.'

Manu obliged immediately. Even the tiniest opportunity to serve Matsya in some way gave him immense delight.

·‖ॐ‖·

They were now strolling in the dusty plains outside the black mountain. The sky was monstrously overcast. The fury that had befallen the Harappan settlements was now spreading its dark loom over far-out lands as well. Manu and Matsya stopped and looked up at the sky as they witnessed what looked like the mass exodus of a million birds, flying in enormous formations against the terrifying clouds and thunder.

'Somdutt does not know the purpose behind this mysterious temple, but he did know that the mountain-guardians are righteous warriors, loyal to both Shiva and to the Surya of Harappa – your great father. He sent you in this direction because he knew this was your only chance of survival,' spoke Matsya, even as he continued to observe the untimely migration of the birds.

'These people were loyal to my father? His influence across these lands never ceases to amaze me. Yet he died without a single friend there with him to offer a shoulder for his last journey,' said Manu bitterly.

Matsya turned to Manu and put an arm on his shoulder.

'Your father will have an impact greater than you can imagine, Manu. The wheels of fate have only just begun to spin. But for now we have more pressing matters to tend to.'

'And what would those be, O great Matsya?'

This time it was the fish-man that sighed. He gazed far out into the horizon visible from between the two steep mountains.

'A great flood is indeed coming, Manu. A deluge so destructive that man has never known, heard of or even imagined, will soon be upon us.'

Manu noticed that Matsya's eyebrows were curled into wrinkles on his forehead. For the first time since he had known this mystical man, he saw worry and gloom written across his otherwise supremely radiant blue face.

'I did not know you were also a soothsayer, Matsya,' said Manu.

Matsya turned to him looking puzzled.

'But I am not a soothsayer, Manu.'

'You are not? How do you know about the impending deluge if you are not an astrologer?'

'That is not important, Manu. What is important is whether you believe me,' Matsya said. He was looking straight at Manu.

Manu smiled and said, 'there is nothing of you that I will not believe, O Matsya. We will gather these men and head for higher ground. We will beat this flood.'

Matsya shook his head in dismay. He looked miffed at Manu's naïve response.

'Are you not listening, Manu? No mountain on Earth is high enough to escape the torrents of this great flood. This flood cannot be survived!'

Manu was a little irritated himself now. Even though the forces of nature carried raw, brutal strength, why couldn't man withstand another flood, even if it was going to be more devastating than ever before? Mankind always found a way!

'But why do you say that, Matsya? Why can't we survive this flood?'

It was now that Matsya lost his cool momentarily, and shouted at Manu for him to grasp the grave reality as it was.

'Because this is no ordinary flood, O son of Sanjna. It is going to destroy Prithvi and all its inhabitants - human, animal, plant, insect – nothing is going to live through this onslaught.

Because what is coming is the ultimate finality written in our ancient scriptures!

What is coming is nothing but PRALAY itself – *the end of the world!'*

Banaras, 2017

THE DARK BROTHERHOODS

It was late in the night. The clock had struck 11.30 pm, which was way past the grandmaster's bedtime. But Dwarka Shastri and Vidyut were in no rush to pack up. What they were discussing was more important than anything else in the world.

'Constantine empowered a secret brotherhood and decided that Christianity was going to be the religion of the New World. I don't think he cared much about which faith takes over anyway. His concern was to ensure that it was one faith, that's all. Given that he was entrenched in Christianity by this time and because it was already a rapidly growing religion, he went with it. But the implications were disastrous. He commandeered this new brotherhood to not only support this one religion, but to spread it with every means available to them. If it meant war, he asked them to wage it. If it meant proselytizing, he asked them to build and unleash an army of missionaries. For him religion was the primary façade behind which his unintentionally nefarious vision was supposed to take shape. Politics and economics were to follow closely behind.'

'So was Christianity always a political tool rather than a spiritual ideology, Baba?' asked Vidyut.

'Of course not, Vidyut. Christianity has always been a profound and giving religion. I have studied the Old and New Testaments, as well as the greatest story every told – the story of Jesus Christ. It propounds nothing but love, equality, forgiveness, devotion and self-sacrifice. Jesus took the suffering of the world upon Himself. How can such a faith be inherently political or imperialistic? Moreover, the magnanimity and compassion of Christianity reflects itself in its innumerable philanthropic organizations and individuals. Why go far? In India alone there are several Christian institutions and people who are working tirelessly towards the uplifting of the poor, towards healthcare, education, sanitation and so much more. So anyone pointing a finger at the religion itself will be making a very big mistake.'

Vidyut nodded in full agreement. It was deeply satisfying for him to see his seemingly orthodox Brahmin great grandfather so well informed and egalitarian about other faiths and their virtues.

'But then where did it all lose the way, Baba? We all know about the violent military Crusades of the Latin Church between the 11th and 13th centuries. The Inquisition, under the reign of which punishments like burning 'heretics' alive at the stake was a common practice, followed the Crusades. Reading about the atrocities and violence meted out during these so-called holy campaigns sends shivers down one's spine. So why did all this happen, if Christianity preaches only benevolence?'

'Exactly where it all goes wrong, Vidyut. The greed of man. The greed for wealth and the lust for power.'

·||卐||·

Their conversation was interrupted when someone knocked at the door.

'Hmmm…' responded Dwarka Shastri in his typical style.

The door opened and Naina entered. Vidyut noticed that even at this hour she looked fresh as a daisy. She smelled like a meadow as she walked past Vidyut to the grandmaster's bedside.

Naina kept a tumbler of warm milk mixed with *haldi* (turmeric) on the side-table of the matthadheesh.

'Thank you, *beta*,' said Dwarka Shastri. 'But why did you trouble yourself?'

'The helpers have all retired for the day, Baba. You have not had anything to eat for hours,' replied Naina with a smile, speaking to the grand old man like a loving daughter. Dwarka Shastri had raised her.

Vidyut could not look Naina in the eye. He had accused her of betraying not only him but also the entire Dev-Raakshasa matth...her home. And he had not yet been able to say sorry.

'*Shubh raatri*, Baba,' she said. 'Good night, Baba.'

Naina left the room and shut the door behind her. Vidyut did not fail to note that she had not even acknowledged his presence in the room.

I have to meet her and apologize for what I did.

And God, she looks beautiful!

·‖ॐ‖·

'His secret brotherhood began to metamorphose into a horrible monster soon after his death on 22nd May, 337 AD. It included some of the richest and most powerful men of that time, and that made the brotherhood grow in influence at a rapid pace. Equally swift was its degeneration in terms of ideology and mission. The vision-statement of a New World Order for the betterment of mankind soon morphed into control over the whole human race based on the doctrines of the brotherhood - a minor difference, when seen from the perspective of the rulers.

The brotherhood first crushed all the voices of dissent and opposition within the faith itself. In 431 AD the Byzantine emperor Theodosius II called another holy Council at Ephesus (near Selcuk in present-day Turkey), which declared an important sect of the Nestorian Christians to be heretics. Little did anyone at the Council know that Theodosius was

a member of the secret brotherhood. He was in fact its supreme commander,' at that time continued Dwarka Shastri.

Vidyut was astounded with the historical prowess of his
great grandfather. Moreover, his curiosity to discover the
truth of the brotherhood was now irrepressible.

'Please go on, Baba. What happened thereafter?'

Dwarka Shastri took a few gulps of the warm milk, shut his
eyes in concentration for a few seconds and began speaking
again. He knew he had to cover nearly fifteen hundred years
of bloodshed, deception, conspiracy, wars, economic crimes
and genocides in a matter of hours. The sequence was critical.

'Like I said, Vidyut, the corrosion of the core values of the
brotherhood was rapid. It soon abandoned religion as the
primary unification goal, even though it continued to be the
mask behind which they committed the most unpardonable
sins in the history of man for several centuries. Then they
became more sophisticated, more ambitious and far more
ruthless.'

'What was this brotherhood called, Baba? Or please let me
correct myself. What *is* it called, Baba?'

Vidyut was a fast learner.

'Good question, my dear Vidyut. When it all started, no one
knew what the brotherhood was called. Advait Shastri also
did not chronicle it in any of the matth records. But soon
the secret society started to expand and establish presence
across more and more countries and continents. What hap-

pened after that is what mostly ensues in cult organizations that lose their Founder and expand beyond a certain scale and size.'

'They split up…' murmured Vidyut. 'They split up, didn't they, Baba?'

'Yes and no,' replied Dwarka Shastri. 'It is hard to trace the exact chronology, but first they got heavily militarized. They were so powerful that no one in the world could turn and question them as to how the faith of Christ now commanded massive armies – the Knights Templar to start with!'

'Wow…' gasped Vidyut in absolute amazement. He knew about the Knights Templar.

'Just like you, most people are aware about the Knights Templar, Vidyut. But very few people know the complete history of this Order, from its origins to its supposed end.'

'I am eager to know everything about them, Baba. Especially because they seem to be deeply connected to this conspiracy spanning millennia.'

Vidyut had not failed to notice that Dwarka Shastri had just said the *supposed* end of the Knights Templar.

Did the Templars still exist in some unknown and dangerous modern incarnation?

·||ॐ||·

'They were known by many names like *Poor Fellow Soldiers of Christ and of the Temple of Solomon*. Also as the *Order of Solo-*

mon's Temple. But mostly they were called the Knights Templar or simply - Templars. When it began it was a Catholic military order, which later received the official blessings of the Church in 1139 AD.

Dreaded by enemies as the formidable fighting force they were, the Templars soon became living legends. Spotted from miles due to their white tunics and massive red crosses on their uniforms and battle-shields, the Templars were the first occurrence in world history when a purely religious establishment boasted of a trained, standing army. This heavily weaponised force did not report into any king or queen. Roughly speaking, they actually served the commandments of a high priest!

Clerics and soldiers had joined forces. Therefore, could religious imperialism be far behind?

Constantine's master plan was taking shape.'

Vidyut nodded and added, 'you are absolutely right, Baba. The Knights Templar played a decisive role in the Crusades, or as the priests of that time liked to call them – the holy wars! The Crusades today seem inexplicable and bizarre if viewed as singularly religious campaigns. Why a faith of peace and sacrifice, as preached by Christ Himself, turned into a bloodthirsty religious war-machine is hard to understand. Christians, who were themselves at the receiving end of a long period of atrocities and violence from the Roman Empire, turned into even more vicious oppressors!'

Dwarka Shastri shook his head in disagreement.

'Correct yourself, Vidyut. It was not Christianity or Christians who waged wars. It was a few vile individuals who misled ordinary folk. Priests of all eras have trumpeted about holy wars. Remember one thumb rule Vidyut. Any God-man who talks about violence is not a man of God at all! The real worshippers of the Almighty, irrespective of which religion you consider, are those who spread the word of peace, love and coexistence. *They* are the real priests.'

The great matthadheesh's beliefs and principles continued to inspire his great grandson. Vidyut could not help but remember how many wars this man and his ancestors had fought. And yet here he sat, speaking with intense conviction about love and brotherhood being the only true channels to God. The last devta recounted how all the battles of the matth and its leaders had been fought to defend this sacred monastery, or to resist the forces of divisiveness and tyranny.

'Then what happened, Baba? What was the next chapter in the history of the Templars? And of the New World Order?' enquired Vidyut, drawing back Dwarka Shastri's attention to the core subject.

'So we had leaders of a faith now bolstered by the power of the Templar sword. What followed was what always follows such nefarious arrangements – money!' said the old grandmaster.

'Money?!' exclaimed Vidyut.

Dwarka Shastri smiled and continued.

'Would you believe it if I tell you that the Order of Solomon's Temple or the Knights Templar were the world's first ever multinational banking corporation?'

Manhattan, New York City, 2017

'EVEN DEATH IS AFRAID OF THE WHITE MASK'

He was among the few men who could afford to reserve the Presidential Suite of the iconic Waldorf Astoria Hotel in New York for weeks together. Nearly every room of the floor in question was booked for him. The entire corridor, decorated with black and white pictures of historically important guests ranging from American Presidents to Indian revolutionaries, was shadowed by his gunmen.

The Maschera Bianca stood at the window of his rich suite, staring out at the glorious Manhattan skyline, smoking his favorite Indian cigarette.

Only today he wasn't enjoying it.

'He looks like a very benevolent God-man, does he not? But it is from the very chair he occupies that edicts for the worst exterminations of humanity have been passed for nearly one thousand years.'

Reg Mariani was sipping on his scotch, wondering why the Maschera was preaching to the choir. If anyone knew the reality of the Big Man, it was he. He was first hand witness and in fact accomplice in some of the recent excesses of the current reigning regent.

'So what now, Maschera? He demands to know. And you are aware he will not take failure lightly. Not from me. Not from you.'

The Maschera's jaw tightened. He crumpled the lit cigarette in his palm and turned to face Reg. He did not flinch when the burning tip of the tobacco scorched into his skin. This burn was a joke compared to everything that the Maschera had been through during his journey from being a murdered hooker's abandoned son on the streets of Milan, to becoming the undisputed king of the European Mafia.

·‖卐‖·

He stabbed the man seventeen times with a long screwdriver. First ten in the stomach and diaphragm, while the remaining seven were in the eyes, temple and groins. He spat on the thrashing body before rolling it with his foot into a gutter.

He had avenged his mother when he was only eleven.

By age sixteen the boy with the cold gaze and nearly feminine features was already ruling several neighborhoods in Milan, under the terror of his infamous weapon of choice. Although he liked to fight alone in the face of even the worst odds, this mindless valour won him several followers. His band grew. His name became more dreaded.

And then one cold night, to the shock and disbelief of the whole of Milan, two policemen were impudently slaughtered in their beat vehicle. One of them had a long screwdriver pierced through his mouth and out from the back of his skull, pinning him to the headrest of the car seat. This horrific twin-murder sent shivers down the spine of the city and its administration.

The green-eyed boy had to leave Milan. But not before he was spotted by the only organization that mattered in that shadowy world of wealth, blood and control.

He was being watched by the *Cosa Nostra* - the fearsome syndicate of the Sicilian Mafia.

Three Mafiosi brothers hired him to run their cocaine network out of Geneva. They made a big mistake. In fifteen years time, the green-eyed boy had become a man - a very dangerous man. He systematically superseded all three of his recruiters, whose bodies were never found from the depths of the Lake Geneva. By age 35, he became the undisputed boss of not only the Sicilian Mafia, but of all organized crime across Europe.

While no one doubted his ruthless talent, there were whispers about his spectacular, meteoric rise. Someone extremely powerful was backing him from behind the shadows. Someone more powerful than governments, more formidable than the CIA and the MI6 taken together. Similarly, there were numerous legends about how and why he came to be known as the Maschera Bianca, or the White Mask. Some attributed his strange and feared title to the colour of his cocaine trade. Others said it was because of the calm paleness on his face when he remorselessly murdered one adversary after another.

Only a few suspected something far more sinister. He was truly a mask, a front hiding somebody who was trying to establish a global order of racial superiority. He was the white mask for the blackest organization to have ever lurked the Earth.

·‖卐‖·

The Maschera Bianca's green eyes were glowering with fearlessness as he walked towards Reg and sat down on a plush sofa.

'Do you know how many times I have faced assassination attempts, Reg?'

Reg shrugged. He knew the domain in which the Maschera ran his illicit empire, he was ruling through the power of a gun barrel.

'One hundred and four times,' continued Maschera in his sophisticated tone, his supremely self-assured smile back on his face. But his eyes were piercing through Reg's soul, who was himself no stranger to death and violence.

'Do you know how many times I have been stabbed, received a bullet wound or strangled to near-death?'

'Why are we talking about all this, Maschera?' said Reg. The Maschera made him nervous no doubt, but Reg Mariani had learnt to conquer anxiety a long time ago.

'Fifty seven times,' continued the Maschera coolly. 'So don't think there is any force on Earth that can scare me.'

He paused for a second or two before leaning forward and speaking again, this time in a terrifying whisper.

Even death is afraid of the White Mask, Reg.'

Harappa, 1700 BCE

RITE OF THE BLUE FIRE

Vivasvan Pujari noticed a frightening change in the faces and bodies of the Saptarishi. They suddenly seemed to appear much older than what they had ever looked. As Sura's vile and bloodthirsty savages stepped closer to the divine sages, the seven of them began to age at an unnerving pace. Their foreheads and cheeks started to wrinkle, their normally calm and serene faces were now distorting into a grotesque expression. With their hair turning grey almost instantly, the seven sages suddenly seemed to have aged by a hundred years!

Is this really happening or am I hallucinating?

For all his cruelty and bravado, Sura too broke into a cold sweat as he saw this macabre transformation in the sages.

His barbaric soldiers also noticed the crumpling flesh of the Saptarishi and gawked to a halt. Prachanda looked at his master with enquiring eyes. *Did he want the assault to stop?*

Sura felt a lump develop in his throat. He had long forgotten what fear was. In an instant he rebuked himself and barked orders with renewed madness. His ambition of becoming the ruler of the entire known world was gnawing at him from within. Nothing could come in his way now. Nothing!

'What stops you, O valiant Asuras? Burn them! Burn these *mayaavi* beings now and please your emperor Sura!'

Bolstered by the aggressive commandment of their de-mon-king, the soldiers of Sura swallowed their fear and charged at the rishis.

A gigantic wood-fire was now stoked-up. The Saptarishi were going to be summarily roasted to ashes.

Or so the fools believed.

'Stop this madness, Sura!' urged Vivasvan Pujari. 'Something is not right here. These are not the Saptarishi. I cannot sense their holy presence anymore. The divine seven have already taken *samaadhi*, and their souls have departed to some place else. Don't you see why their bodies are decomposing rapid-ly and preparing for their final union with the soil of Prith-vi? Without the spiritual presence of the divine seven, these mortal bodies are nothing more than empty vessels!'

'Haarrgh!' growled Sura, with a dismissive gesture from his massive sword. 'They are here in front of me! And I am not going to miss this golden chance to wipe them out from the face of these lands I am about to rule. They shall burn alive in this fire of Sura's wrath!'

The commander of Prachanda's elite regiment grabbed hold of the hair of one of the sages. As soon as his hands closed in on the locks of the decaying rishi, a distant crash was heard. A chilly gust of wind swept the area and nearly froze the Asura contingent.

To the horror of everyone present, the sages all opened their eyes at once. But what lay behind their eyelids were not human eyes. They were just dully glowing stones of white. Either the eyeballs of the rishis had rolled-up into their heads, or some deathly force was peeping out from these ghastly slits on now the thousand year old faces of the seven hermits.

Sura's soldiers were now like statues made of stone. None of them dared to make a move. In the darkness of the night, the only crooked figures visible were those of the Saptarishi, now looking like they were five thousand years old, shriveled lumps of wrinkled, folding skin, but with eyes shining white as a grave shroud.

At the behest of his General Prachanda, the regiment commander summoned all his courage and dragged the first sage to the mammoth blaze. He pulled the hair of the rishi, went around him and kicked him into the burning fire. As soon as the ascetic got engulfed in the flames, something that no one could predict occurred.

The unrelenting yellow fire erupted into a spectacular, dazzling blue, with the condemned sage barely visible.

The distant rumble now seemed to be edging closer.

·‖ॐ‖·

'Bewaaaaaare…O devta of Harappaaaaa…' said a prophesying, haunting voice from the heart of the raging blue inferno. But it echoed like the mountains were talking with pained melancholy.

'Beware Vivasvan Pujari…beware you whose pious soul has lost its path in the murky quagmire of hate and vengeance. Bewaaare…'

The devta of Harappa stood dumbfounded, crippled with sorrow, as he heard the last words of the first Saptarishi and watched his blurred figure turn into dust.

Even before he could react, the regiment-commander had kicked in the next of the sages into the blue flames.

'Vivasvaaaan…I weep for you, you unfortunate devta. Look at what you have become! We scorch and you do nothing. So be it…your calamitous destiny awaits you…'

With these terrifying words the now completely withered, unrecognizable body of the second Saptarishi also burned to ashes in the raging blue fire.

In a matter of moments a catastrophic blizzard tore open the skies, spitting eerie lightning and deafening thunder on all of Aryavarta. It was as if the Mother, the Saraswati, pro-

tested and lamented furiously at the slaughtering of her loving sons.

The blood river was now preparing to unleash the cruelest
curse on all of Harappa, and all of mankind.

·‖卐‖·

Vivasvan Pujari pulled at the hide armour of Prachanda's
regiment leader and threw the bulky commander on the
pebbled ground. He was not going to let this brutal deprav-
ity continue.

'Stop this outrageous blood-thirst, O demon king!' yelled the
devta.

'Get out of the way a-devta,' replied Sura, his eyes transfixed
on the surreal glow of the brilliant blue fire. He was now
consumed with savagery and ambition. The now nearing
rumble in the high mountains, the outlandish chilly winds,
the unnatural sky and the punishing cloudburst...nothing
could hold back the vile king of the Asuras. It was his day,
and he was prepared to wage war - even against the heavens,
should they come in his way.

Before Vivasvan could say another word, he felt the hand of
Prachanda on his shoulder.

'You gave us your word, O great a-devta,' said Prachanda.
'You gave us your word!'

By now the commander had swiftly got up and dragged two
of the sages towards the fire. The remaining Saptarishi had

now crumpled and aged so horrendously, that these two sages weighed nothing more than infants. Laughing like a psychotic villain, the commander lifted the sages by their respective necks and tossed them effortlessly into the incredible sapphire blaze.

The raging fire now erupted into even higher flames leaping towards the sky, as if it were a rapidly growing blue monster preparing to devour everything in its wake. Like the freezing exhalation of an invisible djinn, a mighty hailstorm began sweeping the abode of the seven sages, compelling everyone, including the demon-king and the fallen devta, to cover their eyes. Vivasvan Pujari could sense that this abnormal thunderstorm was emanating from the weeping depths of the Saraswati. The ferocity of the pounding gales was making it hard for the unfortunate mortals to even remain standing on their feet. Sheltering his face behind his forearm and elbow, the Surya of Harappa struggled to peek into the fire.

The two smoldering figures from the core of the blue furnace did not express angst anymore. The proverbial vessel of sins and evil was now full and brimming over.

It was time.

Time for the curse that would change the fate of humanity forever.

It was time.

Pralay was upon all Creation.

Banaras, 2017

VIDYUT

Vidyut decided to take a walk around the sprawling lawns of the matth. The cool morning breeze sprinkled with holy fragrances of marigold flowers, ritual incense sticks, the chant of sacred *shlokas* and the lyrical chiming of distant temple bells, all made a short walk in the Dev-Raakshasa matth an incomparably delightful experience. Every now and then he stopped to touch the feet of matth elders, to kiss the old nannies, to smile shyly at the swooning young girls or to bowl a whizzing delivery to the boys playing cricket with a tennis ball. Vidyut seemed to have dissipated his boundless *praan-vaayu* or life-energy into every pebble of the matth.

By now, it was common knowledge that he smoked. He was the only one permitted to do so in full public view. He wore a simple, black sleeveless vest and grey track pants. Even in these plain clothes he looked magnetic. His unusually radiant skin accentuated his chiseled features and piercing almond-colored eyes. The breeze blew his long brown hair across his face every now and then, which he threw back with all five fingers of his right hand.

Was Vidyut annoyingly perfect? Perhaps. Or did he have flaws? He probably did. Just that those were hard to spot, and never stayed with the devta longer than a few moments.

Vidyut always faced extreme emotional and social reactions from people around him. Those who understood him, loved him. And loved him dearly, unquestioningly. Even those who did not know him closely admired his honest charisma and boyish charm. He did invite envy by those who observed him only from a distance. Not because Vidyut had ever harmed them. He was too productively consumed in himself to ever have to worry about them. But they sometimes disliked him because he was so visibly different. He did not conform. He was not crafted from the standard mold. He was extraordinarily talented, and sometimes infuriatingly independent. He was a gentleman, but never one to back away from taking on a bully. He was wealthy and self-made, but behaved like a university lad with hundred rupees in his pocket. He spent equal time in pumping iron as he did in perfecting Carnatic music. But what gave intense heartburn to his rare detractors was that despite his magnificent appearance, his success, his riches, his talents and his charisma, he was humility personified. *That* was what most people could not come to terms with.

Vidyut did have his share of grey. Was it wrong that he enjoyed smoking, even though he could outperform athletes and martial artists? Was it wrong that he sometimes succumbed to anger? Or to suspicion? Was it *all* wrong for the last devta?

Was it all so wrong for someone who was, after all, half-human?

·||ॐ||·

As he sipped into his hot earthen cup or *purva* of spiced tea to soothe the dryness caused by his last few drags of tobacco, his ears caught a rhythmic sound of jingling *paayal*, the percussion of an expertly played *tabla* and a golden male voice singing *shaastriya* music. A guitarist and a trained vocalist himself, Vidyut was delighted to hear these beautiful notes. He decided to follow the captivating melody.

He knew what it was.

He just didn't know *who* it was.

As Vidyut tossed his cigarette stub into a dustbin and climbed a couple of stairs leading to a high marble corridor, he could spot the half-open door from which the enchanting music seemed to emanate. He walked quietly towards the door so as to not disturb the artists inside and slowly peeked into the music hall.

What he saw took his breath away.

Naina was dressed in traditional North Indian attire of *chudidaar* and *kurta*, all white in color. She was moving gracefully to the beat of the tabla and to the old, silver-haired maestro singing mesmerizing *ragas*. Vidyut caught on instantly to what this beautiful dance was.

Kathak!

The term Kathak finds its origins in the Vedic Sanskrit word *katha*, or story. Dating back to earlier than 400 BCE and finding a mention even in the great *Mahabharata*, Kathak is one of the major traditional dance forms of India. Its popularity is attributed to the ancient bards of Aryavarta who travelled far and wide, narrating the epics in this beautiful art form. Kathak was especially championed during the *Bhakti* movement, where it became a spectacular theatrical form of telling the story of Lord Krishna. The Banaras *gharaana* of Kathak is the apex seat for this glorious cultural treasure.

He could not take his eyes off her. She moved like a goddess, disseminating the splendor of her beauty and illimitable elegance all around her. Vidyut noticed the beads of sweat on her luminescent forehead and the strands of hair kissing her beautiful face as she danced. She tangoed on traditional Indian music like a magical being, the exertion of the rigorous dance not once taking away her beaming smile. Her eyes sparkled like the North Star.

Was it so wrong that the devta could, for once, succumb to forbidden love?

He decided to leave.

'Video!'

Vidyut froze.

This was the first time he had been addressed by this silly yet endearing name since the fateful visit of Trijat Kapaalik. Video! No one besides his closest friends, Bala most of all, had ever called him that. Vidyut was jarred emotionally at hearing this name.

He turned, only to see Naina standing a few paces away from him. She was still panting, breathless from the intense performance till a few moments ago. Vidyut felt he would crumble under the onslaught of this matchless beauty. But more than her physical allure, it was Naina's selfless care that disarmed Vidyut. He would have expected her to sulk for many more days till he begged her for forgiveness. He had wronged her horribly, unpardonably. But here she was – reading his face, caressing his soul. On one end she looked like an incarnation of goddess *Kaali* when in battle, but when in her softer avatar, she was more desirable than anyone Vidyut had known before.

He turned to leave. This was all too overwhelming for him. On the one hand, he loved that Naina had dropped her seemingly high-discipline practice to run out and meet him. On the other, he hated her for calling him Video. That name was dead for him. The man who called him that was dead too. Everything that young, carefree Video stood for lay beheaded that day on the bleeding steel table of the matth prison. Ever since he had set foot into Varanasi, Vidyut's life had changed forever.

'Stay, Vidyut…' cried out Naina.

Vidyut stopped in his path. He knew it was time he faced Naina. More than that, he knew it was high time that he confronted his own inexplicable desire for this *apsara* of a kathak dancer.

She enveloped her soft, artistic fingers around his wrist and forearm, even as they walked on the Tulsi ghaat. It was late morning by this time and it was not totally customary in Banaras for a girl to wrap her hands around a man's arm in a public place. But Naina was not customary. And Vidyut was not just a man.

Vidyut could not help but feel Naina's golden skin brush against his wrists. She was on a trip of unstoppable banter, as most strong girls embark upon when nestled in what they consider to be a secure place. Her laughter sounded like ring-ing bells and the sparkle in her eyes was evident, although visible only when Vidyut dared to turn and look at her.

'*Tum kahaan they ab tak, Vidyut?*' asked Naina with a tilt of her head. 'Where were you till now, Vidyut?'

Her eyes were fixed upon the devta's gaze. She spoke like she owned him.

But who can ever own a devta?

Except for the One who had sent him.

'I'm sorry Naina…' said Vidyut abruptly.

She did not seem to even notice what he had said. She continued walking into the sunny steps of the ghaat, talking nonstop in her chirpy self.

'I'm sorry, yaar, Naina…I really am. I was an idiot to have suspected you like I did. I hate myself for it!'

Now she stopped. She sighed deeply and turned to the devta. She raised her eyebrows as if reminding her man of the most fundamental gesture he owed her.

She succeeded.

'I'm sorry, Nainu…'

East of Harappa, 1700 BCE

THE DEBT

Manu was woken up by the crash of thunder, which was worsening with every passing hour. He had ridden back from the Black Temple the previous night and had decided to rest with the soldiers in black robes, as one among them. Just like they did, Manu had unrolled his straw mattress on the ground.

As he got up from his rugged bed, he noticed that his comrades were up too. No one could continue sleeping when the skies were all but tearing themselves down. It took them some time to realize that the Sun should have risen by now. But it was only a dark and menacing night all around which enveloped them.

The omens of Pralay were imminent. Monstrous clouds had

summarily swallowed the morning Sun.

Aryavarta was going to spend the remainder of its numbered days in total darkness.

·‖ॐ‖·

Matsya rode in with a hundred or so of his band. As Manu saw him approach from a distance in the poor visibility of the downpour that had now become a permanent phenomenon, he noticed something peculiar. Matsya and his men rode in an identical fashion, at the same speed and moving like they were one organism. They looked fearsome, formidable. Some of them carried massive round battle-shields made of some kind of outlandish alloy. The shields glimmered like the eyes of a dragon when lightning reflected off them. Matsya rode at the head of his force, visible only intermittently as the thunder-flash lit up the night into a momentary, frightening blue.

As they came close, Matsya and his men dismounted in one single choreographed action. Their right legs swung high above their horses' heads and they climbed off their saddles in perfect harmony.

They would have trained for years to achieve this level of synchronized precision!

'Pranaam, Matsya,' greeted Manu.

'Pranaam, O king,' replied Matsya, throwing his long wet hair back from his strikingly handsome face. 'Can you please arrange for some warm water for my men and the horses?

They have all travelled through a cold and wet night.'

'Of course, Matsya,' replied Manu, eager as ever to serve Matsya in every way possible.

However, something unusual did occur to him. Every time he had met Matsya, he had provided him with water. A few drops the first time, a canteen-full on the next occasion, a bucket-full after that and now probably several large containers full. Each time they had met, Matsya had requested Manu for larger quantities of water.

Manu smiled to himself and shrugged off the silly thought as a strange coincidence.

It was not coincidence. It was a debt that Matsya was going to repay one day.

·||ॐ||·

After Matsya and his men had washed themselves with the comforting tepid water Manu and the black-robed guardians had offered, they sat down around a glowing bonfire for a hot breakfast.

As usual, Matsya took Manu by surprise. Only this time, it was a very pleasant one.

'You will need Somdutt by your side,' said Matsya, as he took a mouthful of the spiced *poha*.

Manu stopped chewing and looked up in astonishment.

'Sorry…did you say Somdutt, Matsya? Is Somdutt ji alive??'

Matsya looked up for a second, smiled and nodded, before going back into his delicious bowl.

Manu kept his plate aside and folded his hands in a short prayer. Soon after he erupted into a joyous laugh.

'The Gods be praised! The Gods be praised! Thank you, Matsya, for bringing this wonderful news! Why didn't you tell me sooner?'

Matsya did not answer the question. It was he who kept the breakfast bowl aside this time.

'And you will need one more ally, O son of Surya,' he said. He was grinning with mischief. But he knew what he was about to share with Manu was going to change his life forever.

'Which other ally, Matsya?' asked Manu intently. His heart was pounding with anticipation and hope. He knew who was with Somdutt that fateful night. If Somdutt ji made it out of there alive, maybe *she* did too.

'She did, Manu,' said Matsya lovingly. 'Tara made it out too...'

Manu froze. He shut his eyes and let tears of joy trickle down his youthful face.

After a few moments he looked at Matsya and broke into a laugh once again. Matsya responded with a beaming grin. In a jiffy Manu sprung up, jumped towards Matsya and took his hand. He kissed it repeatedly.

'Tara is alive! Tara is alive! *My* Tara is alive, Matsya!' was all he kept saying.

'Oh I see...*your* Tara, huh?' said Matsya naughtily. 'This I did not know!'

There was nothing in this world that Matsya did not know.

Manu blushed.

Matsya winked at him and they both shared a brotherly moment of boundless joy.

Banaras, 2017

THE DARK
BROTHERHOODS- PART II

The group was a little bigger now. The great Dwarka Shastri wanted to step out of his room and get some fresh air. Vidyut and Naina were back from their pleasant walk at the famous Tulsi ghaat, near which the revered poet-saint Tulsidas lived in the 16th century when he wrote the profound *Ramacharitamanas* – the epic story of Lord Rama.

Naina had forgiven Vidyut. How could she not? She was deeply in love with him, and understood the trying circumstances under which Vidyut had reacted the way he did. Trapped in that mayhem of bullets and blood, anyone could have made a mistake. Both of them felt like a mountain had been lifted off their chests.

On the previous day, the matth elders had also undertaken the last rites of Bala. He was given a proper cremation as per *Sanatana* rituals at the *Harishchandra* ghaat. It was tacitly understood by everyone that no police reports about the killing were to be filed. The Dev-Raakshasa matth always fought its own battles. Always delivered justice.

And now they had the prophesied, the awaited protector on their side.

They had Vidyut.

·‖ॐ‖·

Chairs were set-up in one sunlit corner of the vast lawns and tea was served. Vidyut sat directly opposite his grand old man, while Balvanta, Purohit ji and Naina sat with their chairs forming a small circle.

The conversation continued. Vidyut could figure that the three new entrants to the discussion were not actually new. They were listening like they were well versed already with what Dwarka Shastri was narrating. It was Vidyut who was new.

Why did Pa, the great Kartikeya Shastri, and then Baba keep me away from Kashi for so many years?

'The Knights Templar were no doubt a fighting force. But not everyone in the Order was a warrior. In fact, the proportion of non-combatants was much higher in the Templars. As the Order grew rapidly in power and membership, it became the most preferred charity across entire Christendom.

Each knight of the Order took a vow to never build any property or wealth for himself, and devoted his life completely to the cause. The initial insignia of the Templars showed two knights riding on a single horse, in order to depict the poverty of the Order.

However, soon the fortunes of the Templars began to witness a meteoric rise. Shortly after Jerusalem was conquered in the First Crusade in 1099 AD, the Order made itself responsible for the safety and protection of the Christian pilgrims who travelled to the Holy Land to visit the various sacred sites in the city, including the Holy Sepulchre. These hapless pilgrims were often looted and butchered by dacoits and bandits on the way from the coast of Jaffa to the interiors of Jerusalem. And this was where the Knights Templar began their spectacular ascent.'

Vidyut was spellbound by every word coming his way. Constantine, the New World Order, his mysterious hooded ancestor Advait Shastri, Theodosius II and the Knights Templar...

Where is this going?

'It will all make sense soon, Vidyut,' said Dwarka Shastri, as if he were reading Vidyut's mind.

He probably was.

'Saint Bernard of Clairvaux, a powerful Church leader and a French abbot, decided to lend unprecedented support to the Knights Templar. He wrote extensively in their favour and was soon able to get official support for them as the protectors of the Christian pilgrims. That was the windfall.

The Order was flooded with donations, gold, estates and even manpower from high families. The wealth of the Order burgeoned so radically that they began managing Christian finance and issuing money transaction notes to pilgrims. Unlike what most people believe, the non-combatant or accounting staff of the Order far outnumbered the warring Knights.'

Vidyut was now a bit confused.

'Baba this is all vital and eye-opening information about the Knights Templar. But I am unable to understand how all this is connected to the New World Order...' asked a slightly exasperated Vidyut.

Before Dwarka Shastri could respond, Naina spoke up.

'Don't you see what was happening, Vidyut? First, the dominance of one religion was widely propagated as the accepted goal. Then that malicious design was backed-up by heavy militarization. Thereafter the plight of pilgrims was used to plug-in the last missing peace – that of controlling the wealth of the Church, the king as well as the populace at large.'

Vidyut was listening carefully, but did not show signs of full comprehension.

'Don't you get it, Vidyut...one religion, one army, one bank...one government! The Knights Templar were knowingly or unknowingly the greatest weapon of the New World Order!' exclaimed Naina

'What is important to understand about the dangerous men and women behind the New World Order is that they do not plan in months or years. They have an unsettlingly long-term world-vision where they forge strategies that will be executed over centuries, led by generations of this brotherhood. So the Knights Templar were only the first phase of the secret Order,' explained Purohit ji this time.

'Wait a minute please, Purohit ji. With due respect, all this is sounding like too much of a conspiracy theory. The history of the Knights Templar is well recorded. If they were supposed to be working for a clandestine brotherhood, why would they be known all over the world?'

There was a brief silence. Vidyut was looking at the four people around him, who were all looking like they had an ocean of information pent up. Finally, the matthadheesh decided to speak.

'Ever since Constantine commissioned it, the New World Order comprised some of the world's most powerful people – business barons, billionaire entrepreneurs, presidents of states, dictators, bankers, drug-lords, scientists and more. Besides their social, financial and political standing, most of these are individuals gifted with extraordinary intellect, bordering on genius. That is one of the criteria for their initiation into the brotherhood. Do you expect this set of exceptionally powerful and ruthless people to come out in the open? They always use strong, unsuspecting men against weak, helpless men. You don't know who is a part of this brotherhood. It could be the next President of a big country! It could be an Internet tycoon from Silicon Valley. It could be a scientist doing human genome and cloning research in a hidden laboratory in the Swiss Alps. They are everywhere, Vidyut. And yet they are invisible.'

Giving Vidyut a minute to assimilate the information, and taking a sip of soothing herbal tea, the matthadheesh continued.

'If the Knights Templar was such a straightforward unit of warrior monks, why was their initiation ceremony both secret as well as something that fuelled wide speculation and fear? And why were they eventually hunted down and burnt at the stake in full public view?'

Vidyut was not aware of this disturbing detail.

'They were burnt...alive?' he asked.

Dwarka Shastri paused for a moment and spoke calmly.

'Yes they were. On Friday the 13th.'

Harappa, 1700 BCE

CURSE OF THE
BLOOD RIVER

The voices were now not the gentle speech of the Saptarishi that Vivasvan Pujari was familiar with for years. Two horrifying voices now roared from the heart of the blue fire. The devta stood staring into the sapphire flames like a lifeless figure, his single eye wide with horror and anticipation. If anyone really knew what catastrophe the wrath of the Saptarishi could unleash, it was the Surya of Harappa.

The terrifying roar of the voices now reverberated with the distant rumble in the high rocky hills, and seemed to have been amplified by the mourning mountains. Vivasvan Pujari was convinced that what the incandescing sages were now uttering would be audible to every living creature for a hundred miles.

*"Hear this you fallen devta...your sins shall not be forgiven! You...
and all those who partner you in this dark sacrilege...shall soon suffer
the fate your black hearts conjure for others! Before the next rise of
the moon, you shall all turn to dust!*

YOU WILL ALL DIE!"

Hail splattered the face and body of Vivasvan Pujari, as if
the heavens had chosen to stone his decrepit soul. The fear
of death had never bothered the devta even from a long distance. He couldn't care less if he lived or died. Without Sanjna and Manu, his life meant nothing anyway. He stood there,
facing the onslaught of the white rocks smashing against
him, staring into nothingness. He knew in the afterlife his
soul would be lost in the dark realms of the spirit world,
shackled into an endless cycle of birth and death. It would
take him a thousand lives to wash away the *karma* of this
final hour.

His thirst for vengeance grew even more scathing. Those
that condemned him into this hellfire of ceaseless suffering,
lived and laughed even now! They had to pay for what they
had done.

Harappa had to perish...to the last soul!

The savage depredation continued unabated. The fifth Saptarishi was dragged mercilessly on the rough ground by his
hair, before being thrown ruthlessly into the fire. This time

it was the demon-king himself who acted as the executioner. Even though deep down the chilling prophesy of the two sages about imminent death had unsettled Sura, he had to display fearless disregard to his men.

The shriek of the burning sage was even more terrifying than the two voices before. To Vivasvan's disbelief, it was a feminine voice. It was the haunting voice of an inconsolable, angry mother, who mourned the murder of her children. While the other wretches were both frightened and bewildered at this unexpected phenomenon, the Surya of Harappa instantly recognized the celestial voice. He had never heard it before. Yet he was certain who's voice it was.

Sara Maa...

The blood of the demon-king and his wild slaughterers froze as they heard her speak in a voice as loud as a bolt in the sky. It was the sound of cataclysm. The sound of horror, misfortune and destruction. It was the sound of an eternal curse that was to plague mankind forever!

"The Saptarishi loved you like one of their own. I loved you like a son. The Gods bestowed you with divinity and you bore it with grace and worthiness - until your hate became your undoing, O devta! And with your corruption comes the great culling! The Asuras have sinned beyond measure. The Harappans have sinned as a collective. Kings have sinned and priests have sinned. Demons have sinned and devtas have sinned. Humankind compels the universe to unleash the cosmic cleansing! I shall forever forsake this land of immeasurable immorality and return to the holy womb of Mother Prithvi. The Saraswati, the River of the Wise, will fade into legend. But not before She unleashes her final punishment on those who have wronged her.

Bewaaaaare…PRALAY…ESHHYATI…!

THE GREAT DELUGE…IS COMING…!"

Vivasvan Pujari was now on his knees, his eye closed, head bowed and hands folded in devotion. He had studied about Pralay in the ancient scriptures and he knew it was something that occurred at the end of every eon – to restore order and to allow creation to resurrect life from a new beginning. He did not know it would arrive so soon, or that he would be at the epicenter of this gigantic destruction. But again, he did not care. As far as he was concerned, Pralay had already struck his life – incinerating everything he held dear.

The *rakt-dhaara* or blood river was not done yet. The powerful, echoing voice continued.

"Humanity holds in the heart of every individual the potential to become a God. Yet, instead of seeking spiritual salvation within and without, human kind uses its gifts to betray, murder, plunder and avenge. This is the fate your species has chosen! So be it! The Gods will never release you from your hateful destiny. The serpents of violence and bloodshed will never loosen their stranglehold on mankind, which shall kill and destroy each other in the name of the very Gods it has betrayed today! Never shall carnage and butchery leave your side. This is my curse, O fallen devta! Humankind shall hear the shrieks of boundless suffering till the end of time!

I CURSE YOU! I CURSE YOU ALL!"

Tears were rolling down the eye of Vivasvan Pujari. What had happened suddenly to his world? How could everything that was so right till a few days ago, crumble so devastatingly, so cruelly? The Surya that was to ascend to the seat of the chief priest of Harappa was now a one-eyed monster. His home that rang with the trustful laughter of his beloved wife and son was now burnt to ashes. The Saptarishi, whom he adored as guides and brothers, were being massacred as a result of his own connivance. The golden city of Harappa was going to be drowned in the great flood. And the River of the Wise, which he revered as a mother, was now cursing mankind in her demonic incarnation as the blood river.

His silent tears soon turned into heavy moans, and he began crying uncontrollably, his tears sprinkling the hallowed dust of the murdered sages' abode.

The devta did not know then that his tears would fall short given the horrifying last chapter of life that awaited him.

And while he was now desperate to die and meet his maker, he did not know that he was destined to come back…centuries later.

This time truly as the last devta to ever visit the planet.

Banaras, 2017

REVENGE

'I am going to find him and kill him.'

Vidyut was clear what needed to be done with Trijat Kapaalik. It did not matter who was behind the Masaan-raja. The turn of the veiled puppet masters would come later. For now the devta was unrelenting. He had never imagined killing a fellow human being. Even during the most challenging fight at the Dashashwamedh ghaat a few days ago, he had not taken a life.

But that was then. The inhuman murdering of Bala, that too in the sacred precincts of the matth, had convinced Vidyut that they were fighting an indefatigable and ruthless enemy. An enemy that was going to stop at nothing. The failure of Romi Pereira and the mercenaries had not discouraged this foe. Therefore one thing was clear. No half measures were going to vanquish this adversary.

This was a fight to the end. A fight to the death of Trijat Kapaalik and those who were playing this morbid game from the shadows.

·||ॐ||·

'The strange thing is that Trijat has not gone into hiding. Our *guptachar sena* has reported that he has merely retreated into his taantric *yajnashaala* at the outskirts of the city. That premises is a place of rituals only for namesake. It is virtually a fortress. It is Masaan-raja's spiritual and militant stronghold. He knows you will come after him. He *wants* you to come after him,' cautioned Balvanta, the battle-chief of the matth.

'We have to get him, Balvanta dada, even if it means we have to pull him out from the depths of hell!'

'Yes Vidyut. We will get him. But we have to plan this well. We are dealing with the most dangerous man in all of Kashi. We cannot take him lightly. This counterattack will need both courage and valour. But above all, it will require meticulous preparation.'

Vidyut nodded in agreement. Balvanta had more experience in warfare than all of the others combined.

'Why can't we just take all our men and storm their fake *yajnashaala*, Balvanta dada?' questioned an impatient Sonu. 'A hundred of us will be enough to take on his 666 intoxicated henchmen.'

'No, Sonu. An open siege and frontal assault will lead to excessive bloodshed and will draw too much attention. Also, while it is certain that this battle will lead to some loss even at our end, we need to minimize it as far as possible. Lastly, keep in mind that when we confront the maha-taantric himself, it will not be just humans that will fight from his side,' said Balvanta.

There was silence for half a minute before Vidyut spoke.

'So what do we do, dada? If we cannot attack them openly, what other alternative do we have?'

Balvanta was thinking hard.

'There is only one man in all of Banaras who can help us,' he said.

·||ॐ||·

They were walking through the sprawling campus of the reputed Banaras Hindu University (B.H.U.). Established in 1916 by Pandit Madan Mohan Malaviya, B.H.U. is believed to be Asia's largest residential university with over 12,000 students living in its 75+ hostels. Spread over an expansive 1,300 acres, this center of academic excellence teaches over 35,000 students from more than 40 countries.

Balvanta had insisted that Vidyut accompanies him to meet someone he was sure could help them breach the seemingly impregnable bastion of Trijat Kapaalik.

'Professor Prabhat Tripathi is a scholar of Sanskrit and has been with the university for over a decade. He is one of the most accomplished experts on the Vedas, Upanishads and other ancient Indian scriptures. Over a dozen Ph.D students intern under him at any given time. A thorough gentleman, he holds Dwarka Shastri ji in very high regard. He is unfortunately blind in one eye, which is why you will always see him wearing dark sunglasses,' described Balvanta.

'Thank you for sharing this, dada. But how is he useful to us in our present quest?'

Balvanta replied plainly.

'Because before choosing this quiet life of academics, Prof Tripathi was Trijat Kapaalik's brother-in-arms.'

·‖ॐ‖·

They sat over small, canteen cups of tea in the lawns of the University main campus. The simpleton that he was, Prof Tripathi sat crossed legged on the grass. He was not embarrassed to ask his visitors to also make themselves comfortable on the ground next to him. After exchanging a few pleasantries Balvanta broached the topic cautiously.

'Tripathi ji, we have come here to seek your help and blessings. Only you can guide us towards success in our perilous pursuit.'

The professor smiled generously and said, 'What can be perilous for a warrior like you, Balvanta? And how can a man of books and classrooms offer any assistance?'

Vidyut could tell that Prof Tripathi was a genuine, grounded and kind man. It was hard to even imagine him by the side of the cruel maha-taantric!

Balvanta paused for a few moments before hesitantly uttering his next words.

'We need a way to infiltrate the yajnashaala of Trijat Kapaalik…'

The professor's face turned to stone. In a matter of seconds Vidyut could see him trembling with rage. Too civil to express his anger melodramatically, the gentle professor folded his hands in a *Namaste* and got up to leave.

'Tripathi ji…I beg you…please stay…' pleaded Balvanta.

He held the professor's sleeve and implored him to sit down. He was relieved when Tripathi ji yielded.

'You insult me by even mentioning the name of that fiend in my presence. That was a life I left behind a long time ago. It took away everything from me. Everything…

And don't think he does not know you are here. He watches *everything*. He knows *everything!*' said the professor with an eerie fear in his voice.

·‖ॐ‖·

'I spent nine years as an aghori taantric. Trijat was like a brother to me. Or so I thought then. This was much before he became the Masaan-raja and maha-taantric that he is today. We were young. Our penance was bearing fruit and the *siddhis* made us drunk with power. We could caste devastating ancient spells like the *Baglamukhi* on anyone who crossed our paths. But as the months and years passed, something began to change in Trijat.'

The professor was now recounting his days with the evil skull-bearer.

'He was turning more and more cruel with every passing day. His *saadhana* was now less about the worship of Rudra and more about controlling daakinis, pishachas and chudails. He undertook lone, intense penances at public graveyards, and began committing the horrible sin of exhuming the dead for his dark rites. No one knew what he was trying to achieve. But we could tell it was something that should never be done.'

The professor was now visibly disturbed. These recollections were making him sweat. Vidyut offered him a bottle of water, which he gratefully accepted.

'But despite all his efforts, he could never invoke *Smashaan Tara*, the Goddess of the graveyards. *Maa* was not granting him her darshana. This baffled me. Taantrics much less accomplished than Trijat claimed to have found Smashaan Tara. This made me suspicious. And for the first time, I prepared Trijat's *kundali*.'

Prabhat Tripathi was now pale as a ghost. He was clearly transported back into time.

'What did you read in his kundali, Tripathi ji?' asked Vidyut. 'I am sure it told you what an evil man he was going to turn out to be…'

The professor shook his head.

'His kundali did not say whether he was going to be a good man or bad man. It was the kind of horoscope that no astrologer has seen in hundreds of years. I read and re-read it over and over again as I could not believe what I was seeing. Let alone good or evil, it was not the kundali of a *man* at all!'

Balvanta and Vidyut were bewildered. They did not fully understand what the professor had just said.

'Sorry Tripathi ji…I did not follow you,' said Vidyut politely.

The professor was now perspiring with anxiety. He spoke in a frightened whisper.

'Probably Maa Tara was not granting him Her darshana… because…

Trijat was born in *raakshasa yoni* (demonic birth).

He is a raakshasa who has descended on Earth after centuries.'

East of Harappa, 1700 BCE

'ITS LEGEND WILL REMAIN IMMORTAL'

'You will build a giant boat, Manu. A vessel so enormous, that its dimensions will be beyond the boundaries of human comprehension. A ship so gigantic that its hull will rise above the clouds. No one, till the end of time, will be able to visualize this boat in even his wildest imagination. This ark will serve its destined purpose and degenerate naturally with the passage of time. But its legend will remain immortal.

And so will your name, Satyavrata Manu.'

Manu was dumbfounded at everything that Matsya had just said.

If the magnitude of the boat was such that it was beyond human imagination, how am I supposed to build it? How can one create what one cannot even conceive? And why am I the one who has to build it? What purpose was destined for this vessel? And why did Matsya call me Satyavrata Manu?

Matsya could see the bewilderment on Manu's face. He smiled and gestured at Manu to walk with him. As they stepped out of their high cave in the black mountains, they were once again whiplashed by tearing wind and sharp raindrops. The sky looked as unforgiving as it had over the last few days. It was perpetually dark.

Before Manu could ask Matsya why they had stepped out in the storm, he saw a few tired horses trudging up the winding tracks that led up to their cave dwelling. It did not take the son of Surya much time to recognize one of the riders as he passed by a torch protected against the terrifying wind by a translucent lampshade made of cotton yarn.

It was Pundit Somdutt, the chief architect of Harappa and his great father's last friend.

·||ॐ||·

Pundit Somdutt was still wiping his tears. He was overwhelmed with delight seeing the son of Vivasvan Pujari alive, hale and hearty. He was convinced of the truth that he now so clearly saw.

Just like his father, Manu is not an ordinary mortal. Only a devta can survive the kind of wounds he was inflicted with.

Manu had run to Somdutt and nearly pulled him down from

the saddle in an ecstatic hug. He touched the feet of the wise builder of Harappa and held him tightly again, his eyes moist with the memories of his parents. Somdutt blessed Manu repeatedly and could only picture Sanjna smiling from wherever she was, proud to see her son become the man he was today.

He was, however, not so sure about what she would say for her husband.

But that was not for Somdutt to worry about. The souls of Vivasvan and Sanjna were intertwined since time began and would remain so for eternity, until the very end of Creation itself. She was watching her devta. And she knew he was still the man she loved, the greatest man of his time. She knew destiny had put Vivasvan Pujari to a test no man should ever have to go through. She also knew he was now going to suffer several lives till his soul finds its nirvana and merges with the One.

She was going to suffer with him. She was going to be by his side in every life.

They would crossover to the other side…together.

||ॐ||

'I can never repay your debt, Somdutt ji,' said Manu with folded hands. 'You were the only one with my father in his last moments.'

Somdutt did not understand what Manu had just said.

Why is Manu talking about the last moments of his father, when

Vivasvan Pujari is alive?

As he was about to say something, Matsya intervened. His eyes told Somdutt to remain silent for the moment.

'Please join us in our humble shelter, Somdutt,' he said. 'You and your men need a hot meal and some much deserved rest.'

Somdutt nodded, smiled at Manu and proceeded towards the entrance of the high cave.

Manu was watching Somdutt leave when Matsya tapped him on the shoulder. Manu turned to look at Matsya, who barely moved his eyebrows to point at something behind Manu.

Not something.

Someone.

Tara.

Banaras, 2017

THE LOST CIVILIZATION

Vidyut was in deep thought for some time, before he asked the questions that were perturbing him all this while.

'Baba, *why* are they so afraid of us? What makes them believe that we actually have the ability to beat their colossal and organized international network? More importantly, why were they afraid of us right from the beginning? Why did Constantine trust the great Advait Shastri so much?'

Dwarka Shastri smiled.

'They are not afraid of us, Vidyut. They are afraid of what lies hidden in the Black Temple.'

Vidyut sighed, shook his head and then laughed.

'I know you will tell me about the secret of the Black Temple only when you feel the time is right, Baba. So I will save some breath and not ask you what it is!'

Dwarka Shastri responded with a loud, merry laugh. Vidyut was delighted to see his great grandfather laughing so heartily.

'Good to see that you now understand me well, Vidyut,' he said.

'But still Baba, why us? Why a monastery of Indian yogis tucked away in Banaras? How can a monster of a clandestine organization, run by some of the world's most powerful people, find us to be of any threat or significance?'

'Only because we were the receivers and guardians of the greatest treasures of ancient wisdom, Vidyut,' the grandmaster responded simply.

Vidyut grinned and gave a look of skepticism to his great grandfather. He did not fully buy what the matthadheesh had just said.

·||卐||·

'Do you believe in the legend or myth of Manu's Ark, Vidyut?' enquired Dwarka Shastri.

He was not going to unfurl the reality of Vidyut and his own deep association with Manu and the Ark.

Not yet.

'There are thousands of examples around us that point to a lost civilization, Vidyut. Towards ancient wisdom that went missing in the sands of time…or should I say drowned to the depth of the great oceans,' said Dwarka Shastri.

Vidyut was listening intently.

'Think hard and observe carefully, my son. You will see signs of a lost age everywhere. Let me start with some widely known myths and tales. You are a well-read man. You have in-depth knowledge of your epics and scriptures. So tell me, who were the people or characters that were present across both the Ramayana and the Mahabharata, even though these two epics are separated by eons in time?'

After just a few seconds of mentally scanning through the great epics, Vidyut responded, 'Well, there was definitely Lord Hanuman – we find him present in both the epics, the Ramayana and the Mahabharata. He was Lord Rama's greatest devotee and the Ramayana would be incomplete without his tales of valor and wit. Whether it was the burning of the golden city of Lanka or the leaping across vast seas, Hanuman is omnipresent in the Ramayana. He later finds several mentions in the Mahabharata as well, where he crushes the conceit of the great *Bheema* in the form of a small monkey. He eventually places himself on the banner of *Arjuna's* chariot during the great battle of Kurukshetra.'

'Good, but this one was easy. Who else?' enquired Dwarka Shastri, clearly enjoying this conversation.

'Then there is the mighty bird *Garuda* – carrier of none other than Lord Vishnu himself. Garuda comes to the help of

Rama and Lakshman during the Ramayana, when the demon prince *Meghnaad* or *Indrajeet* strikes them with the infamously potent weapon, the *Naagpasha*. Garuda is summoned immediately to devour the poisonous serpents entrenched in the weapon. Then during the Mahabharata, or *Krishnavatara*, Garuda appears again, during Krishna's battle with the raakshasa king *Narakasur*.'

The matthadheesh was smiling. 'I am impressed, Vidyut. Now give me one last example.'

'Baba, then there was the great warrior-saint *Parashurama*. Believed to be one of the ten avatars of Lord Vishnu, Parashurama presents himself at the *Swayamvara* (wedding) of Sita, annoyed with the breaking of Lord Shiva's bow *Pinaaka* by Rama. Later, in the Mahabharata he teaches the art of warfare to the three great warriors – *Bheeshma, Dronacharya* and *Karna*.'

'Excellent!' exclaimed Dwarka Shastri. 'Now tell me this, Vidyut – what do you find common between the three names you have spoken about? What is a shared trait among Hanuman, Garuda and Parashurama?'

Vidyut had no real clue. He thought for a few moments, but could not find any connecting dots between Lord Hanuman, the powerful celestial bird Garuda and the legendary annihilator of evil, Parashurama.

'Sorry Baba, but I am unable to see anything that these iconic personalities had in common. They are all so different in every sense!'

'Yes, they are different. But there is one trait that binds them into one category. And that trait is *speed*. If you remember your epics well, Vidyut, all three were known for their ability to travel faster than *mann ki gati* or the speed of thought. Hanuman travelled at such lightning speed that he had leapt to swallow the Sun. Garuda was chosen by Lord Vishnu as his vehicle because of Garuda's unparalleled velocity. Parashurama enjoyed a boon that permitted him to travel and reach any destination at the speed of thought!'

The grand old man paused for a few moments to allow his great grandson to absorb what he had just explained. After the brief interval, he continued.

'Now do you find it to be a strange coincidence that the three characters that are present across eons of time, are the very three characters that could, proverbially, travel at, or perhaps even faster than, the speed of light?'

'Oh my God!' Vidyut jumped in a Eureka moment. 'Are you saying that their eternally youthful presence across hundreds and thousands of years was possible because they were travelling at the speed of light?! And as per deductions of Einstein's Theory of Relativity, anyone travelling faster than light would experience time passing at a much slower speed than his static counterparts?'

'Precisely, Vidyut!' replied the grandmaster. 'But the real question is this – if Einstein lived and propounded the Theory of Relativity only in the 20th century, how did the ancient rishis who wrote the epics and scriptures thousands of years ago, have any idea about such a modern scientific breakthrough? How did they know that only divine beings equipped with the speed of light could live across eons?'

॥ॐ॥

By now the great grandfather and great grandson duo had discussed and shared scores of clues, insinuations and events from the ancient scriptures that pointed towards a society that was scientifically perhaps even more advanced than the present state of the human race.

'Till telescopes were invented, it was impossible to differentiate between stars and planets. Then how did the ancients know there were nine planets or *Navagraha* in the solar system? In the Ramayana, Lakshman gets annoyed at king *Janaka*'s lamenting about the absence of valor in Aryavarta, and describes how he could toss the Earth like a *ball*. The *Varaha* avatara of Lord Vishnu is described as pulling Prithvi out of the deluge like a globe between its tusks. The earliest recorded mention of our planet being round was in Greek texts dating around the 6th century BCE. It did not become an accepted concept till as late as the 3rd century BCE, after Pythagoras championed it around 500 BCE. Then how did ancient Indians know about it hundreds or thousands of years before this time and describe the Earth as a sphere in the epics?' added Vidyut to all the stunning nuances his great grandfather was pulling out from Indian mythology.

Dwarka Shastri was delighted to see his beloved Vidyut accepting and contributing to what he was trying to elucidate. He walked to his bookshelf and pulled out a volume that looked as if it were a million years old. The matthadheesh opened this prehistoric looking book and flipped its pages to look for some references.

'*Ayurveda*, or the primeval Indian 'science of life', will dazzle you even more, Vidyut. Two ancient rishis, *Sushruta* and *Charaka*, have recorded volumes on sophisticated medicine and surgery. How could people, who had no access to technological instruments to study the impact of medication at a molecular level, execute advanced surgical procedures and offer spectacularly effective prescriptions? The *Sushruta Samhita* lists over 700 medicinal plants. But without elaborate testing laboratories and or even basic microscopes, how did they know these plants had healing properties? How could they perform surgeries as complex as caesarian section, removal of the prostrate gland, fitting of prosthetics...all without modern anesthetics?'

'That is so true, Baba. And do you know, the portrayal given in the scriptures of the aftermath of the apocalyptic weapon *Brahmaastra*, has an uncanny similarity with the description of the atomic bomb explosion given by the survivors of Hiroshima and Nagasaki?'

'Yes, I have read that, Vidyut. There was certainly a plethora of knowledge and scientific wherewithal with our primordial ancestors which got lost somewhere as the centuries passed. A star, which is now called Antares, is the 15th brightest object in the night sky. But the ancients called it *Jyestha* or the eldest or the biggest. Why would they do that, unless they knew that the Antares is indeed the biggest star in the night-sky, about 40,000 times the size of our Sun? Without massive telescopes like the Hubble, this knowledge was not possible!'

The grand old man and his impressive protégé sat there in the matthadheesh's large room. They both had a profound and mystical connection with the ancient wisdom they were now unpeeling, layer by layer.

Like the Greek philosopher Heraclitus of Ephesus had said, the only thing constant in the cosmos is change. The glory of India or Aryavarta that once held the key to the universe's greatest wisdom, was slowly corroded by the passage of time and the connivance of foreign powers in cahoots with a section of its own children.

Magnificent India has always been victim to betrayal by its own creed. Whether it was *Aambhi* who welcomed Alexander to the borders of the great sub-continent or *Jaichand* who conspired against the Rajput king *Prithviraj*; whether it was a *Mir Jafar* at Plassey, or an *Ilahi Baqsh* in the mutiny of 1857; whether it were the landlords who remained loyal to the British or those who propel western imperialistic, anti-national agendas even today - this splendid country, this nucleus of boundless wisdom, has been agonizingly unfortunate.

Harappa, 1700 BCE

SON AFTER SON, GENERATION AFTER GENERATION

Sura kicked the leathery remains of the sixth Saptarishi towards the fire. The icy wind and the punishing hailstorm were wreaking havoc on the morale of the asuras. The curse and the foretelling of the arrival of doomsday had terrified them to the core, their king included. It was only their stubborn madness that made them carry this now pointless slaughtering on. The crashing in the high mountains was nearing at an unnerving pace.

'Stop, Sura! Did you not hear the tormented prophecy of Sara Maa?' screamed Vivasvan Pujari, pointing towards the sapphire inferno that had engulfed five of the divine sages.

'Were your ears deaf to the curse? What do you seek now, O asuras?'

Sura was as enraged as he was afraid. From the moment they had stepped into the abode of the Saptarishi, nothing was going as he had planned. Intoxicated with unbridled ambition and smelling an absolute victory round the corner, he had expected a swift elimination of the sages, paving the way for his unquestioned rule over all of Aryavarta and beyond. But the night had been a haunting one, to say the least. The unexplained aging and terrifying crumpling of the Saptarishi, their deathly white eyes, the raging blue fire, the nerve-wracking blizzard and now the horror of the curse!

Is the universe conspiring against my ascension to the throne of known Earth?

·||ॐ||·

'Back off, O a-devta!' shouted the demon-king.

He walked towards Vivasvan Pujari, prancing purposefully on the rocky surface to accentuate his defiance.

'You knew it, didn't you?' he asked the devta in an accusatory tone.

'I told you Sura, these are just the mortal remains of the Saptarishi. Why do you think they age so horrendously? Because their immortal souls are gone. They are grandmasters of yogic sciences. Using their *siddhi* they have long abandoned their bodies. As we speak, their souls are somewhere else… and I think I know where…' Vivasvan Pujari tried to reason.

Sura ignored every word the devta had said.

'You knew these mayaavi a-rishis would unleash this black magic on us...' he muttered to himself, his eyes darting and looking increasingly insane.

Suddenly Sura turned to his asuras and spoke belligerently, making his announcement like he was already the supreme overlord of everything and everyone around.

'Do not let these dark tricksters fool you, my brave warriors! There is no curse! These wicked sages were master illusionists. All this is nothing more than deception conjured up by these wily wizards!'

The demon-king unsheathed his massive bone-cutter and raised it to the frightening sky.

'*Rise of the kingdom of the mighty Asuras!*' he shouted.

His vicious soldiers responded with their signature savagery. Each one of them brandished his lethal weapon and joined his king in challenging the Gods!

'*Rise of the kingdom of the mighty Asuras!*'

They chanted in deafening unison.

·||ॐ||·

Sura turned to look at the cruel commander of his elite regiment, who immediately understood what his bloodthirsty king wanted. He now tore into the sixth rishi through his back with a massive spear and lifted him on his pike like a hunter picks up dead game. The shriveled rishi let out a painful *aaah*, before he was stoked into the flames, still hanging on the long spear like a lump of meat being roasted. Still alive.

The commander and the fifty savages erupted in wild guffaws.

Just like the five sons of the Saraswati, the cindering sixth sage now spoke, from the heart of the blue embers.

"You make a feeble attempt to stop these butchers with mere words, O devta! And that when you are the possessor of the mighty cosmic weapon granted to you by the Gods! That when you bear the great Ratna-Maru! So be it.

Just the manner in which you have watched the divine Sages burn one after the other on this fateful night, fate will watch your lineage perish violently, son after son, generation after generation. I curse you and your entire bloodline, O fallen devta…

Every single son of your descent will die a death as violent and as horrible as the spectacle today!

I CURSE YOU! AND YOUR ENTIRE BLOODLINE!

THIS CURSE SHALL LAST TILL THE END OF TIME!"

Just as before, Vivasvan Pujari did not flinch. Nevertheless, he was painfully bewildered.

How could the trikaal-darshi Saptarishi not know?

He folded his hands, ashamed and distraught as he was, and

made his submission to the blurring figure of the burning rishi.

'I accept your curse, just as I have always accepted your blessings. I deserve a violent and insufferable end. But you seem to forget, O great rishi…I will have no bloodline. My only son, the best son in the world…my Manu is already dead.'

He sighed and paused for a moment, choking in his tears and sorrow.

'And yes, he probably did die an excruciating death…true to your curse, O rishi…my Manu died mutilated and poisoned!'

Before the sixth Saptarishi softly erupted into ashes, his voice spoke for the last time…this time with more pity than fury.

"You have turned truly blind, Vivasvan. A supreme human that could once gaze deep into the souls of men and into the sands of time, is today oblivious to his own child.

Your son lives, O tarnished Surya! And it shall be he, who will see the first rays of morning after the Great Deluge subsides.

Manu Pujari…will be the protector of all Creation!

AND SHALL BE KNOWN AND IMMORTALISED AS SATYAVRATA MANU…THE GUARDIAN OF ETERNAL TRUTH!

We pity you, you unfortunate father, you corrupted half-God!"

Banaras, 2017

THE DARK BROTHERHOODS-PART III

'It was the US President Woodrow Wilson who first used the term New World Order publicly,' said Dwarka Shastri. 'While it was in reference to the League of Nations that was established after the First World War, many believe it was the day the Order decided to gradually begin revealing its presence and its vision of establishing a totalitarian global government.'

'Baba, before we move on, can you please trace the journey of the Order right from the time of the Knights Templar?' asked Vidyut.

The matthadheesh nodded and spent a minute in collecting his thoughts, as he sat back on a large armchair.

'The Knights Templar amassed such spectacular wealth that they are said to have owned the entire island of Cyprus. Their weapons and battle gear was the finest money could buy. As if their military might was not adequate, the Knights Templar were declared to be above all laws, as decreed by Pope Innocent II.'

'What does that mean, Baba? Above all laws…?'

'It basically meant that the Templars had to follow no local laws, could travel between kingdoms unstopped and unquestioned, had to pay no taxes and could kill at will.'

'So there was a concerted joint effort by the king and the Church to transform the Knights Templar into the world's most powerful brotherhood…' said Vidyut aloud.

'Precisely. But it is not the rise of the Templars that was as dramatic as their painful end. At the dawn of Friday, the 13th of October, 1307 AD, King Philip IV of France ordered the arrest, torture and execution of hundreds of Templars. Fake charges of heresy were slapped, confessions were extracted via inhuman torture and executions carried out swiftly. A brotherhood that dominated Europe and the Middle East for centuries, was crushed brutally in a matter of days.'

'Wow…that's quite dramatic for sure! And nasty. Interesting to know why Friday the 13th is considered by some people to be ill-omened even today.'

'They say King Philip owed so much money to the Knights

Templar, that he used mere allegations as an excuse to summarily destroy the Templars, and therefore simultaneously extinguish the huge debt he had mounted as a result of his war with England. But there is more to it. Once again the Church was deeply involved and the charges made were purely religious. So this time the king and the priest came together to accuse the brotherhood that spent hundreds of years protecting Christianity – of sacrilege! Clearly, at one time the Templars were an asset. Then something changed in the world-view or master plan of the underground society, and the Templars turned into a liability. The forces at play were the same. The same secret puppeteers who built and exploited the Templars, destroyed them in one swift stroke when their work was done.'

'But what do you think could have been the reason behind this brutal annihilation, Baba?'

'Who can say for sure, Vidyut? Like I explained, the secret brotherhood has a global blueprint spanning hundreds of years. A small change in the socio-political dynamics in one part of the world triggers a major revamping of their master plan, to stay aligned to their vision. Do you know the Knights Templar were not even permitted to surrender? No trials were held. No public hearing. The rapidity with which the entire purging was done, points to just one reality –

The Templars knew something that the secret society did not want revealed.'

'So with the end of the Knights Templar, what happened to the secret brotherhood, Baba?'

'Just like a terrifying mythical monster, the clandestine society of the world's most powerful men and women kept shedding its skin, changing its identity and growing in influence. They slowly but surely established some of the world's biggest business barons and banking institutions. They began to control the world economy, and with it everything that mattered – pharmaceuticals, oil, stock markets, weapons, technology and politics.

Their perverted design began to unleash itself on the planet. Decade after decade, century after century they funded revolutions and civil unrests. Some of the world's biggest wars were fought with both sides being funded and fuelled by the secret Order. Human lives mean nothing to them. They believe they are a superior race that is obliged to rule the rest of humanity.'

Vidyut was concentrating hard. He wanted to grasp every word, every fact and every nuance of this mysterious and grim force. A slow realization was seeping into him.

The New World Order had to be stopped.

·||ॐ||·

'What were the other forms and identities that the Order masked itself behind, Baba? You said they kept changing their outward appearance.'

'Yes Vidyut. The most powerful form of the Order after the

Knights Templar was the *Illuminati*.'

Illuminati…I have heard of this.

'And the Illuminati was not the only one – there were several others. There was the *Rosicrucian Group*, the *Skull and Bones Society*, the *Freemasons*…to name the major ones among the brotherhoods.'

Dwarka Shastri sighed. He looked visibly tired.

'I will tell you all about them some other time, Vidyut,' he said. 'That will take a lot of energy.'

Vidyut understood. He kicked himself for pushing his great grandfather too much. He remembered that Dwarka Shastri had recently recovered from a near-fatal illness.

'Of course, Baba. Just one last question…again,' he insisted.

Dwarka Shastri smiled and nodded, permitting Vidyut to ask what he had in mind.

'If this Order is powerful enough to influence global wars, if it is capable of controlling the world's economy, if it has Presidents and billionaires as members, how can they be even bothered about *our* existence? Why would they want to kill a man as insignificant as me? If they have controlled the world for centuries and are set to establish their totalitarian regime in the future, *who are we for them?*'

'That is not one question, Vidyut. Those are many questions. That too questions that will take time to answer in detail. For now know this – these exceptionally gifted, misdirected geniuses have a very deep and intricate understanding of the influence of divinity on this planet. They are privy to ancient secrets and unlike ordinary humans, they know that an umbilical cord connects our world to the supreme power that rules the universe. Like I have said before, they are not afraid of us. They are afraid of what lies in the Black Temple.'

The matthadheesh could notice mild irritation on Vidyut's face. The secret of the Black Temple had not been shared with Vidyut and it was unfair to keep bringing it up. But the time had not yet come. To pacify his great grandson for the moment, Dwarka Shastri decided to share one extra piece of information.

'Vidyut, an ancient prophecy connects you to the Black Temple. What lies buried there for centuries is a secret most precious to all of mankind. It is something everyone has heard of, but no one expects it to really happen. But it will. And the overlords of the Order know this.

If they kill you, they can change the future.'

Harappa, 1700 BCE

THE LAST PRINCESS OF MOHENJO-DARO

She stood at her grand window, staring out into the wailing, frightening night. Her large, beautiful eyes were moist with an excruciating concoction of melancholy, guilt and fear. Ever since the Surya was skinned and tortured, ever since the sand of Harappa was defiled with the pious drops of Sanjna's blood, ever since a young son was pierced mercilessly with poisoned arrows – the heavens had scowled with fury. They wept and showered Aryavarta with unending cloudbursts. The skies were roaring like a celestial demon, ready to swallow the Earth. Birds had flown away from the rooftops of Harappa and dogs howled all night like werewolves. Cries of sleepless, frightened children and hushed prayers of their helpless parents could be heard from every home.

Her face was dripping wet as the rain splattered it. Her enchanting red lips and razor-sharp features looked breathtaking, every time lightning lit her up into a white statue. But she did not believe so. Every time thunder struck, she imagined her face contorted like that of a grotesque daakini. Her self-inflicting illusion was nothing but a reflection of how she perceived herself now.

This is what I have become. A daakini.

News of the mountains of brick and bronze being taken by the asuras had reached her ears. She knew the ghost-like devta leading the mayhem. She had also received a detailed account of what had transpired in the rain of blood.

I am being punished for my sins. My noble husband will share my cursed fate. The people of Harappa will perish for my evil deeds. The kingdom I so craved shall get swept away in this torrent.

I will be the last, wretched queen of Harappa.

I will be the last princess of Mohenjo-daro.

·||卐||·

'Don't touch me, my lord!' reacted Priyamvada, as her husband, Pundit Chandradhar tried to draw her away from the window. She had been standing there, braving the cold rain as if it did not exist, for hours together. Her long, silken hair was drenched, thrown back straight down to her slender waist. Her hands were trembling continuously.

'Come back in, Priyamvada. You will fall sick. There is nothing out there…' said Chandradhar.

She stood still, as if she did not hear what Chandradhar had said. Then she slowly turned to look at him.

'He will come for us, won't he my lord? I hear he has become a ghost. Vivasvan Pujari will come for both of us…'

Chandradhar clenched his teeth to fight his mortal fear. Priyamvada was right.

'He will not, my dear. He has lost an eye, is grievously wounded and our home is defended by five hundred troops.'

Priyamvada smiled crookedly and then broke into a horrible laughter. She continued laughing for several long moments like a lovely yet manic witch. Her laugh drowned under the shattering thunder every few seconds, and she looked haunting with her guffawing head thrown back under the blinding glare of lightning.

'You know we are both dead, Pundit Chandradhar! You know he will tear through these soldiers in no time. We are both dead already, Chandradhar!' she screamed in the midst of her lunatic laugh.

Chandradhar knew Priyamvada was not wrong. No man in his army could stop Vivasvan Pujari.

Except one.

Chandradhar himself.

While he understood he was no match for the devta, he knew he could resist him long enough for Priyamvada to be sent to safety. His beloved wife was all he had left in this whole world.

What Pundit Chandradhar did not know was that Vivasvan Pujari was not going to come after just his queen and him. True to the chilling words the devta had screamed out while being tortured at the Great Bath, he was coming for every man, woman, child, animal, bird and insect of Harappa.

And it was not going to be a sword fight.

Banaras, 2017

'TRIJAT WILL WAKE THE DEAD'

A day later Balvanta and Vidyut were successful in convincing Prof Tripathi to drive to the Dev-Raakshasa matth with them. While the professor resisted initially, the rare chance of meeting the great Dwarka Shastri was incentive enough for him to agree.

Any taantric worth his salt could never let go of this opportunity. Just being in the presence of Dwarka Shastri was a penance of sorts. The aura of the matthadheesh was enough to exponentially multiply the inner energy of a yogi, enough to fill the spiritual kamandal of a taantric or Naga sadhu or even an aghori.

Prabhat Tripathi fell at the feet of the grandmaster. In an

unusual display of affection, the matthadheesh lifted the professor from his prostrate posture and wrapped him in a warm embrace. Vidyut could see they were two people who loved and respected each other. The professor of course was behaving as if he were a devotee in a temple, facing his deity.

·‖卐‖·

'I have advised them against it, guruji,' said the academician from B.H.U.

Dwarka Shastri nodded, as he gestured to Naina to serve some more *chivda-matar* (spiced rice-flakes with peppercorn) snack to Prof Tripathi.

'So what do you suggest we do, Brahmanand?' asked Dwarka Shastri.

Vidyut, Naina and Sonu exchanged glances. None of them could make head or tail of what the matthadheesh had addressed Prof Tripathi as. To make matters worse, the professor seemed to not even bat an eyelid and responded like nothing was out of place.

'Guruji, who can claim to know Trijat better than you? You know he is capable. And you know he is capable of anything. Moreover, in the past I have never known or even imagined him to have the courage to enter the Dev-Raakshasa matth in your presence, let alone commit a gruesome, ritual beheading! Clearly, somebody is backing him. Someone so indescribably powerful that the Masaan-raja feels he can take even *you* head-on. This is not normal, guruji. Something is very wrong here.'

Vidyut was making note of every word, every statement being spoken.

Guruji, who can claim to know Trijat better than you?

What was that? Why will Baba know Trijat better than others?

Ritual beheading?

Brahmanand?

'There *has* to be a weak point, Tripathi ji,' asked Balvanta. 'There always is! You just need to guide us to it and we will do the rest. We will storm that citadel of pishachas!'

Vidyut noticed that the polite professor, the erstwhile aghori taantric appeared to be under visible duress because of this barrage of questions. He decided to ease the one-eyed gentleman into the conversation.

He was also a bit wary of the riddles associated with his great grandfather. How long was it going to take him to uncover all the mysteries and secrets that lurked behind every corner and every individual even distantly connected to this ancient monastery?

'Tripathi ji, why did you part ways with TK?'

The professor's face turned to one filled with hate, but he did not respond. There was an amused silence in the sunny verandah. Half the people in the grandmaster's patio could not understand what Vidyut had just asked. The half that did could not believe how Vidyut could use a casual, bordering on humorous abbreviation for someone as gruesome as Trijat Kapaalik.

None of them had an idea about the primordial fire of vendetta that was raging in Vidyut's heart.

Only Dwarka Shastri did.

And Brahmanand.

·||ॐ||·

With the reluctant permission of the grandmaster, two glasses of *bhang thandai* had opened up the professor like a library book.

Much against the common stereotype of someone like the grandmaster of the Dev-Raakshasa matth, Dwarka Shastri attached minimal importance to worldly pleasures like marijuana, cannabis or alcohol. He knew that any accomplished yogi's soul was far beyond the reach of these ephemeral substances. A true ascetic was in a state of constant bliss.

'You do know that Trijat's yajnashaala is built on a primeval graveyard? It has been laid on a vast burial and funeral ground established as a result of the great battles that raged for the control of this prehistoric, precious city. It is weird how from ancient Indian kings like Ajaatashatru to medieval monarchs like Qutb-ud-din Aibak and Razia Sultana, every emperor had an unexplained affinity to the city of Banaras. Some wanted to protect and proliferate it. Others wanted to raze it to the ground.'

What was it about this city?

'Anyhow,' the professor continued, 'the reason why Trijat chose that place is because it is infested with pishachas and *daayans* – angry spirits of those who met untimely deaths and died in great pain during the wars. He summons them and draws boundless dark powers from the netherworld through them as a medium. So when you think of attacking his compound, remember it will be more than a battle between men.

Trijat will wake the dead!'

Vidyut and his loyal fellowship were quiet. Almost at the same instant, they all turned to the one man that was beyond doubt the supreme occult overlord on Earth. The one man in the world who could summon even a Brahma Raakshasa into himself. The intense yogi who could beckon hundreds of holy men to join forces even in the darkness of the night.

The only *param-taantric* who could vanquish the maha-taantric Trijat Kapaalik.

They all turned to the grand old man – Dwarka Shastri.

The matthadheesh had his eyes closed. He was in deep meditation. An expert yogi could go into meditative trance instantly. An advanced practitioner of *taantric-vidya* himself, Vidyut could see what his great grandfather was trying to do.

He was mentally studying the planetary positions and the *nakshatras*.

He was choosing the perfect hour for the assault.

East of Harappa, 1700 BCE

SATARUPA

'I have read about it in the Vedas, O Matsya – more specifically in the ancient *Satpatha Brahmana*,' said Manu.

'And you still think Pralay is just some theoretical concept, do you, Satyavrata?' asked Matsya.

Manu was a little vexed at this new name Matsya had coined for him out of nowhere.

'Matsya, my friend, my brother, my mentor...why do you address me as Satyavrata ever since this dark night lit up in a blue flash a few times hours ago?'

Matsya stared deep into Manu's eyes.

Because the curse has been spelled out. The sixth Saptarishi has spoken from the core of the blue fire. Vidhi ka vidhaan - the inerasable writing of destiny - has been inscribed.

'That is not important, Manu. Do you think Pralay is a myth?'

'Of course not, Matsya. How can a Veda like the Satpatha Brahmana be wrong?'

·||ॐ||·

Tara had stood motionless when she saw her Manu. She still wore heavy battle armor. Her wounds still bled. She was wet as a fish, and was shivering in the cold, windy night. But her eyes sparkled like they always did – like dazzling gems delicately embedded in a magnificent, sculpted face. She was crying, no doubt, but not really breaking down.

Tara was a very strong person.

Manu and Tara were competitors as children. They competed against each other for everything – archery, riding, Vedic mathematics, unarmed combat, the scriptures…and even for the outdoor games they played with other children of the neighbourhood. Tara always won. She, along with eight other parent-less children, was handpicked by Sanjna to reside at the small hostel within the Shastri household. They were taken care of like family, and were trained and taught by the great Vivasvan Pujari himself. They all grew up into impressive young women and men, having imbibed all the virtues and all the talents imparted to them by the devta.

As they grew from quarreling kids to shy teenagers, Manu and Tara had chosen one another. They never spoke about it, though sometimes their eyes did for a brief moment or two. They never touched each other. Yet they just knew. So did Vivasvan and Sanjna. They could sense the sweetly amorous attraction between these two wonderful youngsters and had wishfully imagined the beautiful Tara as the bride that would knock over the traditional vessel of rice and step into their home one day – to partner Manu as his wife and soul mate.

·‖卐‖·

'You made it, Manu…' she said to the love of her life. 'You made it!'

Manu walked towards her, slowly at first…before breaking into an impatient jog. He ran and grasped her in his arms. He held her in a tight embrace, quietly swearing to the universe that he would never let go of her now. Never!

'My Tara…' was all he could whisper.

Tara could no longer hold her tears back. Seeing her man alive, nestled in his arms and hearing him take her name in a manner as loving as she never knew before, she could not retain her composure. She dug her face into Manu's chest, wrapped her arms around him and wept.

And wept.

Tara was a very strong person.

But she was, after all, also just a nineteen-year-old girl who needed what every human needs most. Love.

Tara and Manu stood on that dark, lonely cliff, against the cruel and frightening sky, braving the lashing rain. They just stood there, soaking in each other's presence.

It was a strange sight for Matsya, who was watching them from a sliver in the cave wall. He had witnessed this before, in another eon, in another galaxy, on a somewhat similar planet in a parallel *Brahmannd* (universe). Over and over again. There were Manus and Taras in all universes. And Vishnu watched over them all.

Love existed across the cosmos as the most potent and indefatigable force. In the middle of all the destruction and all the death around them, despite all that was already lost and all that was being threatened into oblivion, notwithstanding the hate and the violence that surrounded them, irrespective of the fall of devtas and the decimation of cities, they stood there. Immersed in each other's love.

That is when Matsya remembered how and why the Creator envisaged mankind. Why it was God's greatest work, an extension of God Himself. He smiled at this masterpiece of a species that carried within it a trace of God's divinity. Which is why you could take away their homes, their lands, their loved ones, their wealth and everything they held dear. But you could never take away one thing from human beings.

Hope.

·||ॐ||·

Matsya sat at the head of the meeting that was convened

around a comforting wood fire. Somdutt, Tara and their handful of brave companions were by this time fed and rested.

It was time for them to brace themselves for what was coming.

And to play their part.

It was to a packed house that Matsya spoke. The mountain-guardians and their leader, several of the fish-folk from Matsya's band, Somdutt, Tara, their warriors – everyone was present. Matsya had wanted it to be so. And as the radiant blue man had expected, it was with roars of disbelief and gasps of fear that the declaration was greeted.

'It is inevitable, Somdutt. Pralay will destroy everything as we know it. Have no doubt in your mind.'

Matsya was speaking plainly, clearly. He knew this was not the time to honey-coat anything.

It was Somdutt who stood up and urged the gathering to quiet down. While he had heard the most ominous words of his life from this person called Matsya, the great architect was unable to take his eyes off this man glowing a mellow sapphire under his fish skin robes. Somdutt had seen the world. He had met and worked with the greatest of men from Harappa, Mohenjo-daro and Lothal, right up to Kashi, Mesopotamia and even with the great Pharaohs of the far land of the Pyramids. He had had the good fortune of even being a close friend of none other than the devta of Harappa. But even Vivasvan Pujari's luminosity was no match for the inexplicable magnetism of this man. Something told

Somdutt he was something else. Matsya was something more, something greater than any man he had seen. No…he was something greater than even a devta!

'Hear me, O Matsya, as I speak on behalf of all the people in this cave.'

Matsya nodded politely at Somdutt, encouraging him to continue.

'Before I say anything Matsya, please allow me to fold my hands and bow to you. You are not an ordinary man. My old eyes can see it. And if I am right, then please bless me with your grace before I take the liberty of questioning your pronouncement and thereby risk annoying you.'

Matsya was suddenly full of admiration for this fine architect and warrior, who had stood by the side of Vivasvan and Sanjna till the very end. He was convinced he had made the right choice.

The building of the universe's greatest ship was going to take more than architectural and engineering skills. It was going to take character.

Before Matsya could respond, another hand shot up.

'I have a question too!' rang out a confident female voice.

Matsya turned to look around the room but could not place the voice.

'Who is it please?' he urged.

'It is I, Tara,' said she, slowly standing up.

Matsya noticed she was sitting right at the back of the hall, next to his favorite, his protégé…Satyavrata Manu.

'Tara…what a beautiful name,' said Matsya. 'It is as beautiful as you are, my dear.'

Manu beamed with pride. A compliment for his Tara from none other than Matsya!

'That is the name we call her by at home, Matsya. Her real name is something else,' clarified Manu from behind the crowd, feeling strangely shy.

'Really?' asked Matsya, as if there was anything he did not know. 'Then what is her real name?'

Manu turned to look up at Tara. He wanted her to be the one to tell Matsya.

Tara understood Manu. She gave him an almost unnoticeable smile, and turned to Matsya.

'It is *Satarupa*.'

Banaras, 2017

RAKTBEEJ ANUSHTTHAN

'There is a way… a way that might tilt the scale in our favor, gurudev,' said Prof Tripathi.

It had been decided that Balvanta would lead the armed offensive. There was no discussion needed to agree that Dwarka Shastri ji was going to spearhead the battle of the ethereal creatures and black spells.

With blessings and permission from his great grandfather, Vidyut had taken it upon himself to go straight for the Masaan-raja and his two pishachinis. The blunt sickles which dangled around their waists that day at the matth still haunted Vidyut. He knew what weapon had been used to brutally saw off the head of Bala. Despite being a man who admired and respected women deeply as equals, as incarnations of

251

Shakti, Vidyut had let go of the consideration that these two assassins were girls.

They were not. They were demented killers who had no place in this world. Vidyut was going to punish them the way he would have punished ruthless, murderous men.

Evil and brutality had no gender.

'What is that way, Tripathi ji?' enquired Sonu. The young man was rearing to jump into battle. He wanted to pay them back for the serious wounds he had suffered on the Da-shashwamedh ghaat. He wanted to enter and plunder their fortress the way they had defiled his matth, his home. But most of all, he wanted to do everything in his power to protect his beloved devta - his Vidyut dada!

Even now they had to look for the best way to pierce through the guard of Trijat's yajnashaala, to ensure minimal casual-ties on their side. They were relying on Prof Tripathi, or Brahmanand, to provide them with a breakthrough. He had been an insider for years.

'It can be done only on the dark, moonless night of *Amaavasya*...' said Prof Tripathi, suddenly energetic as if he had just bumped into a Eureka moment.

The others were listening.

Even before Brahmanand could complete what he was going to say, Dwarka Shastri was already shaking his head in silent disagreement.

There was a reason why evil spirits were also called *Nishacha-ras* or *Walkers of the Night*.

The moonless night of Amaavasya was the hour when the dead were indomitable.

·‖卐‖·

'There is a reason, gurudev. Every amaavasya, Trijat performs a spectacular yajna, where he lights an enormous ritual fire in a massive pit designed especially for this. Freshly exhumed corpses are submitted to this blaze, along with an endless offering of human and animal blood, skulls of powerful ta-antrics of yore and various other baffling offerings like grave shrouds, rotting meat and the forbidden *ketaki* flowers. But most inexplicably, every amaavasya Trijat pours a generous offering of his own blood into the ritual fire…'

Vidyut was pacing up and down the verandah. He had been a dedicated student of the Atharva Veda, the Garuda Puraana and other ancient scriptures on occult and tantra. But he had never heard of the ghastly ritual Prof Tripathi was describing.

What was Trijat going after?

He turned to his great grandfather. He knew his Baba would know about even this bizarre, cadaverous ceremony.

'Baba, what is this man doing? I have never heard of a taantric ritual such as this one. Please educate us…'

'*Raktbeej Anushtthan*,' said the grandmaster grimly, even before Vidyut could finish his sentence.

Vidyut knew who Raktbeej was. He stiffened as he heard the

next words Dwarka Shastri spoke.

'He is trying to summon an army of raakshasas to Earth.'

·||ॐ||·

'Raktbeej was a mighty demon who was eventually slayed by *Maa Durga* and *Maa Kaali* during their fierce battle against the demon-king *Mahishasura*. Raktbeej was one of Mahishasura's war Generals. The former was the bearer of a unique boon that miraculously spawned thousands of his clones from every drop of his blood that fell to the ground. When any of the clones was slain, his drops would further create more Raktbeejs. It was an endless battle – and Raktbeej could not be defeated!' explained Naina to Sonu, who was the only one who was not aware of the mythical tale of the near-immortal demon.

'Then what happened, Naina *di*?' asked Sonu. 'From what you are narrating, it would have been impossible to slay the demon. In fact, any attempt at killing him would have procreated thousands more of him!'

'Precisely. Which is why Maa Durga summoned Kaali, a fearsome form of the Goddess Herself. They fought Raktbeej as a team, where Durga beheaded the demon and his clones, while Kaali slurped up all the blood before it fell to the ground. So you see why Maa Kaali is always depicted with her tongue outstretched, stained with blood? Slowly all clones were killed by Durga and Raktbeej was left alone, only to be slain himself.'

Sonu smiled in amazement and awe.

'I always wondered why Maa Kaali was shown with a red tongue. Now I know!' he said elatedly.

Vidyut was quiet as Naina completed her narration. He was seriously worried.

'Baba, what is this Raktbeej Anushtthan? It does not sound good.'

'The Raktbeej Anushtthan is a rarest of rare penance that promises to bestow the successful practitioner with unparalleled control over the dark forces, especially over the wandering spirits of primordial raakshasas. Forbidden strictly by all the ancient rishis like Bhrigu, Bharadwaj, Agastya, Durvaasa and even by the first writer of the sacred *Shastras*, Satyavrata Manu, this treacherous siddhi was abandoned centuries ago for a very simple reason.'

Purohit ji, Naina, Sonu, Balvanta, Prof Tripathi and Vidyut were glued to every word Dwarka Shastri was saying.

'What reason...Baba?' asked Naina softly, nervously.

Dwarka Shastri was in no mood to waste time.

'No taantric, however accomplished, ever survived this Anushtthan. Every single one of them not only died, but also died so horribly that this practice was buried forever into the depths of the prohibited arts.

If Trijat is trying to bring this forbidden ritual back to life, there is something he knows that we don't.'

Vidyut felt a chill travel down his spine. If his great grandfather did not know something, how would they ever fight it? How could they win over it?

·‖卐‖·

'I cannot explain the Raktbeej Anushtthan in more detail here and now, Vidyut. All we need to know is that if this is what Trijat is hoping to unleash, we must stop him…at all cost! If that means we need to go in even on an amaavasya, so be it.'

Ever since Vidyut had met the great matthadheesh, he had seen him panic like this only once. That was when the grand-master had sensed the presence of the lethal zippo lighter given by Romi on Vidyut's presence. That had meant sure death for Vidyut. If his Baba was panicking again, there was reason to be worried.

Vidyut went quiet for a minute or two. His mind was work-ing at the speed of a fighter jet. Naina noticed his head was resting lightly on a wall; his eyes were shut, his fists clenched and his jaw tightened. She did not know how to hold herself back from falling in love over and over again with this dash-ing, grounded and supremely accomplished man. She shook away the intense attraction.

The hour was far too dark for her personal desires to matter.

'Tripathi ji, you were going to share something about why amaavasya is the suited time for us to attack. Please shed some light on why you think so,' asked Vidyut as he took his seat again.

'Simply because after the Anushtthan is complete, Trijat is temporarily drained of his otherworldly might until Sunrise. While being the giver of limitless power in the long term, this ritual sucks out the spiritual energy of the practitioner for a few hours. And that is not all. As *prasaad* from the morbid ceremony, a strong concoction of marijuana is consumed by all his aghori comrades.'

Stopping to see if his audience had grasped what he had explained, Prof Tripathi concluded.

'On the dark night of amaavasya, Trijat Kapaalik is at his weakest.'

Harappa, 1700 BCE

EMPEROR OF THE BADLANDS

The last devta of Harappa appeared to have gone completely insane. He wept and laughed simultaneously. He slammed his fists on the ground and yelled to the heavens...all at once. It was as if the devta and the raakshasa within him were in a fierce, final battle.

The proclamation by the sixth rishi that his son Manu lived even now changed everything for Vivasvan Pujari. In the last few bleeding days he had been forcibly suppressing his divine conscience as he committed the killings, connived with the demons and unleashed horrible violence – all starkly against the beliefs and principles of his own righteous self. He was purposefully strangling the devta within himself and feeding the vengeful pishacha. If only he knew his beloved son Manu was alive!

If only he knew!

Even this the Gods hid from me!

Vivasvan Pujari could take it no more. His thirst for vengeance had led to the killing of hundreds of Harappan soldiers. Many of them the devta had personally trained in the better days of the cursed metropolis. But during the battle for his rescue and in their nocturnal raid on the mountains of mayhem, innumerable people had perished. He had lost Sanjna, his beloved wife and timeless soul mate of his karmic journey. His handsome, obedient and valiant son Manu was destined for greatness from the moment he opened his eyes in this world. But instead he had endured his mother's death and the disgracing of his father, before himself becoming a victim to painful machete gashes and poison arrows at the peak of his beautiful youth. The unearthly blue fire had consumed six of his much-loved Saptarishi. Sara Maa, the loving Saraswati, the River of the Wise, had morphed into a merciless rakt-dhaara, and had herself descended and cursed all of mankind to eternal infighting and suffering.

There was nothing left to avenge.

Pralay is going to swallow everything, everyone...

The ancient engravings on the Ratna-Maru gleamed to life

in the blue darkness. The devta had unsheathed his dreaded blade and now stood between Sura and the haunting flames. He rested his entire muscular and skinned frame on one knee, with the other knee raised and both his hands resting on the handle of the legendary super-sword. His head was bowed, his semi-bald scalp reflecting the fire. He looked like a blue ghost.

The commander of this select asura regiment was by now intoxicated with brutality and the unbridled, one-sided killing. In an attempt to please his king, he decided to intervene.

Small men often make big mistakes when fooled by the illusion of power.

'You heard the demon-king Sura, O Avivasv...'

Before he could complete his sentence, the Ratna-Maru beheaded him. His head flew into the darkness of the night and the rest of his body crashed to his knees, his neck spraying blood into the blue fire – as if submitting a repentant offering.

It had not taken Vivasvan more than a split second to tender this sacrifice. And this was the veteran, the manic commander! It was clear to the rest of the asuras what their fate would be if the devta chose to expand the canvas of his death sentence.

But Sura had not become the emperor of the badlands just like that. He drew his sword slowly without saying a word. Fifty other swords were unsheathed instantaneously. The savages of Sura were a suicide squad. In their ferocious tribe they were granted the glorious status of martyrdom when any of them died in suicide operations. They were fooled into believing that they would find heaven posthumously once they laid their lives for the tribe. Fooled by none other than the demon-king Sura, who did not spare a moment before getting these boys and men butchered as sacrifices on his blood-spattered journey to the throne of Aryavarta.

Led by Sura, the savage fighters began closing in on Vivasvan Pujari. The devta did not flinch, and kept sitting in the stance he was in. It was the poised posture that a panther goes into before pouncing like a supreme predator.

As Sura came into striking distance, someone yelled out to him.

'We must stop, my king!'

It was Prachanda.

·||ॐ||·

Prachanda was no less a demon than Sura. He was no less cruel and had fought all the wars shoulder to shoulder with his king. He was feared by his foes far and wide. He burnt and plundered villages without any hesitation or remorse. He conspired and he killed. He was a true asura at heart.

But something had changed today. He was witness to the unspeakable trials of a devta. He had felt a needle piercing his heart when he saw the eyes and the inexplicably hastened aging of the sages. The raging blue fire had nearly hypnotized him and he had heard the curses of Sara and the sixth Saptarishi. He could clearly see that the thunder, the screaming wind, the wild hailstorm…were all unseasonal, unnatural.

Something unheard of, something uncontrollably destructive…was indeed coming. For all of them.

Sura once again turned slowly to look at Prachanda, his eyes burning with fury.

'Are you out of your mind, Prachanda? You attempt to hold back the wrath of Sura's sword?!'

'Forgive me, my lord. But haven't we done enough? We turned six of these mayaavi a-rishis into ashes. But none of them burned like a human. And that…that blue fire is not a trick of any wizard. We heard those voices that were loud as an exploding Sun. No black magician or mayaavi of the world can conjure up something like that…something beyond human imagination!'

'Shut your mouth, Prachanda!' screamed Sura, now trembling with rage.

Prachanda did not relent.

'Let us leave, O king. We have everything west of Aryavarta. Why stay in this land that looks like it is going to be ravaged by both man and nature?. Let us ride back! We don't need this! We are undisputed rulers of the West of Hindukush…'

'*We*? We…are undisputed rulers, Prachanda?'

'Pardon me, O great Sura. You are the undisputed ruler.'

'Stand back, Prachanda, before I kill you first,' said the demon-king.

It is written in the scriptures. When the Almighty pledges to destroy someone, it is by simply taking away the power of good judgment.

Banaras, 2017

THE GREAT
DWARKA SHASTRI

Vidyut saw his great grandfather immersed in books that appeared to be older than the 800-year-old dwaar of the Dev-Raakshasa matth. He flipped pages frantically, moving from one text to another. Most books were written in Sanskrit, while some were in what looked like ancient Egyptian, Awadhi, Latin, English and Hindi.

'What are you looking for, Baba?' asked Vidyut politely. 'May I help you?'

'I am looking for references to the Raktbeej Anushtthan, Vidyut. Cannot seem to find its mention anywhere.'

'But Baba, you already know everything about it, don't you?'

The matthadheesh looked up, took off his heavy-rimmed reading glasses and rested back in the chair.

'No I don't, Vidyut. Once the Anushtthan was prohibited, all available texts related to it were carefully pulled out and expunged by the rishis. Whatever knowledge about this ritual exists with me or a few others today, was passed down verbally.'

'But what is it that you want to study about it, Baba?'

Dwarka Shastri heaved a deep sigh.

'Nothing in specific. Just that I am not happy going in on amaavasya, without complete knowledge of this ancient, abandoned cult ritual. No doubt if Brahmanand is recommending this, he must be right. He is very thorough with his knowledge of the ancient scriptures, including the dark sciences.'

This gave Vidyut an idea.

'Baba, why don't we request Prof Tripathi to come with us as we raid the Masaan-raja's den? His knowledge and inside information will only help.'

The grandmaster nodded, his eyes narrowing a bit as he considered the suggestion.

'Yes, that might help. But why will he come into such hellfire with us? And while he is no less than a maha-taantric himself, he is too meek and distant from all this now. This is not his battle anyway,' said Dwarka Shastri.

After half a minute of silence, the matthadheesh's narrow

eyes suddenly opened up.

'Or maybe it is,' he mumbled.

'What is it that you said, Baba?' asked Vidyut.

'Maybe it *is* his battle!'

Vidyut was confused.

'Why do you say that, Baba? Prof Tripathi was reluctant to even speak about Trijat and his days with him. There is no way he is going to go back there. I don't understand why you say it is his battle also.'

Dwarka Shastri turned to Vidyut fully.

'How do you think Brahmanand lost his eye, Vidyut?'

Vidyut did not want to hear the answer.

'It was plucked out pitilessly with a sickle, even as Brahmanand thrashed in pain and pleaded for mercy.'

·||ॐ||·

The last devta appeared to be deeply disturbed. He sat with his eyes shut and his forehead resting on his clasped hands.

Purohit ji and Dwarka Shastri could see that Vidyut was not relishing everything that was happening around him. Clearly the unstoppable realities of blood and gore were getting to him.

'What happened, beta?' asked Purohit ji, keeping a hand on

Vidyut's strong shoulder.

Vidyut shook his head, turned to Purohit ji and smiled. No matter how strained he was, Vidyut was not one to let his loved ones go through even a stressful minute because of him.

'Nothing, Purohit ji. Just a bit wary of so much malice, intrigue and violence. I grew up knowing well that our matth and our family was not ordinary, but I had no idea that there was a web of deceit, conspiracies and bloodshed at every step.'

Purohit ji grinned empathetically and said, 'even Arjuna felt wary at the beginning of the Mahabharata *yuddha*, Vidyut. There is nothing wrong with it.'

Vidyut smiled again and tapped Purohit ji's hand in a reassuring manner.

Dwarka Shastri was unimpressed. He needed his great grandson to be strong, to be prepared…given the several gruesome battles that awaited him - until the prophesied hour arrived.

Only six more days to go. Centuries of pain, struggle and sacrifice. For this one day.

All for this one golden day.

·‖ॐ‖·

'There is a reason I have called both you and Purohit together, Vidyut,' began the grandmaster.

'Ji, Baba…?' said Vidyut, in his ever so obedient tone.

'My time has come, Vidyut. Purohit and I have been study-ing my kundali for years and we both concur. My end is near, my son. Very near.'

Vidyut did not want to believe what he had just heard. He turned to look at Purohit ji, hoping he would burst out laughing and this was all a big joke. But Purohit looked back at him with tender but grim eyes.

'But Baba, why are you saying this? You have just recovered so speedily. You are hale and hearty. I saw you the day Trijat came. You stood there like a warrior! How can something happen to you suddenly? I am there for you, Baba. I will stand like a wall between you and death. Papa also left me this way! Now you can't leave me like this, Baba…' blurted out Vidyut like a child, ready to burst into tears. He shook his head continuously, refusing to acknowledge what he had been told.

Water trickled down from the great matthadheesh's eyes. It took him some effort to get up from his chair, and he walked a few steps to where Vidyut was sitting. The grand old man lifted his awaited descendent by the shoulders and held him tight.

Vidyut cried his heart out. He had spent nearly his entire life alone, without a family to love him and be with him. He depended on a friend like Bala. That brotherly love was also snatched away from him by the claws of some strange fate he was destined to live out. In the last few days, he had found in his Baba all that he ever wished for. Only to lose him too!

'Baba, you are a marvel. You can do anything that you like. You control the realms of space and time. Save yourself, Baba. You are a devta!'

Dwarka Shastri held Vidyut's face in his large hands, like a doting parent holds a small child.

'I am not a devta, Vidyut. While over all these centuries people have believed that every son and daughter from our bloodline was a devta or *devi*, the truth is something else. Our family, over generations has had only two true devtas. One was the great Vivasvan Pujari, whose tale I have narrated to you.'

The matthadheesh paused for a moment as he admired Vidyut's godly face. His eyes were moist with love and with the longing of someone who was going to go far away soon.

'And the other is you, Vidyut. You are the last devta.

After you, this world will never see a devta again.'

East of Harappa, 1700 BCE

'YOU PASSED THE TEST'

The gathering took a break from the discussion, for each group to huddle and assimilate what Matsya had just announced.

Manu and Tara, or Satyavrata Manu and Satarupa, were walking beside the kind godmother of the mountain-guardians.

'My lady, *who* is Matsya? How do you know him?' asked Manu.

She smiled but did not turn to Manu. As if she expected this question to pop-up anytime and was not surprised to hear it.

'Why do you want to know, Manu?' she said, as they continued to walk.

'He is extraordinary, my lady. His presence soothes the hearts and minds of all around him. On one end he appears to be a fierce warrior. On the other he looks as tender as a loving father. He is fearsome, yet he exudes benevolence beyond measure. When he looks at me, it seems like he is staring at my soul, from this life and all the ones before it. In fact...in fact, I suspect he is an incarnation of Lord Vishnu.'

'He gets impressed easily,' quipped Tara. She knew her Manu, and how emotional and trustful her warrior-prince could get.

The graceful lady laughed at Tara's words. She was delighted to see the bond of pure love and friendship that Manu and Tara shared.

'You have just seen him once...that too from a distance in a crowd, Tara,' she said. 'Wait till you meet him face to face. Also, Matsya decides who finds him divine and who doesn't. You don't begin to love him of your own accord. He chooses the moment for that. He can make you hate him if that fits into his larger scheme of things. No one can say what he has in mind. All I can tell you is that he is as close as it gets to God walking on Earth.'

Manu was not amazed at what he heard. He felt it deeply himself. Tara was a bit skeptical at what she felt was an exaggerated description.

'Tell me this please,' asked Manu, 'if he is who you say he is and I am convinced he is, why did I find him unconscious the other day, thirsting for a few drops of water? How can someone who is so omnipotent, be in such a helpless situation?'

'He was not dying that day, Manu. You were! He is timeless, beyond the captivity of life and death. It was simply his final test for you. He just wanted to be sure that the man he expects the world from, quite literally, was in fact worthy of his trust. By willing to lay down your life to save a fellow human being, you proved him right. You passed the test.'

·||ॐ||·

'But again, my lady, how did you get introduced to Matsya? He does not live here, yet he seems to govern everything. He is not a king but has the aura of a thousand monarchs combined. When he laughs the whole universe laughs with him. When he gets annoyed, the skies lament and weep. Who is he?'

The lady thought for a while and then spoke.

'No one knows where Matsya comes from, Manu. No one knows who his disciples are. It is said he has thousands of them, all dwellers of the water. Some say the mythical sea-monster *Lok-Naas* or the *Destroyer of Men*, an aquatic dragon bigger than a hundred ships taken together, is his tamed servant. Matsya once saved this mountain from the massive forces of a savage warlord. He stood alone on the battlefield, his long hair and his fish robes fluttering in the wind, as hundreds of riders galloped towards him. Matsya simply grinned and raised both his arms in the air. I saw it with my own eyes. The hundreds of horses neighed to a halt, tossing their riders in the air, who crashed on the dust of the battlefield. The horses bowed their heads to Matsya before turning around in retreat.'

Manu and Tara stood there speechless, astounded. The gracious godmother would not ever lie. Someone of her spiritual accomplishment would not hallucinate nor get tricked by a magician.

'Thank you for sharing this with us, my lady. I don't need any convincing about who Matsya is. I think I know who he is,' said Manu, with a faint smile.

The lady nodded. She knew it too.

'Just one question though, my lady...how does Matsya smell of the seas all the time? There is no sea for hundreds of miles from here.'

'Don't you see, Manu...' she replied.

'Matsya *is* the ocean.'

·||ॐ||·

Their voices were raised.

Tara could not believe that even after everything, even with the impending deluge, Manu wanted to ride into Harappa to extract his vengeance.

Upon Matsya's swift counsel, Somdutt had advised Tara not to tell Manu that the devta was alive, and who or what he had become. Tara had resisted wildly. She was not going to hide anything from her man – least of all the news of his father's

273

survival. It was only the safety of Manu that made her agree reluctantly. She knew if Manu found out about Vivasvan Pujari being alive, he would rush to his father's aid – who she was convinced was beyond redemption. All that she knew of the Surya of Harappa was dead anyway. What was left was a murderous raakshasa…and Manu would become one too if he let the fire of revenge burn his soul the way it had scalded Vivasvan Pujari's. She bit her lip at keeping a secret from her Manu, but she had no choice.

'You have to believe in one thing or the other, Manu,' Tara said in a strained voice. She had been trying to convince him for quite some time now. 'You either believe that Pralay is coming. In that case Priyamvada, Chandradhar, Gun, Sha, Ap, those people who pelted the devta with stones, those wretches who spat at him…everyone will perish anyway! And if you don't believe that the great deluge is round the corner, then why are we here on this dark mountain in the first place?'

She made sense. She always did.

'If it is Pralay that kills the men and women who destroyed my family, murdered my mother and took away everything from my father, then shame on the existence of Manu Pujari! It is excruciating pain from the cold blade of my sword that must be the last thing Priyamvada, Chandradhar and those black magicians should feel before they depart from this world,' said Manu frostily.

'And you think that would make your mother, the beautiful Sanjna, proud of you, Satyavrata?'

Manu and Tara noticed that Matsya had walked up to them. The blue fish-man looked at Tara and smiled. Tara's breath stopped where it was and she stood there dazed just as Manu was when he had met Matsya for the first time. She felt the peace that one feels in the sanctum sanctorum of a divine temple. Peace like she experienced in the arms of Sanjna when she was a child. Happiness that her love for Manu gave her. She felt she had seen Matsya somewhere. Or maybe everywhere.

Manu was right… He is Lord Vishnu.

·||ॐ||·

Manu bowed and folded his hands in a respectful greeting to Matsya, who meant everything to him now. He ignored the question Matsya had asked.

'Answer my question, Manu. So you think butchering a woman, along with your very own uncle and three blind men is going to make your parents and ancestors proud of you and your valour?'

'I don't know all that, Matsya. I have to make them pay for making my mother and father suffer. Please don't stop me, I beg you.'

Matsya sighed and walked closer to Manu. Tara was still a statue, soaking in the divinity she was experiencing.

'Don't worry about the Mesopotamian magicians, Manu. The princess of Mohenjo-daro has already thrown them into the mrit-kaaraavaas to rot and die. They will not survive the deluge. But their vile names will. I assure you, the black souls of those scoundrels will never find peace, and they will be remembered by the survivors of Pralay and their generations to follow as harbingers of dark omens. Ap-Sha-Gun will become a term hated for millennia to come.'

Manu did not seem convinced.

'Tell me Satyavrata, what would your mother have you do... save a life or take one?' asked Matsya.

'Of course save a life, Matsya, but that is not...'

'And what would she have you do if it was a question of quenching your thirst for retribution...against saving the whole of *Srishti* and redeeming the entire world?'

Banaras, 2017

'THEY WERE HIS DISCIPLES'

About one hour passed and for most of it Vidyut was inconsolable. He suggested everything from life-saving yajnas to admitting the grandmaster in the best hospital in Los Angeles. He was desperate to hold on to his last, his only family.

But as time passed and Vidyut himself studied the horoscope of his Baba, he began to accept the reality. Intense *Maarkesh*, or the period of inevitable death, was clearly casting its black shadow over his great grandfather's kundali.

If *jyotish* or astrology was to be believed, *no one could save Dwarka Shastri.*

Vidyut's expertise on reading kundalis was far richer than

what the matthadheesh and Purohit had expected. The devta noticed something that stopped his heartbeat.

The kundali of Dwarka Shastri did not just say that his end was near.

It predicted a very painful, vicious death.

·||ॐ||·

'There is something more. My siddhis seem to have faded ever since the battle with the master exorcist from the West. The Brahma Raakshasa certainly served me as he had promised to me half a century ago, but that spiritual exertion took its toll for sure. I could not see the blackened soul of Bala, despite him being right in front of me. Where was my *trikaal-shakti* when Trijat's pishachinis took advantage of our collective focus on him and slipped out to murder Bala? And now, when we embark upon perhaps the last battle of my life, I am unable to see the future. I am unable to recall details of the Raktbeej Anushtthan. I don't even know if I will be of any help to you, Vidyut.'

Vidyut got up, walked up to Dwarka Shastri's chair and sat down on the ground. He took one foot of the matthadheesh in his hands and began pressing it gently – as a sign of his deep love and devotion to his Baba.

'Just your presence is enough to send shivers down the spines of these evil wretches, Baba. Your aura alone will cut their dark powers by half. We don't know what Trijat is going to throw at us. It could be anything. If there is anyone who can protect us from his unpredictable onslaught, it is you.

But having said that, I urge you not to join us, Baba. Please stay here.'

That was never going to happen. Dwarka Shastri was never going to leave his beloved Vidyut alone.

Even if it meant playing out the last chapter of his illustrious but merciless kundali precisely as it was destined.

·‖卐‖·

'Absolutely not, Naina!' snapped Vidyut, as he tried in vain to convince her about the danger involved in their amaavasya undertaking.

'Look, Naina, this time we are going to tear right into the heart of the demon's den. There are hundreds of them, and it is not going to be just a battle of hands and weapons now. It is the kind of battle neither you nor I have ever fought.'

'Then why are you going?' she asked.

'Because I am a taantric, Naina. Deep down under my fancy clothes and my expensive watches, I am a skilled practitioner of occult. I have spent twenty years training...first under Papa, then under the guidance of Gopal, my sanyaasi friend from the Himalayan monastery. I may not be able to out-maneuver Trijat, but I can at least withstand his assault for some time.'

Naina shook her head. She was not going to listen.

'You have got to be kidding me, Vidyut!' she retorted back, equally annoyed. 'The matth is my home! I will not keep out of any fight that concerns my family, my Baba…and you. You…Vidyut.'

Vidyut was looking straight into her large, speaking eyes.

'Naina, you don't…' he started.

'You still don't see it, do you?' interrupted Naina.

She was searching Vidyut's eyes…for answers, for acknowledgement, for one trace of what she wanted to see in them.

'I love you,' she said softly.

Vidyut went numb. He did not know what hit him. She had never looked so vulnerable, so passionate, and so indescribably lovely.

'Wha…?' was all he could blurt out.

'Yes, yes, a thousand times yes…I love you, Vidyut,' she said again, as if pleading for him to hear the story of her heart. As if beseeching him to say what she had wanted to hear - for two decades.

There was a moment of silence - of nothing but a man and a woman feeling each other's presence more intensely than either knew was possible. One was deeply and helplessly in love. The other was almost there, determined not to cross the line.

He could not say he loved her back. But he could not let her heart break. Not after everything. Not after who she was.

On pure instinct, Vidyut's hand slipped around Naina's slender waist as he pulled her towards himself. As their bodies came close and Naina sensed what was going to happen next, she closed her eyes, surrendering to her devta.

Vidyut pressed his lips on hers, which she received gently, softly. A moment passed when they stayed glued to each other's lips, before breaking into a long, passionate kiss.

·‖ॐ‖·

As they stepped out of the matth's dining hall, Vidyut found a moment alone with Purohit ji. He was still dazed at what had happened between Naina and him a couple of hours back.

I will never forget that kiss. Never ever.

'Purohit ji, I could not understand one thing. When Trijat and Baba spoke, it looked like they knew each other from before. The same happened with Prof Tripathi, who Baba has been addressing as Brahmanand. What is going on?'

'You still haven't figured out, Vidyut?' asked Purohit ji, a bit amused at the last devta's question.

Vidyut responded with a blank expression and a mild shrug of his shoulders.

'You silly boy, both Trijat and Brahmanand were disciples of the great Dwarka Shastri. They lived and trained at the matth. How else do you think Trijat could direct his pisha-chinis to the exact location of the monastery's prison cell?

No one in this world can reach the taantric prowess those two have, without the mentorship of the only param-taan-tric left on Earth.'

Harappa, 1700 BCE

THE LAST SAPTARISHI

Vivasvan Pujari slashed the first asura diagonally across his stomach right up to his chest with the Ratna-Maru, ripping him open. At lightning speed he turned around, decapitating the second asura while kicking a third one in his chest, who went flying several feet away into the rocky ground.

These soldiers were no match for the martial prowess of the devta. None of them could take him on.

But there were fifty of them, along with their legendary warrior-king Sura.

In the battle that ensued over the next few minutes, the devta had killed ten more of the savage fighters attacking him from all sides, but not without suffering a few cuts and injuries himself. Given his skinned and mutilated body, the devta could ill-afford any more wounds.

And it was now when Sura called out the names of seven of his best fighters and lifted his own gigantic sword.

Sura was no ordinary trooper. He had been beaten in the past by the devta, but that was when they were in a one to one duel. Nor was the devta in the harrowing physical condition then that he was now. Both these factors were making it hard for Vivasvan Pujari to withstand and repel the barrage of sword and spear attacks that were raining upon him from every direction.

The devta suddenly broke through the ring of adversaries surrounding him and dashed towards a nearby rock. In an elegant and expert move, he pounced on the big stone with one foot, swung around and used the rock to propel him high, giving him the advantage of an aerial attack. The move worked and the Ratna-Maru tore into the head of one of the asuras, who yelped in pain and dropped dead instantly.

But the devta was running out of moves. Sura was now assaulting him with his heavy sword repeatedly, madly, snarling and growling like a wild animal with each powerful stroke.

As the devta repelled the beastly onslaughts from Sura and also deflected hundreds of other blade and pike attacks, he could see a sharp long-sword making its way towards him. He had no choice but to grab it by the blade-end to prevent it from piercing his ribs.

As the devta clutched hold of the sharp sword, it tore his palm and fingers in deep gashes. Vivasvan Pujari screamed in agony. Despite his extraordinary valour and the bodies of fourteen slain asuras scattered around, this was fast becoming a battle the devta was not going to win.

Then suddenly, under the screeching hailstorm, below the crashing in the mountains and amidst the intense battle between the asuras and the devta, the Seventh Saptarishi spoke in a booming, loud voice – one that was not expected from his frail, wrinkled remains of a body.

To everyone's horror, his eyes had opened again, this time glowing blue – as blue as the giant flames.

"Burnish the Ratna-Maru in the blue fire, O devta – and vanquish these perpetrators of evil.

Forge it in the heat of these flames that have been blessed with the sacred remains of the Saptarishi –

and prepare the mighty primordial sword for its ultimate destiny!"

Vivasvan Pujari was still grappling with the menacingly advancing blade with his bleeding left hand and counterattacking with his sword in the right when he heard the pronouncement of the last Saptarishi. The distraction caused by the loud, roaring voice gave him the sliver of opportunity he needed. He was only twenty feet away from the celestial fire

There was no way the asuras could prevent the devta from

covering this short distance.

The sight was something that even Mother Earth would forever remember. How could Prithvi forget the union of the human and the divine? How could the hand of God reaching out to alter the course of destiny not remain etched in her eternal memory?

As the devta thrust his sword into the inferno, the flames first dipped into a hush, as if extinguished. In the very next moment, with a startling whoosh they leapt into the skies like a flaming column of blue fire! Sura and his men could feel mortal fear creeping deep into their cruel hearts. They first exchanged frozen glances with one another and then raised their eyes and heads to fathom the height of this dazzling column - only to see it originating from repeated blue lightning from the heavens.

Someone beyond the realm of Earth was intervening.

The One in the skies was fuelling this supernatural phenomenon.

Vivasvan Pujari stood next to the blazing column like a primeval warrior, his head thrown back, his legs apart and his muscular arm outstretched deep into the pillar of fire. His eye was shut and his lips moved in prayer, invoking Shakti, the Goddess of all creation. In the darkness of the stormy night, he looked as blue as the fire itself.

Slowly the column began to subside. It first reduced back

to the giant blue fire, before sagging further into a regular flame, glowing yellow. The rain and hail were going to soon extinguish this ordinary, Earthly fire.

But something still glowed a glittering blue.

It was the devta's sword.

Outskirts of Banaras, 2017

KAALCHAKRA

Brahmanand was terrified.

It was after much persuading by Vidyut and Balvanta, and the firm instructions of the matthadheesh that coerced Prof Tripathi to agree to join them in their raid on Trijat's den. Vidyut sensed that for all his protests, somewhere it was the latent yearning to avenge the blinding of his eye that made the professor agree. He could not have hoped to draw his revenge from the Mritak-naath on his own. But with help from the great Dwarka Shastri, Vidyut and Balvanta, he could smell a real payback chance.

The squad was ready. It was to be led by the grandmaster himself. There was Balvanta, Sonu, Brahmanand, a hundred or so of the matth's choicest fighters…

...and Vidyut.

·‖ॐ‖·

They looked heavily intoxicated. The aghori taantric guards on duty outside the yajnashaala were gently swaying as they stood in the pitch-dark, moonless night of amaavasya. Prof Tripathi was right. They appeared to be under heavy influence of a very strong narcotic.

Trijat Kapaalik's yajnashaala was about forty kilometers out of the main city of Banaras. It was situated at an unusually remote area that was normally ignored by the local police, given both their fear of, and their incomes from, the sinister Masaan-raja. Local villagers avoided passing by that area completely, as they knew about the medieval burial grounds. They believed that entire tract with the mysterious citadel in its midst was haunted.

They were not wrong.

·‖ॐ‖·

A thicket of trees surrounded the yajnashaala of Trijat Kapaalik from all sides for several hundred metres. In the darkness of the night, as Dwarka Shastri sprinkled sanctified water from his kamandal on the ground around the wicked yajnashaala, Vidyut and the others were stunned to hear angry shrieks of some strange beings. The shrieks were human all right. But they sounded like they came from deep inside the womb of the Earth.

The feudal graveyards were coming to life.

As they made their way stealthily on foot, progressing closer to the high walls around the perimeter of the dark priory, something inexplicable stopped them. They heard the eerie wailing of what sounded like scores of women, weeping in pain and eternal longing. No one could be seen around.

Sonu turned to Vidyut, his eyes wide with horror.

'Daakinis,' said Vidyut calmly.

Just as he said those words, Dwarka Shastri lit a massive multi-tiered ceremonial lamp – similar to the ones used by the priests during the Ganga *aarti*. Its camphor flames erupted high into the darkness. As soon as this sacred torch was lit, the wailing turned into a cacophony of hisses, gnarls and shrieks. As the matthadheesh began chanting mantras, wind swept the dry leaves off the ground and trees began to sway - as if caused by the chaos among the otherworldly beings that resided in that ancient burial ground and served the Masaan-raja.

Vidyut was right. Even in his tired and faded self, the grandmaster of the Dev-Raakshasa matth was formidable. Only this param-taantric could repel a whole army of pret-aatmas in their own stronghold.

They were now very close to the giant black gate that guarded the entrance to Trijat Kapaalik's yajnashaala. Vidyut could see his Baba was under tremendous strain. Every step closer to the ghastly citadel was making the angry spirits stronger and Dwarka Shastri weaker. Invisible shadows seemed to lurk in the trees, as if waiting to unleash their true horror as soon as the aura of the mantras subsided.

'Baba, should Prof Tripathi and I join in the chanting? The three of us will be stronger than you taking them on alone!' asked Vidyut, worried for his great grandfather.

Dwarka Shastri refused and gestured to Vidyut to attack the black gate.

Vidyut turned to Balvanta, who drew out both his short swords. It was going to be a combat with blades, spears and fists. Both sides knew better than to draw the attention of the police with gunfire, when they knew this was going to be a bloodbath. The fighters of the matth were now ready to storm the fortress of the dark forces.

·||ॐ||·

Just as Vidyut was about to dash towards the yajnashaala, Dwarka Shastri turned to him, looking extremely anxious.

'Something is not right, Vidyut. The pishachas and daayans appear to be as daunting as I had expected them to be on amaavasya. But there is something more I sense…something far more terrible than we can imagine. This night is not going to turn out the way we have been hoping.'

Vidyut did not know how to react. This hour had been recommended strongly by Prof Tripathi and retreating now would mean waiting till the next moonless night.

Dwarka Shastri understood Vidyut's dilemma.

'Go on, Vidyut. The dead are awakened already and it is too late to retreat. Just look after yourself, my son...'

The devta saw pain in the grandmaster's eyes. The way he said the last sentence sounded like a farewell.

·||࿕||·

By now the guards of Trijat had spotted the matth's militia and had raised an alarm.

'We must leave...now!' Balvanta yelled out to Vidyut.

Vidyut did not want to leave his great grandfather. There was so much unsaid, so much love and reverence still not shared.

'I will come back for you, Baba...I promise! I will come back for you!'

Dwarka Shastri smiled and nodded, as tears welled up in his holy eyes. He remembered another time, another battlefield, where a loving son had promised the same to his mother. The continuum of karma was in no one's control. The wheel of time was always turning, presenting human souls with the same trials.

Kaalchakra was ceaseless.

East of Harappa, 1700 BCE

SATYAVRATA MANU

'Harappa will be the first to get swept away by the great deluge,' said Matsya.

They were now back in the cave where Matsya was addressing the large group. Everyone appeared flustered at the grim prospect the leader of the fish-tribe had spoken about.

In the group meeting before this one Tara had decided to question Matsya as to whom he was, and how he was in a position to make such a bizarre, cataclysmic prediction. But that was then. Tara had never seen a man like Matsya. One close glimpse of him and she was convinced that he was no ordinary man. He was someone else.

Just like the leader of the mountain-guardians had said, it was Matsya who chose how and when you embrace him as your own, admire him like a God and love him like you were his own child.

She was not going to question him. Every speck of her body, her mind and her soul was eager to submit to this bluish phenomenon of a person. Her Manu and she were going to follow him.

Blindly.

·||ॐ||·

'Harappa will not last beyond a few hours. Tomorrow, in the darkness of the night, the rakt-dhaara will consume the entire metropolis.'

There was stunned silence in the cave, glowing dimly under torchlights. Despite the cold and wet evening, each one from the gathering broke into a sweat.

The flooding of Harappa meant certain death for hundreds of thousands of innocent people.

'There has to be something we can do, Matsya,' exclaimed Somdutt, with a deep sense of urgency in his tone. 'We have a few hours. We can ride into Harappa and warn the citizens. They can save their children, Matsya! They can save themselves...'

Matsya did not respond. He kept looking at Somdutt, as if picturing the futility of the effort in his mind.

'Say something, O great Matsya,' pleaded Somdutt. He too was mesmerized by the divine fish-man. He somehow, deep down, believed it was all in the hands of Matsya. That Matsya could singlehandedly salvage the world from the impending death and destruction.

It was now the turn of Manu to rise and speak.

'With your permission, we ride to Harappa in the next hour. It was indeed that city and its people that took away everything from my family and me. It was the soldiers of Harappa whose arrows pierced the heart of my mother. It was the citizens of that city who pelted my father with stones, laughed at his torture and spat on him when he bled. And yet, I say we ride. We ride because if we fail to protect the people now, we are no different from the black-hearted scoundrels who perpetrated all that hate. We ride because every human life is just as precious as that of my beloved mother and my great father.'

Matsya's eyes could not help but admire the character and moral fabric of this young man, with great satisfaction at the choice he had made.

Only Vivasvan and Sanjna could have raised such a fine human being, a gem among men.

'Have you both not been listening to me carefully, Satyavrata, Somdutt…?' asked Matsya, looking at the two men who had just offered to risk their own lives to save the others. Riding into Harappa would mean instant arrest and execution for both, and yet they were willing to bet their lives for the sake of fellow human beings.

'What is the point in trying to save those who are destined to perish in the great cleansing that comes? The deluge will devour everything, everyone!' he continued.

'Be that as it may, O mighty Matsya, we cannot just give up,' said Manu respectfully. 'If Pralay has to engulf everything, there is nothing we can do against the will of nature. But till there is even one breath left in me, I cannot sit back and see people drowning in their own homes.'

Matsya shook his head, helpless in the face of such a determined stand taken by Manu.

'So you think it makes sense to risk your life to save those who are going to perish no more than a few months later?' he asked.

'Yes it does, Matsya.' This time it was Tara.

'If it means even a day more of life for so many people, it is worth the risk,' she spoke firmly, righteously.

Matsya now grinned, and everyone in the room felt a breeze of bliss waft across the cave. He gave in.

Free human will.

·||卐||·

It was decided that Manu, Somdutt, Tara and a handful of mountain-guardians would leave for Harappa immediately. If they galloped non-stop, they could reach the gates of the cursed metropolis a few hours ahead of the predicted disaster. If they succeeded in evacuating the city hastily, innumerable lives could be saved.

At least for now.

But even before they could begin their fateful journey, Matsya sought to convene a meeting of a smaller group. He invited the graceful leader of the mountain-guardians, Somdutt, Tara, Manu and a few of his own tribesmen into a smaller cave-room.

'You are very stubborn, Satyavrata,' said Matsya, as they walked towards their meeting destination.

Manu stopped and held Matsya by the arm, forcing the fishman to halt too. Matsya turned to look at Manu, amused at being held back in this manner.

'Why do you address me as Satyavrata, O Matsya? My name is Manu.'

Matsya laughed and started to move, but Manu tightened his grip and pulled him back.

'You are not going anywhere till you answer my question!' Manu said in jest, but not letting go of his friend and guardian anyway. By now they shared a bond strong enough to permit Manu to take a few liberties.

'See, I told you that you were stubborn!' replied Matsya, now turning to Manu.

He stretched out his arms and held Manu by his shoulders.

'Tell me, Manu…what does Satyavrata mean?'

Manu did not have to think.

'It means someone who has taken the pledge to speak the truth, Matsya. Someone who is the guardian of the truth.'

Matsya smiled and his eyes surveyed Manu's face with great affection.

'Precisely. You will be the only one to take the truth with you to the other side of the deluge, Manu.

You will be the only Satyavrata.'

Outskirts of Banaras, 2017

A HUNDRED RITUAL PITS

Vidyut shot a kick that landed like a cannonball into the ribs of the aghori who had charged at him with a trident. The man squealed in intense pain. His ribcage was shattered.

The devta was in an unforgiving frame of mind, something very rare for a man with a heart as golden as Vidyut's.

The next two men were equally unfortunate. Vidyut's fist smashed the face of one of them into a pulp. The other lunged at him with a butcher's knife. The devta dodged the assault, grabbed the attacking wrist of the aghori with one hand and his other hand strangled the throat of the attacker. Vidyut then smashed his forehead on the aghori's cranium, who crumbled under this merciless punishment.

Several other men from Trijat's cult faced a similar fate as

Vidyut made his way towards the black gate of the fortress. However, one thing was bothering the devta as he fought through the aghoris.

These men don't seem to be intoxicated, as they were supposed to be tonight.

·||ॐ||·

Vidyut and Balvanta could not believe their eyes as they stepped into the courtyard of the Masaan-raja's yajnashaala. It was the most morbidly repulsive place either of them had ever stepped into, or even imagined in their worst nightmare. They stared momentarily at each other and then at Prof Tripathi, who looked like a living cadaver.

The large central atrium had over one hundred taantric ceremonial pits, each surrounded by low, cemented seating platforms. The pits were burnt black with soot over years of dark rituals. Trijat's aghoris could perform a hundred sacraments at any given time...all at once. Vidyut could only imagine the invincible spiritual traction something like that would unleash. The four corners of the atrium had magnificent but fearsome looking statues made of black marble. Vidyut instantly recognized what those statues were. Or more importantly, *whose* sculptures they were. The entire premises was strewn with pieces of flesh, bloodstains, chopped animal limbs, country liquor and bones of all kinds. But it was the presence of one particular accessory to their rituals that made this aghori priory truly abhorrent.

Corpses.

Some still wrapped in their white shrouds, tightly bound by rough jute ropes. The others twisted in rigor mortis, their eyes rolled up and their jaws contorted. Scores of dead bodies lay scattered around the vast field of pit-fires.

The stench of death and human decay pervaded the air of this sickening raakshasa monastery.

·||ॐ||·

The fighting continued. Young warrior-monks of the Dev-Raakshasa matth had followed their devta valiantly and were now in a gory battle of stabs, punches and blood with the savage followers of Trijat Kapaalik.

Vidyut's eyes were darting across the compound, searching for the demon that had violated the Dev-Raakshasa matth. He was looking for the black-magician that had orchestrated the killing of Bala. He was scanning the ritual ground to find the raakshasa who was colluding with a dark, global organization and had brought that lurking monster right to the doorstep of his home, his matth.

His eyes were searching for the deity of the dead – Trijat Kapaalik.

Even as he longed to catch a glimpse of his target, Vidyut noticed Balvanta surveying one of the black marble statues. It depicted a muscular man with wings like those of a prehistoric dragon. The face of the statue was handsome, but not pleasant.

'Balvanta dada, we need to find Trijat,' said Vidyut, as he

tried to pull the war-General of the matth out of his stupor.

Balvanta took a moment but was back with Vidyut, ready for battle again.

As they stood shoulder to shoulder, surveying the ritual ground and the corridors and rooms lined around it, Balvanta could not help but ask the devta.

'Whose statues are these, Vidyut? Who is this strangely powerful yet menacing creature? I have never heard of him in our scriptures.'

Vidyut remained silent.

You have not heard of him because he is not there in our scriptures.

'Tell me, Vidyut…' insisted Balvanta.

Vidyut turned to the war-General.

'I don't know what is going on, Balvanta dada. I don't know who these people are and what they seek. I always thought Trijat was a taantric from Kashi. But these statues tell a different story. They should not be here!'

Balvanta did not fully grasp what his devta had just said.

'*Who* is this, Vidyut?' he asked again.

The devta took just one name. Perhaps the most feared name in the entire western world.

'It is *him*, dada. It is Satan.'

Balvanta understood nothing. He just repeated what Vidyut had said, without any comprehension of it.

'It is Satan?'

'Yes, dada,' replied Vidyut.

'It is Lucifer!'

·‖ॐ‖·

Finally, Vidyut saw him. He looked terrifying, and disturbingly splendid.

They did not call him the king of the graveyards just like that. He stood like the emperor of the dark realms that he was, surrounded by gigantic followers with ashen faces and blood-red mouths.

And then Vidyut saw them.

The two pishachinis. Their eyes were transfixed on the devta. They breathed as heavily as they did when Vidyut saw them first.

Breathe. Breathe because you breathe your last today.

The Masaan-raja locked his eyes with Vidyut's. He fearlessly gestured to the devta, inviting him to follow, as he turned around to leave and disappeared into what looked like a stairway going into the basement of the complex. His followers and the two witches left with him.

Vidyut clenched his teeth to control his rage and charged towards the Masaan-raja. Only to be pulled back by Prof Tripathi, who grabbed hold of the devta's arm.

'Don't Vidyut! He is beckoning you into the belly of the underworld. It is where he performs the Raktbeej Anushtthan.

He is luring you into the heart of the primordial abyss.

He is luring you into *Paataal.*'

Harappa, 1700 BCE

THE DEVTA OF HARAPPA

Sura rested on his knees. His head was dropped as if looking with disbelief at the massive, glowing sword that had torn right through his chest, its pointed end protruding from the other side, dripping with the demon-king's blood.

All his life Sura had hated Vivasvan Pujari. He hated the Saptarishi and he despised Aryavarta.

Little did the emperor of asuras know that it was to be in the heart of Aryavarta, at the behest of the last Saptarishi and by the sword of Vivasvan Pujari that he was to meet his end.

Destiny had drawn the legendary demon-king all the way across the ravines of the Hindukush.

To die.

·‖ॐ‖·

The brilliance of Vivasvan Pujari's sword had no parallel on Earth. It had taken the devta not more than a few moments to slay the demon-king and each one of his henchmen. The only asura still standing was Prachanda, who had tried to put a stop to the savagery of Sura.

The last Saptarishi lay on the rocky riverbed, broken and aged, breathing his last. Vivasvan picked him up reverently in his arms and sat him up gently against a boulder as backrest.

The distraught devta now fell at the feet of the last Saptarishi. He had had enough. His soul rejoiced at the thought of his beloved son. His conscience wept at what he had become. All Vivasvan Pujari wanted now was liberation – and to unite once again with Sanjna, wherever she was.

'Forgive me, O pious rishi! Forgive me if you can…' said the devta, as his tears of intense pain and indescribable remorse fell on the sacred ground of the abode of the sages.

The sage did not respond. His eyes were shut in a meditative trance.

The devta sighed and nodded to himself.

My soul is beyond forgiveness, beyond reclamation.

Vivasvan drew out his dagger with the lapis lazuli grip.

'Hear me, O great sage. Your fallen servant is aware that *aatmaghaat* (suicide) is one of the greatest sins that a man or a woman can commit. It alters the cosmic cycle of birth and death. It insults creation that bestows us with the precious gift of life. But I see no other path to redeem myself. No lesser punishment shall suffice. Forgive me if you can, O divine rishi.

I, Vivasvan Pujari, offer my life to you. May the death of this blemished devta be his final submission to you and to the Gods he has let down!'

With this the blotted Surya of Harappa placed the tip of his dagger against his own belly. Prachanda stood witness to everything. He was too dazed, too overwhelmed to intervene.

The devta closed his eyes and placed his hands on the handle of the blade. He offered his last prayer to Lord Rudra.

But this was not the manner in which the greatest man of his era was meant to die. A split moment before he plunged the knife deep into his gut, the last rishi spoke.

"Lament not, O Surya of Harappa! You have sinned no doubt, but your soul is not beyond redemption. Its work is not yet done. You will return, O devta…in another age, in another time."

·||ॐ||·

Vivasvan Pujari sank to his knees and rested his hands on his thighs. He shut his eyes in mild reprieve and gratitude. It was for the first time during this horrific night that he had heard the familiar, tender voice of the Saptarishi he once knew.

'Let me go, O rishi. How you remain benevolent when I have just caused the death of six of your brothers is beyond me! I can only seek your forgiveness and lay down my life as a feeble offering,' said the devta with folded hands.

You have not killed the Saptarishi, Vivasvan. Who can harm those who are one with creation itself? As soon as you had set foot here, the devta in you had sensed that our decaying bodies did not house the rishis anymore. You were right. The Saptarishi are eternal, immortal...and we now reside in the chambers of the Black Temple, that glow blue with the radiance of our penance. Our souls shall now dwell in new, divine bodies. And your son, Satyavrata Manu, shall be accompanied by us.

Vivasvan Pujari felt as if his agitated soul had suddenly been immersed in an ocean of calm. His suffering conscience found itself peaceably unburdened. He knew what lay hidden in the heart of the Black Temple. He knew if Manu and the Saptarishi were there, they were all safe. Safer than they could be anywhere else in the universe.

The devta now gathered the strength and courage to plead with the Saptarishi. To beg him for one last mercy.

'Free my son from the curse, O generous sage. Free his children from it. And theirs. Make me suffer as I have sinned. Condemn me to pain that is beyond human endurance. Tear my mortal body into shreds. But spare my son. Please... spare my children.'

What was causing the grinding roar in the mountains was now visible. A colossal landslide was hurtling towards the riverbed. Small pebbles had already started showering all over the land already being ravaged by rain and hail.

In a matter of minutes the battlefield, where the devta had fought the asuras, was going to be submerged under the crashing mountain.

·‖卐‖·

What has been spoken cannot be taken back, O devta! The curse cannot be undone. But you demonstrated the righteousness of your heart, the goodness of your soul when you fought to save me, the last of the sages. So I repay this debt, O Surya of Harappa. Your son, Satyavrata Manu, shall remain untouched by the curse.

And your descendants shall all live to achieve greatness, but true to the curse – they will all die violently! They shall be the guardians of the Black Temple, till the time you arrive on the planet again.

Send the Ratna-Maru to the Black Temple, O devta, in the hands of the last asura. Prachanda shall return to the kingdom of Sura and rule over a new dawn for his kind. Leave now, Vivasvan Pujari, for the mountains come forth to shroud this land forever!'

The devta of Harappa bowed to the last sage. The Saptarishi had granted him almost everything his shattered soul could have hoped for. He pulled out his sword from the demon-king's torso and washed it reverentially in the waters of the gushing stream and with the droplets of the incessant rain.

'Take this to the Black Temple, O Prachanda. I will guide you to it as we ride out. Take this magnificent sword to its rightful place,' urged the devta.

Prachanda accepted the sword respectfully and reassured Vivasvan Pujari.

'It shall be done, O great devta. I shall return beyond the Hindukush, with the fable of Sara, for all generations of asuras to worship and learn from. Being here with you tonight has been the defining moment of my life. You truly are half-human, half-God.'

Before the holy abode of the Saptarishi was buried under mounds of stone and dust, the voice of the last rishi echoed above all the noise.

"Your name shall become immortal, O Vivasvan Pujari. You will be born again, thousands of years from now - to fulfill a destiny greater than anyone to have ever walked this planet.

You will be reborn to protect the secret of the Black Temple in its final hour. It shall be you who will unfurl it in the Rohini Nakshatra of a particularly pious purnima, millennia from now.

You are the chosen one, O great devta."

Outskirts of Banaras, 2017

PAATAAL

Even Vidyut's heart skipped a beat as he climbed down the winding stairway that led into the basement of Trijat's yajnashaala.

It was a massive hall with not even a ray of natural light. It appeared to be a medieval cave of sorts, lit only by the flames of hundreds of torches that were framed into the walls. Scores of human skulls mounted on iron pikes were lined all around the hall, their mouths open, their hollow eyes gaping into the darkness. Vidyut knew their purpose. Taantrics attached great importance to the remains, skulls in particular, of ancient taantrics and yogis. They believed they could draw unearthly power from them.

The far corners of the cave had giant statues of the Goddesses – Maa Kaali, Maa Baglamukhi, Maa Smashaan Tara and others. The Masaan-raja knew no anushtthan in the realm of the dead could be concluded without the blessings of these incarnations of Shakti. Vidyut instantly realized what a big mistake Trijat was making.

No force of evil can ever vanquish the good under the watchful eyes of the Goddesses. Trijat will not win tonight.

But what astounded the devta most was the giant pit that raged in the central area of the cave. It was perhaps fifty feet long and twenty feet wide. Vidyut had never even heard of such a ritual fire. The pit was sunk about five feet into the floor of the hall and was filled with burning, glowing coal embers. The heat emanating from this fire was unbearable, and the entire place was sweltering. Vidyut noticed that the pit was not filled just with coal. He almost threw up when he spotted pieces of human limbs and bones baking in that fire of evil, and realized that the gross air of the place was actually the stench of incinerating human flesh.

If there was any hell, any paataal on Earth, Vidyut had stepped into it.

·||卐||·

'Welcome to my humble yajnashaala, O devta!' shouted Trijat from the other end of the pit without looking at Vidyut. He was pouring blood from a clay pot into the pit-fire. The red glow from the sea of embers burning below him was making the Masaan-raja appear even more ominous than he otherwise looked. They were quite far but Vidyut instantly recognized the two figures that sat like zombies at the maha-taantric's feet.

Pishachinis.

Slowly Trijat's giant aghori guards emerged from the dark corners into the orange hue of the pit. The heat was excruciating and Vidyut was drenched with sweat. Keeping his eyes fixed on the armed aghoris that were slowly surrounding him, he quietly unbuttoned his black shirt, took it off and tied it around his waist. The chiseled, muscular frame of the devta's torso glistened in the dim, fiery lighting.

By now Balvanta, Prof Tripathi and Sonu had clambered down to the hellish basement and joined Vidyut.

The battle was about to begin.

·||ॐ||·

Vidyut dashed forward, breaking into a swift run. The speed at which he moved took the aghoris completely by surprise. In a split second the devta leapt up and crashed his foot into the chest of one of the massively built guards. Even before the other aghoris could raise their weapons, Vidyut had landed an aerial kick into the skull of the next guard. Both these men crashed to the ground like falling timber.

As he turned towards the rest of them, Vidyut noticed with the corner of his eye that Trijat was now pouring blood from the same pot over the two pishachinis - who appeared to be in a trance of some kind. Balvanta and Sonu had also charged into the enemy by now, and the war-General of the matth drew first blood. He had hacked off the forearm of one of the attackers.

This fight was not going to last long. And that was worrying Vidyut.

This is too easy. Is this all the Masaan-raja has to throw at us?

And then he saw it.

Vidyut shook his head to check if he was seeing right. What appeared like two ghostly auras were now emerging from the pit-fire. These looked like they were made of thick, grey smoke, but the devta could see two figures within. Two terrifying figures. As they suddenly turned to look at Vidyut, his sweat turned cold. They were the most chilling, the most ugly and most grotesque faces he had ever seen. Their horror was beyond human imagination. They were primordial daakinis that Trijat had summoned from the depths of the realm of the dead.

The two pishachinis sat at the edge of the pit, with their eyes rolled-up and their mouths open, panting profusely. Trijat Kapaalik was incessantly chanting dark spells that spoke to the angry daakinis. The two frightening figurines floating in the grey smoke were inching slowly towards the pishachinis.

Vidyut now knew what the maha-taantric was doing. He was summoning the daakinis into the bodies of his two assassins. If he succeeded, even Vidyut would not be able to withstand their demonic attack.

"Oum beejam;
Namah Shakti;
Shivayeti Keelkam…"

Vidyut, Balvanta, Sonu, Brahmanand…all turned to see the massive shadow of the towering figure of Dwarka Shastri flicker on the walls of the underground cave's stairwell. Vidyut and Prof Tripathi knew what the grandmaster was chanting.

It was the most potent, the most powerful mantra against dark ethereal forces since the beginning of time.

He was chanting the giver of Lord Shiva's divine armour, the unstoppable — *Shiva Kavach!*

The two haunting auras scowled in protest. Their shrieks were so horrendous that Sonu crashed to his knees, trembling with fear. He covered his ears with his palms, looking away from the daakinis.

They twisted, scowled, screamed…but in vain. It was clear that they were retreating. Going back into the blackness they had emerged from.

No daakini or pret-aatma could withstand the Shiva Kavach.

But Shiva's divine armour could not defend a man from another man's deceit.

Vidyut felt his head had been split into two. The pain was excruciating and his vision was clouding. The devta clasped his head with both hands. His fingers were instantly drenched in his own blood that was oozing profusely from the deep gash on his scalp. Moments before passing out he turned around to see what had struck him.

In his fast blurring view he saw a one-eyed monster and rec-ognized him instantly. Grinning like an insane psychopath, the glasses of Prof Tripathi were gone. His blind eye showed the pink flesh of his hollow socket. He looked as gruesome as the daakinis.

As Vidyut fell unconscious, he heard the last words from Brahmanand echo.

'Paataal mein tumhara swaagat hai, devta!'

Welcome to hell, devta!

East of Harappa, 1700 BCE

MANU'S ARK

'But what kind of a boat do you want us to build, O Matsya? And why do we have to build a new one? There are thousands of large ships at the ports. If we reach there in time, we can acquire several of those vessels.'

Somdutt was bewildered when Matsya had asked him to be the chief architect of a giant Ark.

There was silence in the room. Manu, Tara, the leader of the mountain-guardians and everyone else present appeared to agree with Somdutt. The need to build something anew when the skies were so unrelenting, when keeping eyes open against the lashing wind was impossible, when the hearts of both man and beast were frozen with fear, was something they did not concur with.

Matsya got up and looked out of a natural window in the rocky wall. He saw the thunderous sky that was turning increasingly red. Raindrops pattered on his stunning blue face.

The time has come.

·‖卐‖·

'As far as Aryavarta is concerned, it is the end of the world.'

Matsya knew the time had come when he shared with everyone else what he had briefly described to Manu.

'Pardon me, but what do you mean by end of the world, Matsya? The Earth is more vast than any of us can imagine. Surely there would be regions that are out of the grip of this deluge?' enquired Somdutt, quite logically.

He was forgetting that the cosmos was created millions of years before human logic appeared on the scene. That the logic of the Creator who oversaw billions of galaxies and trillions of planets like Earth, was a bit more comprehensive and all-encompassing than his own.

Matsya turned around from the window. Lightning lit up the sky into daylight, as if bowing to Matsya and illuminating the words he was about to speak.

This deluge is nothing like Aryavarta has seen before. Or for that matter this whole world. Nothing will be spared. No human, no plant, no animal, no bird, no insect, no home, no temple, no mountains, no forests…

Pralay is the cosmic force that shall cleanse Aryavarta of everything.

*Waves higher than the tallest mountains shall rise and devastate every-
thing in their wake.*

*Yes some regions will be spared. But no one from Aryavarta would
make it to those far corners.*

*The skies will turn a blood red. Torrential rain will not cease for
months, brimming the oceans over and inundating the entire known
Earth.*

Cities will be swallowed in moments, millions of lives culled in hours.

Pralay - The Great Deluge…is coming.'

·‖卐‖·

Manu was speechless as he saw them.

Matsya pointed towards the high cliffs further above their cave.

Seven hermits sat meditating up in the mountains, unflinch-
ingly braving the rain. They glowed in a soft blue hue. From
what Manu could tell when thunder lit up the rocks, these sages were nothing more than young lads, perhaps even young-
er to him! They were delightfully calm, infectiously peaceful.
Their skin was radiant as if they had just emerged from some
divine womb.

They had.

'These are the Saptarishi, Manu. They shall be your companions in the arduous journey you embark upon. They will guide
you, handhold you. You will do the same for them. Together,

you will welcome the new dawn of Creation, the age when humans will conquer the depths of the seas, fly the skies in silver chariots and step on the Moon. The golden age.'

Manu turned to Matsya.

'What do you mean the Saptarishi will guide me? Won't you be there by my side, Matsya?'

Matsya laughed. But this time it was not merry. It was a laugh that said they would soon have to part ways.

'I will always be by your side, Satyavrata. I will always be there for the dwellers of this precious planet. It may be with a different name, in a dissimilar appearance, in some other land far far away...

But I will always be there.'

Matsya now stood on a sharp, high cliff, towering against the backdrop of the merciless skies. Manu, Tara, Somdutt and several others had gathered to hear what the celestial fish-man was going to say next.

Wind swept violently at the leader of the fish-tribe. His long hair and loose robes fluttered in the air. Drenched in rain, the magical man stood with his arms outstretched by his sides. His face looked up at the heavens as once again thunder greeted this divine marvel. Matsya now glowed a brilliant blue under the white flashes of lightning.

'He is a prophet...' whispered Tara to Manu.

But Manu knew better.

'No he is not, Tara. He is the One who *sends* the prophets.'

'Gather tens of thousands of men, women and children from Harappa, Mohenjo-daro and all other settlements. Collect more from the mountains and the forest tribes.

In the few months that remain before Pralay consumes everything, build the most gigantic boat to ever float on the oceans of this planet.

An Ark so colossal that its mast scrapes the heavens. A ship so mammoth that tens of thousands of people take refuge in it. An Ark that can carry a million plants, birds, animals and seeds.

Gather the alchemists, the physicians, the architects, the farmers, the musicians, the writers, the traders, the teachers and the priests.

Take with you the Vedas, the scriptures, the metals, the yarns, the medicinal herbs, the tools and the gems.

You will rebuild the world, recreate civilization and keep kaalchakra spinning.

This Ark, Manu's Ark…will be remembered till the end of time!

The immortal giant-boat will serve the universe's most noble objective.

It will survive Pralay.

It will save Creation!'

Harappa, 1700 BCE

VIVASVAN PUJARI

He was the only human for miles. He could hardly see in the dark of that unusually fearsome, stormy night. Especially with the heavy trickle of his blood, tears and sweat mixed with the muddy waters of the unseasonal, torrential rain blurring his vision. In the pitch-black night the bald, bare-chested Brahmin struck with his axe back and forth at a feverish yet futile pace. He was attempting to cut at least one of the thick jute ropes that bound one pillar of the freshly built, man-made mountain of brick and bronze. Although made with the objective of diverting the course of a river, the enormous mound of stone, brick, metal and wooden blocks appeared threatening enough to alter the assault of even the bold tsunamis of a rogue sea. But then the river under question was no less than the mighty oceans themselves.

Muttering to himself under the roar of the downpour, like a man possessed, he used every ounce of strength from his body hardened by years of penance and Vedic discipline. He pounded the cable-like rope furiously even as his fingers splayed and started to bleed. When he couldn't breathe anymore he threw his head back and looked up once to let the heavy raindrops slap his face angrily. With the unsympathetic water washing the red mud off his eyelids, he let out a ghastly, sky-piercing scream. It was perhaps an attempt by his recently blackened soul to make the Gods hear his indescribable angst. But he knew it was too late. The Gods were horrified at his deeds and would not forgive him. Or anyone.

He started cutting the rope with his short axe again, more menacingly than before. He knew he had been trying to cut one coupling knot for over an hour now. The ropes were specially made, upon his own instructions. He knew there were 998 more brick, bronze and stone pillars held together by thousands of similar rope-knots that forged the unbreakable mount. And that it would take weeks to disassemble it if a thousand men worked day and night. The 999 strategically engineered and reinforced pillars were built as per his own careful architectural and astrologic guidelines. *What was he doing? Had he gone mad?* He knew he could not undo the giant mound even one bit. And yet he fired away his axe incessantly, hopelessly.

A solitary figure in the lonely miles of empty land ravaged by a mid-night cloudburst, Vivasvan Pujari, a man worshipped for decades as a devta (half-human, half-God), revered as the Sun of Harappa, looked liked a ghost. He felt extreme pain and a sinking regret at the sinister consequence he knew could not be averted. He kept weeping, kept mumbling and kept chopping away. And then he heard it.

It had begun.

The ominous rumble of the mighty river gushing into an unnatural course, somewhere distant but not too far, made his blood curdle. The once generous, loving and nurturing Mother River had incarnated into a thirsty rakt-dhaara (blood-river) lunging towards devouring her very own children. The River of the Wise was betrayed by one of her favorite sons. She was betrayed by her devta son, Vivasvan Pujari.

The once righteous and indomitable Vivasvan Pujari let the axe slip from his hand and it fell on the slushy mud with a wet thud. He stood frozen gazing towards the direction he knew his now-manic Mother would appear in her demonic form. He knew it then. He knew this night he was going to be the first blood at her altar. Suddenly, he wanted it that way.

He slowly felt a sense of ease and relief spreading within him. He felt hope. Maybe his Mother would claw out his life but spare the millions of others. He dropped to his knees, stretched out arms in submission by his sides and opened his palms. The rain washed his taut and wounded body as if finally helping him cleanse his badly knotted conscience. As if pitying Vivasvan Pujari and offering him his last bath.

'Take my life, O mighty Mother! I have earned your wrath. And I submit myself to thee!' he yelled out as the night sky lit-up with an angry clap of thunder. It was as if the Gods were rejecting this fallen devta's plea.

He screamed again, this time his voice splitting with desperation and heavy sobbing, *'Do you not listen to your crestfallen son, O mighty Mother?! Take my life but forgive the others! They have not sinned as your son has. Take me!!'*

The sky lit up again. It was nearly daylight for a few moments. The silent lightning flashed on Vivasvan Pujari's bleeding, sweating and deranged face. And then it followed. The delayed noise of the thunder was as loud as an exploding sun.

The Gods were saying NO!

Vivasvan Pujari felt a powerful gust of wind on his face as he saw the giant water-mountain appear from the corner of the far mound, turning directly towards the path where he sat crumbled on his knees. It looked like an enormous hydra dragon turning its head towards its prey. The din of the river was louder than the thunder that roared a few moments ago. Vivasvan Pujari sat there dazed, as he looked up at the mountain-high torrent casting a looming shadow even in the darkness. He appeared as small as an ant would in front of Mount Sumeru, as the sky-high tsunami of his Mother River was all but a few moments away from engulfing him.

Vivasvan Pujari had faltered in the last few days. He lost the glory of a lifetime in a few days of the blinding revenge he sought. But he was Vivasvan Pujari. A devta! Like all men of advanced *yogic* learning, he instantly summoned and centered his soul within his *kundalini*, he froze his heartbeat and prepared his mortal body for death. Even as he did that and was getting swept off the ground with the force of the invading water, he whispered a calm, last prayer.

"Mother, forgive them. Don't let them perish for my sins. Forgive them,

Mother!"

The devastating river swallowed the devta Vivasvan Pujari like a mammoth tornado erases the existence of a dry twig. The Gods, the murderous blood-river, the dark night, the thunder of Indra (the God of lightning and storm), the vast expanse of land and the merciless rain stood witness to the end of the greatest man of his time. But the death of Vivasvan Pujari was not going to be the end of his impact on this planet. It was the beginning. He was going to live on in hatred, deceit, conspiracy and violent conflicts for thousands of years. He would haunt not just Aryavarta but the whole world with never-ending bloodshed and killing in the name of the very Gods that abandoned him. Even his death would not liberate him or human kind from the curse.

She maintained her unrelenting course. Despite Vivasvan Pujari's dying plea, the blood-river was not going to forgive them.

The *Saraswati* was going to devour the mighty city of Harappa, along with every last one of its inhabitants.

Outskirts of Banaras, 2017

DEV-BALI -
THE SACRIFICE OF A GOD

The heat was unbearable, as if he were on fire. His arms and legs were being pulled like they would rip apart. His head was reeling with intense pain. His wrists and ankles felt as if they were being cut into by metal.

Vidyut was in unbearable agony and completely disoriented when he began to gain back his consciousness. As he opened his eyes, for several seconds he could not gather where he was and what was happening to him.

He felt like he was floating in the air, overlooking a giant fire that was scalding his skin.

He was right. Within moments Vidyut remembered where he

was and realized the gravity of his situation.

He was hanging horizontally ten feet above the center of Trijat Kapaalik's pit-fire, his face and unclothed upper body getting scorched from the raging heat below. His hands and legs were spread in all four directions, tied by long iron chains to high hooks in the cave's walls. During his unconscious state, the Masaan-raja, the monstrous Brahmanand, the pishachinis and the maha-taantric's remaining henchmen had chained and suspended the devta right above the sea of burning coal and flesh.

·||ૐ||·

'Look...look at this devta!' screamed out Trijat Kapaalik, walking around the ritual pit, mocking Vidyut. 'Is *this* the devta those white-skinned men are so afraid of?'

Brahmanand laughed in evil ecstasy. 'We have done it, Trijat! It is done! He who was feared for centuries hangs in front of us like a roasting duck!'

Balvanta and Sonu were both tied with ropes and sat kneeling on the ground. Sonu wept as he saw Vidyut in extreme suffering. But that was not what was most disturbing. Dwarka Shastri's hands had been tied up too, and he had a blunt sickle pressed against his neck. The pishachini breathed heavily like a goblin, thirsting for blood.

'Let them go, Trijat...' said Vidyut, his voice shaking with pain. 'You are a blot on the ancient name of the aghoris. You are an insult to the spiritual philosophy of aghora itself. True aghori taantrics are worshippers of Lord Rudra, devotees of *Dattatreya*, and they are the givers of blessings. They are denouncers of worldly materialism and true seekers of the truth. You are not an aghori at all, Masaan-raja! You are *not* a true taantric! Now, it is me you want. Kill me…but let them go.'

'Kill you?' asked the Masaan-raja, unfazed by Vidyut's rebuke. 'You really don't know then, do you?' He turned to Dwarka Shastri enquiringly before looking back at Vidyut.

'You have been kept alive for years, O devta. The Rohini Nakshatra is not far. The Black Temple shall rise! It is only thereafter that you shall die…for sure.'

The maha-taantric now slowly closed his eyes and raised his head, as if submitting a prayer to some dark force. A few seconds later he suddenly opened them. With manic cruelty and lust for power dripping from his ashen face, he pointed to Vidyut.

'Uss prahar issi anushtthan-agni mein Dev-Bali chadhegi!'

That hour a God will be sacrificed in this very ceremonial fire!

·‖ॐ‖·

'Trijat…this is a golden chance,' said Brahmanand. 'To add unprecedented power to our anushtthan.'

Trijat turned to look at Brahmanand, curious to know what the one-eyed professor had in mind. He knew his aghori brother well. It had to be something devilish, something savage.

'Look around you, Trijat…we have spent years collecting the skulls of accomplished taantrics. Every kapaal adds to our reach into the dark realms. Some of them were maha-taantrics as well.'

The Masaan-raja was listening intently, but did not follow what his partner was suggesting.

Brahmanand's eye twinkled. He leaned forward to Trijat, but spoke loudly enough for everyone to hear, including Vidyut. He gestured in the great matthadheesh's direction.

'Imagine Trijat…what power the kapaal of the world's only param-taantric will bring us!'

·||ॐ||·

Trijat nodded at the pishachini. She threw her head back and rolled it slowly, readying herself for the pleasure that was to follow.

'No…! Stop…!' screamed Vidyut, as he strained his arms and legs against the chains that held them. But they were too strong.

Vidyut knew he had very little time. He pulled again, this time with all his strength. His chest muscles stretched like iron cables and the veins on his powerful arms were ready to explode. The devta's desperate struggle was awe-inspiring for Sonu and Balvanta, who looked at this heroic effort with moist, hopeful eyes.

Vidyut was indeed a devta.

To the horror of Trijat and Brahmanand, the iron hook that held the chain tying Vidyut's right hand, began to give way. Cracks started to appear at first. Moments later the rocky surface of the cave wall started to crumble.

As he pulled the chain and his right hand free from the shattered wall, Vidyut's eyes, glowing red as embers reflecting the inferno below, darted towards Trijat Kapaalik. The maha-taantric was now trembling with disbelief.

'You made a big mistake, O Masaan-raja!' cried Vidyut, his voice splitting with pain, rage and hate.

With this the last devta broke free his right leg as well, now swinging like a flying God just above the bed of fire.

'You forgot, Trijat!

I am half-human, half-God!'

TO BE CONCLUDED...

TO BE CONCLUDED...

KASHI
SECRET OF
THE BLACK TEMPLE

ABOUT THE AUTHOR

Vineet is a first-generation entrepreneur. At age 22 he started his company Magnon from a small shed. Today Magnon is among the largest digital agencies in the subcontinent, and part of the Fortune 500 Omnicom Group.

He has led the global top-ten advertising agency TBWA as its India CEO. This made him perhaps the youngest ever CEO of a multinational advertising network in the country.

He has won several entrepreneurship and corporate excellence awards, including the *Entrepreneur of the Year 2016*. He was recently listed among the *100 Most Influential People in India's Digital Ecosystem*.

Vineet's second company talentrack is disrupting the media, entertainment & creative industry in India. It is the fastest-growing online hiring and networking platform for the sector.

He has written three bestselling management & inspirational books – *Build From Scratch, The Street to the Highway* and *The 30 Something CEO*.

His first fiction novel *Harappa – Curse of the Blood River* is a national bestseller. It has also won rich critical and literary acclaim.

www.VineetBajpai.com
facebook.com/vineet.bajpai
twitter/Vineet_Bajpai
Write to Vineet at vb@vineetbajpai.com